SEDUCTION IN THE MIST

"The longer I know you," Claire said in a voice she reserved for her most scathing sarcasm, "the more I'm convinced that your mouth is not the deadliest weapon in your arsenal against women."

Graham shrugged his powerful shoulders, a lazy ripple of muscle. "There are many women who would disagree with that assessment."

Damn him to Hades, but he was probably correct. Every blasted time she looked at him she remembered the way he'd kissed her, so rough and so... acutely arousing. Such an uninvited kiss should have enraged her, but instead she had near melted all over him.

"Yer mouth, on the other hand," he said with an irrepressible smile, "is deadly indeed."

Please turn this page for reviews
for Paula Quinn and her novels...

LORD OF TEMPTATION

"Features a sinfully sexy hero who meets his match in a strong-willed heroine...An excellent choice for readers who like powerful, passion-rich medieval romances."

—*Booklist*

"Will enchant and entertain...Passion, danger, treachery, and heartbreak fill the pages of this splendid novel...don't miss *Lord of Temptation*."   —*RomRevToday.com*

"Quinn's lively romance...offers two spirited protagonists as well as engaging minor characters...The sharp repartee and dramatic finale make this a pleasant read."

—*Publishers Weekly*

"Quinn wins readers' hearts with a light touch, even as she invokes strong themes of slavery, freedom, and the need for independence."

—*Romantic Times BOOKreviews Magazine*

"A truly magnificent tale...Dante is a perfect hero and lover and Gianelle is special—perfect for each other. The passion is fantastic—unbeatable!"

—*RomanceReviewsMag.com*

LORD OF DESIRE

"4 Stars!...fast-paced and brimming with biting, sexy repartee, and a sensual cat-and-mouse game."

—*Romantic Times BOOKreviews Magazine*

A Highlander Never Surrenders

PAULA QUINN

FOREVER

NEW YORK   BOSTON

Book design by Stratford, a TexTech business.

Forever
Hachette Book Group
237 Park Avenue
New York, NY 10017
Visit our website at www.HachetteBookGroup.com

Forever is an imprint of Grand Central Publishing.

The Forever name and logo is a trademark of Hachette Book Group, Inc.

Printed in the United States of America

First Printing: August 2008

10 9 8 7 6 5 4 3 2

Daddy . . .
I will love you always.

Acknowledgments

A special thank you to the wonderful people of Metropolitan Jewish Hospice for all the special, loving care they gave to my dad. It made a difference.

To Chris Capaldi for helping me bring Graham alive, and to Teresa Fritschi of Thistle & Broom for all the great pictures.

Chapter One

It has all gone terribly wrong. What I feared most has come to pass.

The stench of cheap wine and ale filled the tavern like a dense fog and settled onto the table where Graham Grant, first in command of the mighty clan MacGregor, sat watching his friend, the eleventh Earl of Argyll, drain his fourth cup of ale.

"This business with Connor Stuart weighs heavily on ye."

Robert slapped his cup on the table and raised his heavy-lidded gaze to him. "Why do you say that?"

"Ye're getting drunk, and ye brood more than I can stand of late."

"I've only had four cups," Robert countered with a scowl. "I've seen you drink more than twice that amount."

The mocking curl of Graham's half smile needed no

explanation, but Graham gave one anyway. "I'm a High-lander," he said and raised his cup to his mouth.

"I can drink as much as any of you." Robert swung around on his chair, teetered, caught himself, and tried to catch the attention of a swarthy serving wench.

He succeeded, but the deep-cleavaged lass's eyes swept past his and settled on Graham's. Graham looked her over from foot to crown, thinking what a pity it was to have to send her away, but the last thing his friend needed was more ale. A subtle shake of his head was all it took for her to move on, pretending not to have seen Robert motioning for her.

"Damnation," Robert swore, then waved to another wench.

"Rob."

"What?"

"Look at me," Graham said seriously, and Robert obeyed. "Not being able to find Stuart is naught to be ashamed of. The man's as elusive as Callum. Find yerself a wench fer the night and ferget yer duty."

Robert pushed his cup away, raked his hand through his dark hair, and gave Graham a look that said his friend could never understand what he was feeling. "Graham, General Monck commanded me to find him. Since I was a boy I've wanted to serve the realm. Now, when I've been granted the honor, I have failed."

"Who have ye failed, Rob?" Graham asked him and winked at a bonny wench who caught his eye. He stretched his long, bare legs out in front of him, crossing his boots at the ankles, and downed the rest of his ale. "Oliver Cromwell is dead. His pacifist son Richard has been ousted from his seat by military tyrants who claim to hate despotism, yet fight fer power to rule the country."

"But someone needs to lead us, Graham. General Monck was one of Cromwell's most fearsome warriors of the New Model Army."

"Aye," Graham agreed caustically. "So great were his victories over the Royalists in Scotland, the old Lord Protector named him governor over the country he had so skillfully subdued. Yer country." Graham added, giving his friend a pointed look.

"That was many years ago," Robert pointed out. "He's been fair to our people and has refused to support the dissolving of Parliament."

Graham yawned.

"Besides, the most likely to gain the title is John Lambert. Remember, he commands all the military forces in England."

A vision caught Graham's eye, thankfully distracting him from his friend's tedious passion for politics. The lovely Lianne. The lass had stolen into his thoughts several times since she left his bed the night before. He flicked his simmering gaze over her form as she approached his table, toting a pitcher of ale.

Now here was the kind of passion Rob needed. When Graham left his home on Skye two years ago with the newly confirmed Earl of Argyll, it was with a vow to teach the peach-faced lord how to balance his duties with pleasure. Robert had yet to experience the pleasures a lass could offer. Graham narrowed his eyes on him. What the hell was he waiting for? Love? Graham almost snorted out loud. There was no place for it in a warrior's life. A man was either a husband or a great warrior. He could not truly be both. Graham had made his choice long ago. He was a great warrior because he did not fear death. He had naught to lose, no one's life to destroy. Hell, he'd seen it so often throughout his life. Lasses made into widows, bairns left to go hungry, without a father to look after them. He did not want to carry that fear, that vulnerability, when he faced his enemy.

He motioned for Lianne and she practically flung herself into his lap.

"More brew, m'laird?"

"Nae, my lovely," Graham coiled his arm around her waist and fitted his palm neatly over her buttocks. "My friend has had enough." Hearing him, Robert shot him an irritated look. "He could use a wee bit of distraction from his troubles, though," Graham continued, ignoring him. With a gentle nudge, he pushed Lianne off his lap and in Robert's direction, then leaned back in his chair to watch.

"Is that so?" The golden-haired wench rested her tray on the table and swung her tattered apron over her shoulder, readying herself for what she did best. "I've been waitin' all day to be of some aid to such a fine nobleman as yerself."

Robert barely looked up. He rested his elbow on the table and sank his head into his hand. "I fear, dear lady, that you cannot help me."

She slid down Robert's chest until her rump reached his knee. "Dinna be so hasty, sir. Ye've no idea what talents I possess."

Graham did. He smiled, accomplishing his mission, and spread his gaze around the crowded tavern in search of another wench to help him pass the night while Robert became a man.

"I . . . ehm—" The sound of Robert stumbling over his words reminded Graham just how much he still had to teach the young earl. But first, where had that swarthy wench gone off to?

"We can retire above stairs, ye and I." Lianne's voice dipped to a lusty whisper.

"But I thought you . . ." Robert paused and swallowed audibly when Lianne leaned forward and into him. "I thought you fancied my friend."

"Aye, yer companion is a sinful creature, indeed." Her pale blue eyes settled on Graham and deepened with pleasure as if the most decadent memory had just swept across her thoughts. "But tonight," she returned her attention to Robert, "I want an angel in m' bed."

A shadow rising above him drew Graham's dimpled grin off the seduction of his friend and upward. Very high upward.

"Ye're supposed to be at my table tonight, Lianne. I paid in advance." The Highlander was enormous. His soiled plaid stretched across his broad chest when he grazed his eyes over Robert and then to Graham. The challenge in them was unmistakable before he turned back to Lianne. "Now get yer arse where it belongs."

Hell, Graham thought, mildly disappointed for Robert. He could get up and fight for Lianne's company tonight, but the brute *had* paid, and he was quite large. As long as Robert did not open his mouth there was still a chance they might find themselves spending their energy on something more thrilling than fighting tonight.

Unfazed, Lianne left her seat and slapped her apron along the man's arm as she passed him. In response, the angry patron gave her a shove between the shoulders before he, too, turned to leave.

"You there, the ugly one."

Graham's shoulders crunched around his neck as Robert rose from his chair.

The giant pivoted slowly, his black expression a prelude to murder. "Are ye talkin' to me?"

"Aye," Robert assured him coolly. "Though I'm astonished you posses the intelligence to have surmised it."

The patron's volatile gaze narrowed. Graham couldn't help but smile, suspecting that the brute was either wondering if he'd just been insulted again, or deciding which of Robert's limbs to sever first.

When the Highlander grinned, flashing what few teeth he had left, Robert met the baleful challenge with a slight hook of his mouth. Graham set his gaze heavenward and shook his head. This was as bad as traveling with the MacGregors.

"I pray for your sake that you also possess the wisdom to believe me when I tell you that if you lay your hands on that lady again, I shall take you out of doors and beat you senseless."

The confidence in his promise might have convinced the other patrons who were watching that the smaller lad fully intended to keep his word. But Graham knew better. Having naught to do as a young lad but practice weaponry in the fields of Glen Orchy and study the words of bards and poets, Robert Campbell had grown into an excellent swordsman—and an overzealous knight who was constantly getting them into fights defending someone's "honor." But for all his training with a sword, the young fool had trouble connecting his fist to someone else's face.

Sadly for Robert, the murderous Highlander only laughed, took a step forward, and swatted the table that stood between them out of the way.

Graham stepped aside to avoid getting struck in the head with the flying wood. He grimaced as a huge fist felled Robert to the floor. He wanted to help, but the earl needed to learn how to fight without his sword, and now was as good a time as any. Still, he pushed his cap back from his bronze mane of curls, readying himself for the fight. He would intervene if the ogre pounded his knuckles into Rob's face one more time.

"Are ye goin' to stand here and do nothin' while Atard beats yer friend to death?" Lianne charged, rushing to Graham's side.

Graham figured she meant to get him moving with her admonishment, but when she patted the creamy mounds of her bosom with her apron, he was sorely tempted to leave Robert to his own defense and carry her above stairs.

"My friend does well." His dimples flashed, as frivolous as his concerns. "He is once again standing upright."

Robert's body countered that opinion as it hurled past Graham's shoulder.

Muttering a curse under his breath when the earl landed hard against the wall, Graham turned to the advancing giant. He bent to pick up a leg from the shattered table and swung, cracking the wood in half against Atard's face.

Stepping over the Highlander's body, Graham knelt beside his motionless friend. "Rob." He slapped his cheek gently. "Wake up."

Robert stirred, lifting his heavy lids. "Where is he?"

"Afar off," Graham assured, then gave him a hard look. "How many times must I tell ye not to fight with drunken Highlanders?" He shoved his hands under his friend's arms and lifted him to his wobbly feet.

"The ruffian mishandled the lady."

Lianne offered the knight a grateful smile, but Robert's already swelling lip prevented him from offering her one back.

"What can I do"—Lianne's smile changed into something more obvious when she took a step toward them—"to persuade ye both to stop in again on yer way back from where ye're goin?"

Graham's languid grin sent a flame straight to Lianne's groin. Aye, she thought, melting before him, this one's mouth was as deadly as his sword, a sword he knew what to do with. Ah, but he was a feast for the eyes. His lips were full and fashioned for heathen delights. His eyes sparkled in the light like emeralds set aflame from within. The threat of prettiness was vanquished from his features by an edge of rugged masculinity, and a nose that looked as if it might have been broken a time or two.

She let out a small gasp when he snatched her up by the waist, hauled her against his hard angles, and swept his mouth over hers. His kiss was like sin, tempting her to abandon any last shred of decency she possessed and beg him to take her with him.

"I'm persuaded," he said, releasing her with a smack to her rump and a lecherous wink that promised he would return.

Feeling like a silly spring maiden, Lianne waved them farewell, then tossed her apron over her shoulder and headed for the patron calling for a drink.

"Ye look like hell."

Robert slid his gaze to Graham, riding alongside him, as they left the town of Stirling. Everything else pained him too much to move. "I feel like I was tossed into it."

"Ye needn't fret about that, Rob," Graham said, readjusting his cap forward over his brow. "Hell wouldn't have ye. Which is fortunate fer me. I don't want to spend eternity with ye."

Robert didn't believe his friend would spend an instant in that fiery place. If anyone could find a way to convince God that he belonged in His good graces, it was Graham. "Though you lack any kind of honor when it comes to women, bedding them is not a sin deserving of eternal damnation."

The doubtful crook of Graham's mouth convinced Robert otherwise.

Robert smiled, then cringed and lifted his hand to his jaw. "Then for your soul's sake, find a lady to give your heart to and let her make a decent man of you."

Graham cast him an askew glance and laughed. "I fear yer books about the courtly ways of love have led ye far from the truth. Ye ferget I have eleven sisters, most of whom are wed to miserable bastards who began as decent men." He held up his palm when Robert would have spoken, cutting him off. "Lasses are fer caressing, bedding, and leaving. Else ye'll find yer ears pricked by constant troubles, and yer manhood as useless as yer battle sword."

"Mayhap the fault lies with your sisters," Robert pointed out. "Callum is not miserable with Kate."

"Aye," Graham conceded, watching the bruise below the young earl's eye turn purple. "Yer sister is a rare jewel. But even the Devil MacGregor has traded in his claymore fer a sprig of heather clutched in his fist."

Robert sighed and shook his head. He had much to say on the matter, but his jaw felt like it had been hit with a mace. Besides, he'd had this argument with Graham a dozen times and each time his words had proved fruitless. Graham held fast to the belief that the only things lasting and tangible on this Earth were battle and death. And he was determined to enjoy his life in betwixt the two.

"We should have taken my army," Robert said after a moment of silence. "If Connor Stuart were standing in front of us right now, I fear I couldn't pull my sword from its sheath."

"I told ye, Rob, yer army would only have alerted him to our search. Stuart is cunning. 'Tis why he is the leader of the Royalist rebellion. Remember 'twas he who set the ambush upon General Lambert's army after they crushed the rebellion in Cheshire a pair of months ago. I am familiar with his brand of strategy. The tales of his prowess grow each day. According to some at the inn, Stuart fights even Monck's men now. He attacked a legion of the governor's garrison not far from here. He is well skilled and trained to sense danger days before 'tis upon him. We'll find him faster with just the both of us. Trust me in this."

"I do. For I still recall your cunning in breaching the walls of Kildun when MacGregor came for my uncle two years past. But I am out of time, my friend." Robert worried out loud, rolling his shoulder to loosen the cramp setting in. "In a few short days I will have to face General Monck empty-handed."

At first, Robert had considered it an honor that General Monck had commanded *him* to find the Royalist rebel, Connor Stuart. Since there was no longer anyone formally "in command" of the three kingdoms of England, Scotland, and Ireland, the Royalists' campaign to return Charles II to the throne was rampant. Stuart was cousin to the exiled king, and the leader of the resistance of the English army's occupation in Scotland. Monck wanted him found, but the man was as elusive as the wind.

"I will not find him unless he comes to me. And he will not do that."

"Nor would I if the Roundheads were hunting me."

"Some would consider me a Roundhead," Robert reminded him, realizing once again how precarious their friendship was.

Graham shrugged his shoulders, keeping his eyes on the path ahead. "Aye, ye support a Parliament that has recently been expelled by the military. 'Twas better here in Scotland when we had a king."

"You are a Royalist, Graham, I understand. But should I forget my allegiance to the commonwealth?"

"Yer commonwealth is ruled by generals who fight amongst themselves and who suppress our people. Even Parliament does not trust them."

Robert ground his jaw with frustration over his own uncertainty. The Campbells had served the law for generations. Whether that law was handed down by one man or a house full of them made no difference. To turn his back on the realm was treason. Still, he knew Graham was right in his thinking. The return of a sovereign power would be better than the complete anarchy in England now. "Why do you aid me in finding Stuart if you believe in his crusade?"

Graham looked over his friend's swollen face and sighed. "Because I'm afraid he'll kill ye."

"Your confidence in my skills is warming." Robert attempted a sardonic smirk, which Graham answered by grimacing with him.

"I'd be more confident if ye'd thrown a punch in return."

Robert shook his head, painful as it was to both his shoulders and his pride. "I think the bastard broke my jaw."

Chapter Two

We have all been betrayed.

Satan's balls, she wasn't going to die this way! Claire Stuart glared at the man's head buried between her breasts. With a final tug that confirmed how tightly her wrists were bound to the oak behind her, she gritted her teeth and then sank them into the mauler's shoulder.

"Ahh! You bitch!" Her attacker reeled away gripping his bloodied wound. "I'll kill you for that!" He lunged for her, mindless that her legs were free. None of the men had thought to secure her feet to the tree. After all, it was her arms that had wielded a sword so expertly against them, killing six of his comrades when they came upon her this morning. But her attacker realized his oversight an instant after, when she kicked him square in his nether regions and sent him straight to his knees.

"You're a feisty wench." Another man strode toward her with an arrogant swagger. Claire silently promised to rid him of it the moment she was free—if she could just get her damned hands loose! "Brave . . ." He stepped over his writhing companion and, with a smile of purely naked male intent, pointed the tip of his blade at her throat.

". . . and foolish enough to travel alone. Mayhap I shall bring you back to London with me. Surely General Lambert would grant me a wife for all my years of service."

"Lambert?" Claire glowered at him while she struggled against her restraints. "What are Lambert's men doing in Scotland?"

"We are paving the way for our leader, and killing a few Royalists along the way. Someone must fulfill the task, since Monck sits idly in his castle doing little to stop them." He dipped his eyes to the creamy swell of her bosom, half exposed by her torn shirt. Then lower, to her shapely hips and legs, encased in snug-fitting trews and boots. "Strange attire for a lady," he said, meeting her fired gaze. "What is your name?"

Hell, he was as dense as a wall. Did he think she would give him her true name if she was a Royalist? Which, being the king's cousin, she was. She gave him an exasperated sigh. How long were these two going to waste her time? Her sister could be being forced to marry some despicable Roundhead soldier at this very moment. "I am a Campbell, and if you release me now I will beg my father to spare your worthless life."

"She's lying, John. No Campbell would let his daughter ride alone." The man she'd kicked staggered to his feet rubbing his injured groin. "Kill the bitch. Better yet, let me do it after I shove my cock up her arse."

"Touch me again," Claire's voice was a low warning growl, "and I'll cut out your innards and then strangle you with them, you filthy son of a whore."

He came at her quickly, and pushing John's sword out of his way, cracked her hard across the face.

"Geoffrey, stand down!" John commanded, stepping

away from Claire's treacherous boots. "If she is a Campbell we'll be flogged for striking her." He angled the edge of his sword against her throat to keep her still, then lifted his other hand and swept a strand of flaxen hair off her cheek. "We'll take her back to camp and find out who she is." John inched closer to her, so that when he spoke his breath touched her clenched jaw. "If she is lying, I will take her first and then give her to the rest."

Claire closed her eyes, sickened when he spread his tongue over the seam of her mouth. She beseeched God and all His saints to give her the opportunity to kill these two Puritan Roundhead bastards quickly. She had to find her sister.

Dear God, Anne. Poor Anne. She'd been taken from their home by General Monck's army, but how long ago, Claire did not know. She'd been at Ravenglade Castle, awaiting her brother's return from England, when she received word that he had been killed. Immediately, she'd gone home to Anne to give her the terrible news, but her sister was gone. A message left for Claire, written in Monck's own hand, told her that he had promised their guardian that he would keep them protected from the fanatical Independents in England. Claire did not believe it. Not after what had happened to Connor. The General had the audacity to add in his missive that he believed their lives were in danger, and he'd come to take them to Edinburgh.

He was going to marry them off. With Connor now out of the way and the king exiled in France, the Stuart lands could be given to a man of Monck's choosing. No. She would never obey the man behind her brother's death. She was going to kill Monck first and then rescue her sister.

She cursed herself for meeting with the resistance at Ravenglade, and not being home to protect Anne. Her sister was delicate and mild-mannered. She didn't have the blood for fighting the way Claire did. After Charles was banished from Scotland, she never showed the slightest bit of interest in the rebellion. Anne had refused to lift a blade, even after their parents were killed. Instead, she locked herself away with her books, never complaining to her elder siblings about their long absences from home.

They were supposed to protect her, and Claire had failed. She prayed it was not too late, else she'd have to make her sister a widow. All she had to do was get rid of these two dimwits and she'd be on her way.

"Geoffrey," John turned to his companion after getting no reaction from her. "I'll get the horses. Do not untie her until I return."

Claire stood alone facing the grinning soldier. Geoffrey stepped closer, pulled her dagger from her belt, and traced the tip along her cheekbone. "Not so bloody fierce now, are you. Think you will still want to kill me after I fuck you bent over backward?"

Every muscle in Claire's body ached with the need to end this pig's life. "I'm certain I will kill you just for breathing on me."

He raised his fist to strike her again, but a powerful command to halt stopped his hand in midair.

Claire looked over his shoulder to see two men mounted on great black warhorses approaching cautiously, one surveying the six dead men scattered along the ground, the other surveying her.

"Release that lady at once, and give me an account of what happened here."

"Who are you to command me?" John gained his saddle and trotted toward the two men with his hand poised on the hilt of his sword. Claire saw the reason for his caution. One of the men was a Highlander. They were easy to spot, these warriors of the north, they were bigger than the English in their belted plaids and bare legs.

"I am Lord Robert Campbell, Earl of Argyll." While he spoke, his rougher-looking companion slipped off his mount and began walking toward her and Geoffrey.

What was a Highlander doing traveling with a Presbyterian Campbell? Another traitor to the throne, Claire thought sourly, giving the earl a look of black contempt, and then turning it on the Highlander. She was only mildly aware of John's sputtering voice asking if she belonged to the Campbell house, as she took in the full sight of the warrior fast approaching. He moved without pause, his shapely calves tight with muscle, his boots pounding a path straight for her. His hard gaze was made even more threatening beneath the shadow of a brimmed bonnet of deep indigo wool, much like her own. As he grew closer, he tilted the bonnet jauntily over his mop of honeyed curls.

Claire raised her chin in direct challenge as his potent green gaze swept over her from foot to crown, lingering momentarily on her barely concealed breasts.

She'd been correct to think Geoffrey a dimwit, for he brandished her meager dagger at the intruder, readying for a fight. His bluster ended with a swift, bone-crunching fist that shattered his nose and sent him reeling backward, unconscious.

Seeing the fate of his companion, John drew his blade and swung it at the Earl of Argyll. The Highlander produced a dagger from a fold in his plaid, sliced it across the rope binding Claire's wrists, then hurled it end over flashing end into John's·chest.

Finally free, Claire stepped closer to the warrior who'd just rescued her.

"Graham Grant," he introduced himself with a sensual grin as deadly as his reflexes. "Commander of . . ." While he was speaking, she snatched his great claymore from its sheath and turned the other way. When she reached Geoffrey, she raised the sword in both hands then brought it down with a resounding thump into his chest.

After retrieving her dagger from Geoffrey's lifeless hand, she strode back to the Highlander, and offering him neither smile nor thanks for freeing her, shoved his bloody claymore from whence it came. Boldly, she tilted her gaze to meet his, expecting to see the disbelief and disapproval of men when they saw her fight. But this one's eyes glittered with approval. Pity there was no time to spare him another moment, she thought, stepping away. She had to keep moving. Forgetting him, she began searching among the dead. When she found the one she was looking for, she snatched up the cap he had shoved into his pouch and tucked it under her belt.

"Were you harmed, lady?" Grant's companion asked.

"That is no concern of yours, Campbell," she said, checking for bloodstains on the shirt of one of her earlier victims. Finding the fabric unsoiled, she bent and yanked it over the dead man's head. When she straightened, her gaze slid back to the Highlander. She glared at his blatant inspection of her backside. He smiled in return, muddling her senses with two recklessly sexy dimples.

"On the contrary. It is my duty to protect the defenseless."

Claire cut Robert Campbell an inconsequential glance and pulled the shirt she'd retrieved over her head. When her head poked out of the neckline, she cast her eyes over the ground and then offered Robert a smile that suggested he was as dense as the dead men around him. "I can assure you I am not defenseless." With a flick of her wrist, she released her long wheaten braid from under the shirt. It dangled like a thick rope to her hips. With little or no regard for the two men watching her, she slipped her hands beneath her new shirt, unlaced the torn one beneath, and wiggled out of it. She knew how to change her clothes in front of men. She'd done the like many times when she rode with Connor and his army.

"You expect me to believe you killed these men?" Campbell asked, dismounting while she began searching again.

"Would you like me to prove it to you?" She spotted what she was looking for a few feet from the tree and bent to pick it up. The sword was rapier thin, its hilt wrapped within worn leather. Blood from an earlier fight glistened along its steel edge. With a graceful sweep of her arm, she positioned the blade flat over her other elbow, pointing its tip at the earl. She arched her brow, waiting for his reply. Her hard gaze inspected him from the tips of his dusty boots to his sable hair. He didn't look like a Roundhead. His hair was not closely cropped round the head in the fashion that gave Roundheads their name. But he was a Campbell, and Campbells were supporters of Parliament. "Tell me why I shouldn't kill you now."

"Lower yer sword, lass."

Claire swung her gaze to the Highlander. His voice was gentle, but the warning in his striking green eyes was anything but. She had no time for another altercation, and the Highlander didn't look as if he would go down easily.

Straightening, she backed away. "Your duty is done. Be on your way." She wiped the bloody blade on her torn shirt before tossing the shirt away, then sheathed the sword in the scabbard dangling from her slim waist. It fit perfectly.

"What happened here?" Grant asked.

Claire found it almost impossible not to let her gaze linger on him. The soft honeyed curls peeking out from beneath his cap captured the sun's rays, giving him an almost angelic look. His mouth . . . Hell, his mouth was hypnotic, with full sulky curves that beckoned her careful attention. Everything else about him was warrior hard. Beneath his tunic and belted plaid, his body was tight and built for speed and fighting. His shoulders were broad and his legs strong. The deep bronze shadow along his cheek and jaw—that did not do enough to conceal those blasted dimples—added to his rugged virility.

"These are Lambert's men. I . . ."

"Why have Lambert's men returned to Scotland?" Campbell took a step closer to her. She took a step back and rested her hand on the hilt of her sword.

"They are here to do the same thing you do, Round-head. Kill Royalists."

"I've killed no one," the earl defended. "Why were they holding you prisoner? Who are you?"

Claire wasn't about to tell him. "I am but a servant. They came upon me this morn and thought to ravish me."

"Ye were alone?" the Highlander asked, looking around at the dead, then back at her.

"How does a servant, a woman servant at that, know

how to wield a sword against half a dozen men?" Campbell asked, looking just as skeptical as his companion.

"My brother taught me how to fight," she said, peering fearlessly into his gold-green eyes. "Do you not believe me?"

"I do," the young earl replied. "I often practiced swordplay with my sister while we were growing up."

"This isn't swordplay, Campbell," she said letting her gaze drift over the bruises on his face. "Mayhap you should have practiced more seriously. You look as if you've been tossed into the side of a mountain a few times."

She was surprised by his reply, expecting him to bluster about and boast of his great skill, as any other man would do.

"My fight, though I lost it, was a noble one."

She almost smiled. "So was my brother's."

Chapter Three

Would that I had known the truth. Now there is naught I can do but think on his death.

The lass intrigued him. Graham watched her mount a snorting chestnut stallion with a single, graceful leap and his blood scalded his veins. He had never thought a woman could look so alluring in man's garb. Her close-fitting trews accentuated the tantalizing swell of her backside, the maddening curve of her hips. Her legs were long and coltish, fashioned for running . . . and wrapping snugly around a man's waist. Everything about her was a stark contradiction. She wore the face of an angel, pure as freshly fallen snow, yet she had killed six men and then rummaged around their bodies like a battle-hardened warrior, completely unaffected by the blood she'd spilled. Her form was delicate, utterly feminine, yet she moved like a feline predator. He knew he would be haunted for months to come by the look of her when they'd first come upon her. The spark of rage that colored her blue eyes to smoldering indigo. Strands of buttery blond hair eclipsing her flushed cheeks. The helpless look of her tied to a tree, half naked and ready to be devoured . . . the brazen satisfaction that fired her eyes when she returned his sword to his sheath.

"She's no servant," Robert said, gaining his saddle a moment after Graham gained his. "She's lying. Why?"

"I do not know," Graham said, keeping his eyes on her riding up ahead. "Let's follow her and find out."

"Nae, I cannot. I must get to Edinburgh, Graham."

"And leave the lass to her own defenses?" Graham asked, knowing full well which weapon to use to persuade his friend into compliance. "Where is the honor I've come to value so highly in ye, Rob?"

Robert gave him his foulest look. "That's low, even for you. I will not tarry because you have found yet another woman to your liking. We don't know who she is or where she is going."

"Lass," Graham called out. When she turned slightly, his chest tightened at the beauty of her profile. He swore if she had announced her destination was France he would not have paused. "To where d'ye ride?"

"To Edinburgh," she advised over her shoulder.

Graham grinned at Robert. "We, too, are headed fer Edinburgh. We shall ride with ye."

"Hell," Robert groaned, and shook his head at the heavens.

"Nae, you shall not," she answered back, and quickened her horse's pace.

"As much as we admire yer skill and courage," Graham said, taking off after her, "we cannot allow ye to travel alone."

Suddenly she wheeled her horse around and faced him fully. Graham let his gaze soak in every inch of her. Hell, she was bonny. Her thick plait cascaded over her shoulder and down her breast. She wasn't as buxom as the maids he usually took to his bed, but he did not care. The spark of fearlessness in her eyes excited him. She would be a challenge, this one. He smiled at her. She did not smile back.

"You have no choice."

"And what will ye be up to in Edinburgh, alone?" Graham asked her, unable to think of anything save the intoxicating shape of her mouth and how all that thick hair would feel coiled around his fists while he pulled her head back to ravish that creamy throat.

"I'll be rescuing my sister."

He raised a tawny brow. "From whom?"

"From General Monck."

He would have laughed, but the curl of her mouth and the glint in her eyes was such a direct challenge, he almost believed she could do it.

Robert's reaction to her statement was quite the opposite. He nearly choked on his words when he spoke them. "General Monck, the governor?"

"Aye." She sighed, tapping her fingers impatiently on the pommel of her saddle.

"Are ye going to free her from servitude, then?" Graham inquired, enjoying the daring look she flung at him. She did not care if they knew she was lying. And Graham did not care how many men she'd killed this morn, she was reckless and foolish if she thought she could fight a full regiment by herself. "Have ye ever been to Edinburgh, lass? There are hundreds of guards patrolling the battlements. Ye cannot fight them all, and ye cannot simply walk into Monck's home and rescue yer sister on yer own."

"And yet that is exactly what I intend to do."

"We will come with ye," he insisted.

"You will be a hindrance to me."

Now Graham laughed. Damn, she was arrogant. Her confidence stirred his blood. The way she met his gaze head on without even a trace of blush made him more eager for her surrender. He was not about to let her go. "Come with us and we will discuss yer sister's release civilly with the general. If she's but a servant as ye say, my friend here can—"

"Nae, I want no aid from a Roundhead."

"I am beginning to take offense at that word," Robert muttered, then he shook his head, fearing he was going daft for even having this conversation. "You are no servant. My guess, from the way you continue to insult me, is that you are a Royalist. One with skill and more weapons on her body than any woman should know what to do with. Whatever you are planning, I ask you not to be a fool. You will die."

"So be it." She shrugged. "I will save my sister first."

"Is she in Edinburgh against her will?" When she nodded, Robert raked his hand through his hair. "Why is she there?"

The lines of her face grew rigid, bearing the evidence of belligerence no servant possessed. "She is there to face a fate worse than death." Without another word, she turned her horse to leave them again.

"You will fail her," Robert called out. "Let me save her."

Graham turned to grin at him, and Robert ground his jaw before taking off after her. Aye, he was daft. He didn't need to be reminded of it.

"Why would you aid me, Campbell?" she called over her shoulder. "You do the Parliament's bidding."

Catching up to her, Robert directed his steed in front of hers, cutting off her path. "My sister was once abducted by the MacGregors. Like you, I was ready to rescue her alone."

"From the MacGregors?" She sized him up with a flicker of new appreciation in her eyes. "That was brave, but foolish of you."

"Precisely," he said, waiting for her to understand.

When she did, her expression darkened. She snapped her reins, but he blocked her route again. "I do not serve the military, my lady. But I do serve Parliament, and though my head may be put to the chopping block for this when it is restored, I understand what you want to do, and why you want to do it, no matter what position you hold."

"Why should I trust you?" she threw back at him, misgivings clearly written on her face. "Campbells kiss the arse of whomever rules." She turned on Graham next, her eyes lit with accusation. "And you, Highlander. The Grants have fought for years at the king's side, and yet here you ride with a Roundhead."

"Think what you will of us," Robert said, sharpening his tone to let her know arguing this point was useless. "Right now, honor dictates that I help save a maiden in distress."

She dipped her brow at him and then turned an incredulous look at Graham. "Does he jest?"

"Nae," Graham answered, coming up beside her. "I believe it has been his lifelong desire to surpass even Sir Galahad where honor is concerned."

"I see." She cast a wry smirk back at Robert. "Are you pure of heart, then?"

"You know of Pendragon's knights?" Robert asked

her, looking more doubtful than he had when she told them she had killed six men.

"Not I, but my sister knows the tales well. Once, when she was a child, she pretended to be Guinevere and made everyone in the household call her by that name. She refused to answer to Anne for a full year." The memory brought a delicacy to her smile as she angled her face to Graham. "And you, Commander? Are you pure of heart as well?"

He could not lie to her. Not when her lips took on a challenging slant that told him she already knew the answer. "Alas," he said, not sounding repentant at all. "I fear I am as depraved as Satan himself."

She stared at him long enough to make him doubt his declaration. "My thanks for the warning," she finally said, then yanked on her reins hard enough to make her stallion rise up on its hind legs. Robert had no choice but to move out of her way lest he be struck by the beast's front hooves. "Farewell, Roundhead and rogue!" she called as she thundered away. "For your sakes, may our paths never meet again."

Graham and Robert watched her go, each at a bit of a loss after her swift rejection of their aid and her arrogant threat.

"She doesn't like us," Robert offered in a somber tone.

Graham turned to him. "She doesn't like *ye*." Then, with a mischievous glint in his eyes that Robert knew all too well from the pair of years he'd spent in Graham's company, Graham dug his heels into his mount's flanks and took off after her.

Chapter Four

Would that I were with you, to ride once again by your side, and to warn you . . .

Claire muttered an oath against the wind cutting her teeth. She chanced a quick look over her shoulder while her horse raced across an open glen, its hooves tearing chunks of earth from the ground. The two men were still behind her. Damn them to Hades! She'd done everything to lose them in the past hour, pushing her poor steed to its limit. They had crashed through streams, bounded over farm walls, and thundered through two villages, but her would-be champions remained hot on her heels.

She had to find a way to rid herself of them. If she needed men to help her with what she meant to do, she would have brought her closest ally and Connor's dearest friend, James Buchanan, and a few of his guardsmen along. Hell, James was going to be furious with her for leaving Ravenglade without telling him. But there was no reason to get him killed, which was exactly what would happen if she arrived in Edinburgh with the new leader of the resistance. Besides, he never would have gone along with her plan, and she loved him too much to battle him on the issue. If all went well she would rescue Anne without even having to unsheathe her blade save to slice Monck's throat. That is, if she could just shake the two pests behind her.

She imagined they meant well. At least the Roundhead did. Aye, he was a Campbell, but there was something in those wide hazel eyes of his—a total lack of guile, a genuine sincerity she hadn't seen in many men. Galahad, indeed.

His lecherous friend was another matter entirely. She knew his kind well enough. She'd practically grown up in the company of men, who for many years had regarded her presence in her father's practice fields as nothing more than a pleasant distraction, a *woman* whom they ached to tame, claim, and conquer. None ever did, and many still bore the scars of their attempts.

The forest loomed before her. Patting her mount's lathery coat, she dug her heels into the weary beast's flanks and sped toward the trees. She must lose her followers within the labyrinth or be forced to stop her exhausted horse and speak to them again. If they discovered she was a member of the royal household and a promised bride to one of Monck's men, they would try to take her into their custody and deliver her to the general's feet.

Determined on her quest, she plunged through the dense forest, her ears pricked to the panting snorts of horses behind her. Darting through a stand of oak, she fled south, toward her destination. She would not be stopped from saving Anne—and herself—from arranged marriages to their enemies. At least, that's what she was telling herself when her steed slowed its pace, then finally stopped running.

She tried to get the horse moving again, but it was no use. She had pushed him too hard. "Forgive me, Troy." She slid from her saddle and bent her forehead to the horse's neck. "But 'twas urgent, dear friend. I must . . ." Her apology was interrupted by the sound of her pursuers coming to a halt behind her. They were to blame for this. Grinding her teeth, she lifted her face and turned to them. "If my horse dies," she dragged her sword from its sheath and pointed it at them, "I shall impale you both on my blade."

The Highlander cut his gaze to her horse, then leaped to the ground. He strode directly toward her, his plaid swinging about his knees, and pulled the cap back from his head. Claire stood motionless while a lock of deep gold fell over his brow. When he reached her, he slapped her blade out of his way, discounting her threat as if she were no more dangerous than a badly behaved child.

"He needs rest," he said, stepping past her and examining the animal's coat and mouth. "And water." He grasped Troy's reins and moved to lead the horse away. Claire took a step forward, reaching for the bridle to stop him, but his fingers closed tightly around her wrist. "Ye were careless with yer steed, lass. If the beast dies, ye have only yerself to blame."

She did not try to free herself from his steely hold, though his accusation enraged her. The attempt would be futile, and she refused to give him the satisfaction of seeing her struggle against his strength. Instead, she took a step closer to him and tilted her face to meet and match his cool gaze. "Either way, I will need another horse. Yours looks fit enough."

His eyes flashed with a hint of mischief Claire was

sure lent to his devilish reputation. His mouth pursed with the arrogance of a man confident in his power to take up any challenge she presented. Indeed, he welcomed it.

"Two on my mount would slow us up considerably." His voice deepened to a husky murmur as he leaned down over her. "Though the prospect of having ye nestled between my thighs all the way to Edinburgh is tempting enough to make me dispose of yer horse myself."

Claire gave him a cheeky smile and blinked innocently into his gaze. "Which is precisely why you will be dead when I leave."

Laugh lines crinkled at the outer corners of his eyes as he drew back. But the amusement in his expression was appreciative, not mocking. Claire did not know what to make of it. Men usually took offense at her threats. Even if they did not believe she could carry them out until it was too late, they hated being challenged by a woman. This one was arrogant indeed.

"Why didn't you halt your horse sooner?"

Claire turned to toss a scowl at Robert Campbell, still seated upon his mount. He regarded her with large, disarmingly innocent eyes before he came to some conclusion that did not please him.

"We only sought to protect you, my lady."

"I do not—" Her charge was cut short by a dagger whistling past his nose, and by Grant lifting her off her feet and tossing her behind his back.

Gripping her hilt in both hands, Claire glared at his shoulders, which blocked her view, then stepped around him to stand at his side. He cut her a hasty side-glance, but spared her no more than that as he dragged his claymore from its sheath. Together, they set their eyes on the small group of men stepping out from behind the surrounding trees.

"Thieves," Claire muttered, noting their tattered garments and the glint of appreciation in their eyes, aimed at the horses.

"About two and twenty," the commander agreed.

"Twenty," Claire corrected, noting with a certain amount of appreciation his fine battle stance.

"Nae, lass, there are two behind us."

Claire glanced over her shoulder to find he was correct.

"Hand over them beasts and there won't be any killin'," one of the pack called out while he advanced.

Bracing her legs, Claire watched the miscreant's every movement over the edge of her blade. She'd had just about enough for one day. She refused to allow a few parasites to postpone her task another moment. "Take the beasts," she replied. "The horses are mine."

The soft chuckle from the unwanted companion at her side drew her glance to him. Graham Grant believed her confidence foolish, her threats meager.

Every man's error.

She proved it an instant later when two thieves lunged at her, their swords aloft, their legs swift. Bending her knees, she swept her blade across one man's belly, then brought it back in a flashing arc beneath the second man's chin. He remained upright for a grisly moment while the rest of his comrades attacked. Then he fell backward, blood spurting from his neck.

Claire did not pause to see if her champions needed aid, but blocked a crushing blow over her head, then another slice to her legs. Three clean swipes of her sword shredded her assailant's dirty tunic, and his chest beneath. Another thief, about to raise his weapon to her, took off running instead.

With no one to fight at the moment, she spun around— and looked up into a slanted grin that made her arms feel heavy and her head feel light. Her body went alarmingly soft. There had been but one man in her life who smiled at her the way this Highlander did, with appreciation and respect for her skill, rather than disdain. She offered Graham a slight nod, and then watched, silently appraising the strength and speed of his arm as he smashed his fist into the last remaining thief's face.

Dismounting, Campbell came to stand at his friend's side and tossed the unconscious outlaw at their feet a disheartened glance. "He went down quickly."

Graham agreed and patted his back. "We'll practice more, Rob."

"Practice what?" Claire asked, sheathing her sword.

"Fighting with fi—"

"Ehm," Campbell interrupted, looking as if he'd just swallowed a pebble. "That is of no importance."

Claire smiled at his sudden unease, and at the cuts and bruises marring his handsome face. It was obvious the poor man did not know how to fight. Pity she'd have no time to teach him, since his companion had clearly failed at the task.

"You fought extremely well." The earl's compliment caught her a bit off guard, but before she could thank him, he spoke again and her smile faded. "You said your brother taught you?"

"That's correct," Claire replied, meeting his scrutinizing gaze with a stoic one of her own. He might not be a warrior, this one, but he was sharper than she had first credited him with being.

"May I ask the name of such a competent warrior?" he inquired, as innocently as one might ask about the weather.

"You may not," Claire answered, just as politely. "He is dead and I prefer not to speak of him further."

His eyes on her softened. "I'm sorry for your loss."

She nodded and began to turn away, ready to leave, when the Highlander stepped into her path. "Tell us yer name then."

She thought about refusing his request. She could not tell him who she was and expect to leave with her wrists unbound. Worse, they would know Anne was not a simple servant, but the sister of the most wanted rebels in Scotland. Even if Grant had no quarrel with the royal family, the Campbells certainly did. She might be able to fight them both off and escape, but the moment they arrived in Edinburgh, the earl would alert Monck to her intention to rescue the king's cousin.

Still, even while her logic screamed to give a false name as she had done with Lambert's men earlier, her mouth betrayed her when she looked up into the Highlander's twinkling emerald gaze.

"My name is Claire."

"Claire," he intoned in the softest of whispers, as if he'd never heard a more profound word. Reaching for her hand, he slid his fingers beneath hers and brought them to his lips. "We are at yer mercy."

Claire pulled her hand away from the warmth of his breath and fought the titillating tremor rushing through her muscles. Damn the man, but he hadn't stated an untruth when he claimed to be wicked. He was a rogue warrior, the embodiment of pure male temptation. The plump pout of his mouth and his slow sultry smile warned of pleasures no gentle lady should ever ponder.

But Claire Stuart was not gentle, and most who knew her did not consider her a lady. That had to be why she could ponder naught at the moment but how he might taste if she stroked her tongue over those lips.

"My horse needs water," she said, stepping away from him and reaching for her reins. What the hell was she thinking? She was used to men trying to win her favor with lusty smiles and pretty words. This man was no different from the others she'd been rejecting since she was four and ten. She refused to give his mouth, or any other part of him, another thought. "Thank me swiftly for fighting with you rather than against you, and let me be on my way," she said over her shoulder.

She gritted her teeth and closed her eyes in frustration when she heard the two men pick up their pace to follow after her. She had to save Anne and she couldn't do it with General Monck's men on her tail. Satan's balls, they were leaving her with no other choice.

She was going to have to kill them.

Chapter Five

. . . Be wary of the fox's snare.

Graham would have enjoyed walking at her side where he could enjoy the indignant tilt of her chin, the beguiling curve of her jaw. The thought of tracing his lips, his teeth over the creamy allure of her throat made his body tighten. But hell, keeping his stallion a slow pace behind her while he enjoyed the view was satisfying enough. He took his leisure sizing up the plump, perfect roundness of her buttocks, tantalizingly caressed by her soft woolen trews. Her manly attire only accentuated the maddening sway of her hips, the feminine grace of her long legs.

An elbow in his ribs snapped his attention to the man beside him.

"Do you know who she is?"

"If I have my way, she will be my bedmate fer the next sennight."

Robert looked up as if beseeching the heavens to anoint him with some great gift. He leaned in closer to Graham and whispered. "Nae, she's Claire Stuart. Connor Stuart's sister! The king's cousin!" He darted his glance toward her to ensure she hadn't heard his enthusiastic discovery, then continued in a hushed tone. "Their parents were killed a year after Charles II was banished. John Stuart, I'm told, refused to pledge his loyalty to Cromwell and was summoned to London to meet with Parliament. He and his wife never returned."

"Stuart was foolish to trust the English," Graham murmured, sweeping his gaze over the lass a few paces away. Damnation, he couldn't take his eyes off her. "But what does any of this have to do with her?"

"Stuart and his wife were survived by their three children, Connor, Claire, and Anne."

Now Graham turned to him, his brows knit with the memory of her words to them earlier. "Her sister made everyone at the keep call her Guinevere. She refused to answer to Anne for a full year."

Robert nodded. "Monck must have taken Anne to force Connor to come to him."

"But Connor's dead."

"So says she," Robert pointed out with another quick look aimed in her direction. "There is a price on Connor's head, paid for by what she is wont to call me, Roundheads. Should her true identity be discovered, what better way to end the search for her brother than by claiming him dead?"

Graham mulled it over in his mind as he stepped over a fallen branch in his path. "What you say cannot be true." He turned to Robert again. "Connor Stuart has spent the last eight years fighting the English army. Whether ye agree with his position or not, whether ye believe his efforts have been foolish or valiant, he was no coward."

Robert paused, and setting his eyes to the woman ahead, the pleasure of his discovery faded from his features. "He would not have sent his sister to do his work." He spoke Graham's thoughts aloud. "She speaks the truth then. Connor Stuart is dead."

" 'Twould seem so," Graham agreed, then lowered his voice. "Would Monck have sent others to find Stuart when ye had no success, and mayhap 'twas them who killed him?"

"Nae, Monck wanted Stuart alive."

So, the general might not know Connor Stuart was dead, Graham concluded as they came upon a fern-filled glade with a thin stream running through it, its current dappled by sunlight streaming through the sparse canopy above. At the stream's mossy edge, Claire draped the reins over her saddle and smoothed her palm down her steed's long neck. Graham watched the delicacy of her movements, the tenderness in her touch as she comforted the heaving beast. She tilted her face upward and a splash of sunshine graced her softly curving mouth. Like a blissful angel, she basked for the space of six of Graham's stalled breaths, then she angled her head and looked at him. No angel there. Graham's mouth hooked into a grin. 'Twas the flash in her eyes that revealed her true nature, and intentions.

"Say naught of her identity, Rob," Graham said, under his breath. "She is earnest in her quest and we are already a hindrance to it."

The scalding venom of her glare would have given another man cause for concern, but the thought of going to swords with her titillated Graham's imagination. He wanted her in every way possible, in his bed, in the woods, upon his horse. He wanted to feel her lithe body beneath him, resisting him like a wild mare until her ragged sighs gave him leave to claim her.

"Ye look ragged and dusty," he said, coming up to stand beside her. The fire in her blue eyes flashed. He smiled. "Why d'ye not slip out of those garments and wash up?"

"Is that your best attempt to see me unclothed?" she queried with a sudden—and adorable, to Graham's way of thinking—quirk of her brow. "Really, rogue, you disappoint me. Your skills of seduction are as weak as your friend's fighting arm."

Instantly, Robert sputtered his defense, but Claire's gaze was fixed on Graham's, and on the sun-kissed halo of curls tumbling about his face when he tugged off his cap. He unclasped the plaid at his shoulder. The heavy wool slid down his chest, stopping at the belt above his hips. She watched as he pulled his tunic over his head, exposing a tight, rippled belly and sleek, chiseled chest. She lifted her gaze from the small brown nipples that suddenly made her mouth moisten, and beheld his lecherous dimple as he reached for his belt. He turned his back on her as the wool crumpled at his feet, giving her a splendid view of his backside as he stalked toward the water's edge, kicking off his boots.

Claire blushed three shades of scarlet and spun around, ready to give Campbell her attention and douse the heat searing her blood. It was too late. The Roundhead had stalked to one of the trees surrounding the glade and had already closed his eyes for a nap.

Claire had seen naked men before when she'd meandered into Ravenglade's gatehouse while the men were changing for practice. None of those bodies had affected her. She was there to practice with them, and after she demonstrated her skill and determination by almost severing a few arms, most of the men accepted her in their presence. But this lout undressed for her pleasure, slowly, sensually. He challenged her mocking assessment of his ability to seduce her with a body crafted for war. Even Connor's men, tireless as they'd been in their efforts to win her, had never been so bold.

Hearing the splashing behind her, she refused to look anywhere but at the treetops. The man was daft for bathing in the middle of autumn! It was true then, the men of the north were less affected by the cold. When the Highlander's footsteps behind her alerted her to his exit from the stream, she closed her eyes. Certainly, the scoundrel lacked no confidence in his appearance. How many weak-kneed wenches had he seduced thus? Cocky bastard, she thought, gritting her teeth.

"The water's brisk, but it served its purpose well."

The amusement in his voice raked on Claire's last nerve. She knew the meaning of his crass observation. Connor had often quipped with James about the consequences cold water had for a man's . . . extremities.

"Not well enough, I fear," she replied, with calm detachment she didn't feel. He infuriated her. He set her nerve endings aflame, and she hated him for it. "You did not drown."

Catching the Campbell's faint smile while he rested, Claire suspected it was the first time he'd heard a female utter something other than *take me to your bed* to his companion, and he was enjoying it. If such was the case, she was about to make the young earl shout with joy.

"It is a pity you're a Roundhead." She feigned a despondent sigh when Campbell lifted one lid to look up at her. Curling a stray lock of flaxen hair behind her ear, she stepped closer to where he sat propped against the tree trunk. Both of his eyes were opened now. "I find your humility a refreshing respite from untrained hounds that bark arrogantly at a wolf."

Robert's eyes lit with amusement as he lifted them to his friend dressing somewhere behind her, and then back to her. "Aye, wolves are crafty."

Claire nodded and tilted her head at him, wondering why he used the word crafty, when the nape of her neck went warm from the Highlander's breath above her.

"But does not even the fiercest wolf fall prey to the hunter?"

It could have been his melodious burr, or the husky cadence of his voice grazing her ear, or mayhap it was simply the way he made his query sound like a promise that made her heart accelerate. Pivoting around, she found her nose inches from his damp, clingy tunic. She looked up from his chest, and with a smirk as coolly confident as his own, said, "Not this wolf."

Stepping around him, she sauntered back to the edge of the stream and checked on Troy. The young steed appeared to be faring better than she. She didn't realize her hands were shaking until she lifted them to Troy's bridle. Her breath felt strained, her flesh warm against the cool breeze. Damn him for possessing a smile so shamelessly sinful, Satan himself would slap him on the back with delight. That he cast that smile on her every time she challenged him both infuriated and excited her. Claire loved a good fight, but she had no time for overconfident rogues. It was a pity though that the Highlander wouldn't be around long enough to suffer his defeat. She would have enjoyed humiliating him with rejection. Ha! The lusty fool had no idea who she was, or how many suitors she had refused without so much as a glance in their direction. She had defied her father and even her brother at first, and chose to live in a man's world. She was immune to their charms, impervious to their affections. She cared only for her kin, her country, and restoring Charles to the throne.

Angling her head, she glanced at Graham Grant while he adjusted his plaid over his wet body and spoke quietly with the Campbell. As if sensing her eyes on him, the Highlander looked up and winked at her.

Satan's blasted balls, she thought as her toes curled. She had to get away from him. And fast.

Chapter Six

I am plagued by the flower of Scotland crying, save me!

"Where d'ye think ye're going?" Graham asked, watching as Claire fit her boot into her stirrup.

About to leap up, she paused with her hands on the saddle and cut him a glacial glance. "Where do I *think* I'm going? I'm going to Edinburgh. Alone."

"'Twill be dark in a few hours and there's naught fer leagues but woods. We'll make camp here fer the night and—"

Her laughter cut him off, but when she stepped off the stirrup and strode toward him, her sneer turned murderous. "Do you truly think to order me about, you insufferable lout?"

Graham pushed off the tree he was leaning against just before she reached him. His gaze couldn't help but examine and admire the hellfire in the sway of her hips. She was a saucy wench, aflame with purpose, and seemingly resistant to his attentions. He told himself that he wanted to remain with her to keep the determined lass from getting herself killed. But she made his blood sear hot through his veins like no lass before her. She ran rampant through his thoughts, inciting his curiosity for more. Normally, a chase, such as the one she presented, would have been enough. But he didn't want her to run, and run she would if he cornered her.

"I would not dare to order ye about," he amended softly. "I am giving ye a choice. If ye ride away now, be assured that I will remain hot on yer tail throughout the night." One corner of his mouth lifted slightly, suggesting he meant something far more provocative than following her. "If ye wait until the morn, I will bid ye farewell."

Claire stared at him, searching his expression for the truth. Would they both leave her to her task if she but stayed until the sun rose? Would they truly stay out of her way? She shifted her gaze to the earl, now on his feet, as well. His word, she would be more inclined to believe.

"Do I have your promise on this, Campbell?"

He cast his friend a tentative glance, ground his teeth, and then turned to face her. "I believe it best that we stay together. I hate thinking what would have become of you had we not been with you earlier."

"I believe I've given you no cause to ponder such things," Claire returned steadily, confident in her own abilities.

"I admit you wield a sword even better than my sister," the earl allowed easily. "But I must ask you, what sort of brother does not teach his sister to fear the forest?"

A fair enough question, Claire decided, since he knew naught of her or Connor. This man was a supporter of the Republic, unacquainted with the hazards of living life as an outlaw. She could not judge him too harshly for his ignorance, so her reply was simple. "The kind of brother who taught her how to stay alive in them. Now do I have your word?"

His features grew taut with reluctance to concede, but finally he nodded and strode away.

Claire watched him go. When he reached the edge of the stream, he knelt and dipped his hands into the dappled current. Mayhap, she hoped, washing his hands of her. Sensing another pair of eyes on her, she shifted her gaze to the Highlander.

Saints, he was handsome standing there with his shoulder propped against the tree, his arms folded across his chest, and an irritatingly triumphant smile curling his sensual mouth. She decided that if she were ever to take a man, she quite preferred his companion's quiet humility over the warrior's unabashed arrogance. But when she turned from him, prepared to spend whatever time she had with the less intolerable of the two, her thoughts remained behind her. Why was a Catholic Highlander traveling with a Presbyterian Roundhead? Which one of them was betraying his allegiance? Probably the rogue, she thought, kicking the dirt. The devilment that made his eyes shimmer like polished emerald facets proved his scoundrel's heart. His loyalty and devotion belonged to no one. Mayhap, he was a mercenary, paid by the noble earl to protect him on his journey to Edinburgh. Grant had likely been hired after Campbell's face was pummeled.

"How did you fall to Lambert's men this morn?" The earl's question drew her attention from her thoughts and she looked down to find she'd reached him.

She looked out beyond the stream and into the opposite tree line. "They came upon me while I slept. I killed three of them, but the others came at me from every direction. I managed to take down three more before the rest grabbed me. They took my sword and dragged me to the tree where you found me."

"Truly, I've never known a woman such as you."

Hearing the regret in his compliment, Claire dropped her eyes to him.

"You speak like a warrior," he said.

"And you disapprove?"

He shrugged shoulders encased in an indigo tunic and veiled his gaze beneath long sable lashes. "I believe it is a man's duty to protect a lady."

Claire fought the urge to smile. Such an earnest declaration did not deserve mockery, even though it was clear that he could not protect himself, let alone a lady. The Earl of Argyll possessed ideals born of another age, and as endearing as they might be, they were foolish in the present. "Did you not teach your sister to fight?"

"There was not much else to do." He raised his large eyes and watched her as she knelt to sit beside him. "We were raised by soldiers and servants after our father died. I practiced my skills in the field each day, and Kate just came along at first. Then Amish and John taught her, as well."

Resting her elbows on her bent knees, Claire studied him while he spoke. He was a Roundhead, an enemy of the monarchy. He, like many other nobles of Scotland, had traded his fealty to the king for a title and lands. But sitting here with him amid the serene sounds of rushing water and rustling leaves, she found him quite likable. "You've been practicing since you were a boy and you still cannot fight. Is that why you hired the Highland commander to keep you safe?" Before she could stop herself, she turned and looked at Graham. Rogue. He was lounging beneath the tree as if he hadn't a care in the world, his cap pulled over his eyes while he rested, his long legs sprawled before him.

"Graham?" the earl asked, following her gaze. "It's true he saved my life on more than one occasion, but I can fight well enough with a sword. I just don't think it necessary to kill everyone who comes against me."

Claire turned back to him and gave him a puzzled look. "A contrary belief for someone raised by soldiers. Tell me, then," her gaze hardened, "what you think of the armies who torture those who do not adhere to their generals' ways of thinking?"

"General Monck is a fair man. I know of no—"

"General Monck is even worse than the others," Claire interrupted, with passion's sting in her voice. "They lead men to war. They know nothing of loyalty or governing kingdoms. Should we trust the good of our nation to bloodthirsty men who care not for its people, but only for power?"

"And the Royalist resistance would stop them by killing them all?" Campbell questioned her in return, his tone neutral, his eyes keen yet dispassionate upon her. "Is the man who leads them to war any less bloodthirsty?"

Claire bristled at his unfair judgment of her brother but caught herself before rushing into battle. It was obvious that she was a member of such a resistance, and Claire did not care if Campbell knew it. But that was all she was willing to expose to his watchful gaze. "We refuse to accept that which is forced upon us," she answered coolly. "We have no other option but to fight. Your Highlander should understand that."

"He does."

Claire arched a curious brow at his brief response and stared at him, waiting for more.

"Graham fought at the side of the MacGregors for many years. He remains a loyal friend to them, despite the proscription and its consequences to sympathizers."

Every nobleman south of Aberdeen knew the Grants had allied themselves with the MacGregors for many years now, even claiming them as kin. But Claire was surprised to hear of Graham's steadfast devotion to the outlawed clan. She believed him to be committed to no one. Hell, he had told her with his own words that he was a shameless knave, and stripping naked before her eyes confirmed his claim.

Fighting the urge to look at him again, she wondered what compelled such faithfulness in a self-avowed scoundrel. And more, if he was truly a friend to the MacGregors, what was he doing with a Campbell? "You said your sister was once abducted by the MacGregors. How is it then that you ride with their ally?"

"He is more than just their ally. He is their commander."

Claire raised her brow, impressed.

"Kate is now wed to the MacGregor laird and there is peace between Argyll and their clan."

"Peace is fleeting," Claire scoffed, and bent forward to dip her hand into the stream. She scooped some water into her palm and splashed it across her face. "I heard my brother often tell of the laird of the mist. A great warlord who fought against the laws that would oppress him. He is rumored to have killed Duncan Campbell, the earl before you, and you expect me to believe there is peace now between your kin?"

"The laird of the mist did not kill my uncle."

"How do you know he did not?"

"Because he is my sister's husband, and I was with him and my uncle when they fought."

Claire laughed. "Your brother in marriage is the Devil MacGregor?" When he nodded, she cast him an understanding look. "You did not succeed in rescuing her, then. That must weigh heavily upon you, knight, but I will not suffer the same failure."

"I did not fail my sister." Robert leaned back in the grass, canted his arm behind his head, and closed his eyes. "And if yours is anything like you, Monck and his men are likely the ones suffering right now."

Claire flashed his tranquil features a heated scowl, then poked him in the side with her finger. "Do not speak unkindly of my sister. Anne is nothing like me."

He yawned. "What's she like then?"

"She's quiet and . . ." she paused, searching for the truest word to describe her dear Anne. "Wistful. Demure, and so much more elegant than I. She is secretive, but her emotions play so openly upon her face, it is easy to read her thoughts." Claire smiled and then remembered the man beside her. She looked down and was surprised to find him still awake and staring at her.

"What else?" he asked.

Claire didn't mind speaking of her. In fact, it helped her focus on her quest. She had lost her brother. She would not lose her sister, as well, even if it was to marriage. The thought of it stilled Claire's heart. She would die before she or Anne were wed to a Roundhead. As the king's cousins, she'd always known their future was written on the whims of the monarchy. She didn't want to take a husband and give up the life she'd chosen as a warrior.

But if she had to marry, it would be to someone of King Charles's choosing.

"She has hair like my mother's, arrow-straight and painted in deep shades of vermilion. Her eyes are the color of the sky before a storm, and looking into them is like looking into the eyes of a falcon."

"She sounds very beautiful," the earl said, sounding as if he truly believed she was.

"She is," Claire agreed quietly. "And she is as dutiful as I am rebellious. She will go before the priest, and though her heart silently protests, she will wed whoever General Monck chooses for her."

The earl sat up, his usually pleasant features marked now with consternation. "She is in Edinburgh to be married?"

"Aye, and to a Roundhead. Now you see why I make haste to save her."

He stared out across the water for a moment, his furrowed brow casting a shadow over his eyes and the warring thoughts within. He was quiet, and then ran both hands through his thick brown hair and said, "We will leave for Edinburgh at first light."

"We?"

He cut his gaze to her. "Aye. We. I will—"

"What will you do? You serve Monck," Claire snapped at him, angry that he had broken his word to her. The fool would ruin everything when he alerted all of Edinburgh that he had arrived to save the damsel, Anne. "What will you do when he refuses whatever silly *request* you put to him? Will you defy him? Fight him? Mayhap kill him if your hand is forced? Nae, you will not! So, tell me, knight, how you will be of any aid to either of us?"

"I will bargain with him."

Claire almost laughed right in his face. "And what do you have that he wants?"

"Connor Stuart."

Her face went rigid. When he reached a hand to her, she sprang backward. "Claire," he said, holding up a palm as if to stop her from taking off, which was exactly what she meant to do. "General Monck doesn't know that your brother is dead. I will promise him Connor for Anne."

He knew. The bastard knew she was Connor's sister the entire time. With her hand on the hilt of her dagger, she considered the best way to injure him without rousing his friend. "I should kill you."

"I would prefer it if you didn't."

She looked around. The Highlander hadn't stirred. Her horse was close by. She could strike the earl and be gone in seconds. But first, she would hear why he believed what he said. "Why do you think the general doesn't know my brother is dead?"

The Campbell's gaze dipped to her hand. "Because," he drew in a deep breath and then lifted his eyes to meet her murderous glare, "he sent me to find him."

Chapter Seven

Save me from the kiss of the devil!

Claire's dagger flashed in the filtered sunlight as she came to her feet. "I knew you were not to be trusted." She lifted her hand to strike at him. "Your search ends here."

Broad fingers closed around her wrist, stopping its descent with painful force. With a twist to her arm that nearly sucked the breath out of her, she was spun around and butted up against the hard, taut body of the Highlander behind her. His expression was dark, his gaze inscrutable as he secured her wrist against the small of her back. A harsh yank drew her body closer and her arm up higher along her back. She ground her teeth together in an effort not to cry out.

"Drop it," he warned, with another slight twist to her wrist.

Glaring at him, she opened her fingers and released the dagger.

He snatched her sword from its sheath next and tossed it aside. His eyes never left hers, nor did he relax his hold. She struggled against his steel embrace, but he only slanted his mouth into an infuriating grin and lowered his face to hers.

"There will be nae more of that, lass." The low timbre of his voice brought a strange quiver to her spine. He was at least two heads taller than she. His body encompassed hers, enveloping her in raw strength and heat. Her body went almost limp. He loosened his grip just a bit.

And then he crumpled to his knees, cupping his groin with both hands.

Now on his feet, Robert watched Graham go down with agony twisting his features. When Claire spun around, Robert took a cautious step back and let her run toward her horse, unopposed.

That is, just until her fingers reached for her reins, and then she, too, went down flat on her face. Still on his knees, Graham lunged for her, shackling her ankles an instant before his face hit the grass. With a forceful grunt, he pulled her back, flipped her over, and crawled atop her.

"Ye think his honor is mine," he wheezed heavily, straddling her. He held her hands firmly above her head and let his gaze rake boldly over her panting bosom. "Ye're mistaken. Lift a weapon to either of us again, and that includes yer knee, and I'll bind yer hands, yer feet, and yer—"

Her teeth sank into his arm, changing his threat to a howl. She tasted blood, and then she was hauled upward, her body floating in midair. He set her on her feet with a rattle that disengaged her teeth from his flesh. He looked at his bloody wrist, then at the warning gleam in her eyes, and then he hauled her into his arms.

Claire had been kissed before; a chaste peck given to her by Kenny, the tanner's son, when she was twelve, a stolen kiss from Sir Rupert the knave while she practiced with him, and then set him abed for a sennight. And from James, before he had left for England with Connor. But she'd never been kissed like this before. This mouth was demanding, utterly ravishing. These lips molded and caressed with such masterful skill it sapped the strength from her body. He stroked her deeply with his tongue, and the feel of it was so erotic, so intimate, she shuddered in his embrace.

He withdrew with two shorter, but no less arousing kisses before his eyes settled on hers.

"You leech!" she hissed at him. "If you ever dare—" Her eyes opened wide as he tore the left sleeve of her shirt from the shoulder. The right sleeve followed. Too stunned to speak, Claire watched him tug the sleeves over her balled fists and begin to bind her wrists. She tried to kick him, and he tied her ankles next.

"You son of a bleating goat!" she shrieked at him. "I will see you—"

"Fair warning, wench," he cut her off in a low, deadly voice while he dug his fingers into her shoulders to keep her from falling over. "I will bind yer mouth next with the remainder of yer shirt."

The remainder of her shirt included the part that covered her, and since she didn't doubt his threat, she clamped her lips tight. Her nostrils flared with rage. Her eyes blazed with the promise of retribution.

"Sit."

"Rot in hell."

His hand cupped her nape and he heaved her mouth to his yet again, kissing her senseless. She was vaguely aware of his arm cradling her lower back, and her feet coming off the ground. When he released her, Claire found herself seated on her rump in the grass. Her lips tingled and her head felt light. Standing over her, the High-lander swept her with a warm, yet conquering gaze, then turned his back and strode to his friend.

"We'll need a fire."

"And some food," his companion agreed. "We don't have enough left for three."

"Aye, see what ye can find. I'll get a fire going."

Claire watched the earl leave the glade and then looked around for anything that might aid her in escaping. Her dagger lay a few feet away, her sword even farther off. She glanced up at Troy, chomping at the grass. No help there. Finally, her eyes came to rest on her captor. Loathsome bastard, she cursed inwardly, while he stretched to pluck a thin branch from one of the surrounding trees. As if sens-ing her eyes on him, he looked over his shoulder at her, noted her murderous gaze, and chuckled. Claire bristled but said nothing, lest he force his mouth on her again. The thought of it sent an unwanted fissure of heat down her spine. Good God in Heaven, he knew how to kiss! No doubt he had kissed countless women with the same blistering ardor, sealing their fate—to pine after him like kittens mewling for warm milk.

"I am not a damned kitten," she muttered.

"Did ye say something?" He dropped a handful of twigs into a pile a few feet away and turned to face her.

Against her will, she surveyed the length of him. From his soiled leather boots to the flare of his shoulders, he was a lean, muscular masterpiece.

"I have nothing to say to you, save that I have never hated anyone as I do you."

"Ah, that would explain the fire in yer kiss, then." He shoved his hand into the pouch hanging from his belt and pulled out a small piece of birchbark and a bit of dried peat moss.

"What you felt was my repulsion."

He gave her a doubtful look before returning his attention to getting the fire started. He worked in silence, squatting to chafe the wood and ignite the tinder. Pursing his lips, he gently blew his breath into the wispy tendrils of smoke until the tiny flame grew stronger.

Claire grew mesmerized by the shape of his lips. Oh, but they were carved for pagan pleasures, achingly full and soft . . .

"How did yer brother die?" he asked suddenly, adding twigs and sticks to the burning tinder.

Claire blinked. "Enjoying the fleeting pleasure of my humiliation is not enough for you? Would you know the details of Connor's death so that you can mock him, as well as me?"

His gaze on her softened as he straightened once again to his full height and moved toward her. "I mock neither of ye. I've nae doubt 'twas he who nurtured such fire in ye fer yer cause. Yer skill and yer fortitude reflect well upon him. I wish to know how a man such as he met his end."

Claire looked up at him while he sat at her side, her gaze following the shapely length of his legs as he stretched them out before him and crossed them at the ankles. All that body, she found herself thinking—helpless to stop, all that muscle pulsing against her when he forced his kiss on her.

"He was betrayed," she told him, hoping now that she had told him, he would take himself somewhere else. When she saw that he was not leaving, she heaved a sigh. "What does it matter to you, truly? You hunt him with a

Roundhead. Were you not willing to deliver him to General Monck to be hanged in Edinburgh?"

He didn't answer her, and she nodded, knowing he couldn't, and turned away from him.

"How was he betrayed?"

"A meeting had been agreed upon between my brother and Lambert's cohort, General Fleetwood. But it was a trap."

Graham leaned in a bit nearer to her, touching her bare forearm when she wouldn't look at him. "Claire, yer brother was a radical patriot. Why would he agree to sit with his enemy?"

She shook her head and laughed softly, as if at herself. Then she turned her head to meet his gaze. "Because General Monck asked him to do so."

"Do you think it a good idea to trust her behind those trees?" Robert chewed on a root, grimaced at its bitter taste, and tossed it into the flames.

Sitting across from him, Graham passed his hand over the rest of the roots Robert had gathered and reached for the stale bread instead. "She had to relieve herself."

"And you gave her back her weapons." Robert peered into the shadows looking for her, but it was too dark to see. "If you live through the night, tell my sister I love her."

"She will not kill us, Rob." Graham laughed and popped a berry into his mouth.

"She trusts no one."

"And with good reason." Graham looked at him over the crackling fire. "Yer General Monck betrayed her brother."

Now it was Robert's turn to laugh. "You believe her tale that Monck is considering restoring King Charles to the throne?"

"I believe the general convinced Connor Stuart that he was."

"It makes no sense!" Robert argued. "She tells you Monck and her brother were allies, but if the general was that close to Stuart and he wanted him dead, why did he not just do it himself?"

"I will tell you why." Claire stepped out from beyond the trees and into the light of the fire. "My brother and his supporters fight for independence from English occupation. Their cause is valued highly by many. While the other generals fight over who is to be the next Lord Protector, General Monck bides his time quietly here in Scotland. He will make his move soon, though, when the others are at their weakest. But he will need the support of the people. Killing their champion would only gain him more enemies. So he had Lambert or Fleetwood do it for him."

"I do not believe it." Robert shook his head at her as she sat beside Graham. "The governor does not covet the title of Lord Protector. He cares for Scotland and will not leave it."

"Aye, nor will he lose it to a restored king. He fought hard to gain it, lest you forget." Claire gave him a pointed look over the fire. "He took Stirling in four days. Dundee, in two."

"My uncle told me of the general's victories under Cromwell," Robert acknowledged. "But that was many years ago. Since then, he has sided with the other generals in nothing. He supports Parliament, not the military."

Claire smiled faintly. "He has you duped. Just as he

had Connor and James duped. God only knows what he has told Anne. She does not know of his involvement with Connor's death."

"Who is James?" Graham asked, and then took a swig of water from his pouch.

"A dear friend."

The pouch paused leaving Graham's lips. His eyes flashed at her above the glimmering light. "How dear?"

"Very dear." Claire didn't bother to look at him but kept her attention on Robert. "Monck swore to my—"

"Is he also dead?"

"Is who also dead?" She turned to Graham, a bit exasperated by his interruptions.

"This James, who is verra dear to ye."

Claire narrowed her eyes at him, trying to read his expression. He appeared calm enough, but his voice was tense, his question brusque. "Nae, he is not dead."

"Thank the saints, aye?" he asked, watching her reaction.

"Aye," she said sincerely. "I do, each day."

"Good." Graham smiled and flung his bread into the flames. "I'm pleased to hear it."

After a moment of listening to the crickets around them, Robert directed his next question to his best friend. "Are you done?"

Graham's lethal glare was all the answer Robert was going to get.

"Very well, then," the young earl continued. "Let me ask you this, my lady. Why did Monck send me to find your brother if he knew Connor was dead?"

"Mayhap that is a question you should put to the general when you see him."

"I intend to," Robert assured her, then glanced at the sword in her lap. "We should get some sleep. I will take first watch." He caught the faint grin on Graham's face as his friend settled into his plaid. Let Graham think him a fool for not trusting that she wouldn't slice off their heads in their sleep. She had every reason to want them dead, and she had it in her to do it. He eyed her as she set her head to the ground. He could see clearly why Graham was so attracted to her. She was fair, and self-sufficient. Too self-sufficient for his liking, though. He thought of her sister and how they could be so different. Why was the governor forcing Anne to wed?

"Lady Stuart?" He listened for her drowsy response. "When did the general send Connor to England?"

"Monck did not send him. Connor was already there fighting Lambert's men in Cheshire when Monck sent him word of the meeting. He was killed on his way to London." She shifted uncomfortably, then grew quiet again.

Robert thought the matter over in his mind. Something did not sit right with him. So many things made no logical sense. And then something occurred to him. Something that apparently struck Graham as well, for he sat up, and together they looked at Claire.

Connor had fought with Lambert's men in August. If he had been killed two months ago, then who had attacked General Monck's men outside Stirling a few weeks ago?

Chapter Eight

How shall I escape that which keeps me from my utmost duty?

In the lavender stillness moments before dawn, Graham watched the low firelight flicker over Claire's sleeping face. He took his leisure studying the impudent curve of her nose, the fine lines of her cheekbones, and the alluring slopes of her lips licked by shadows and light. The taste of that plump, parted mouth and the fervor in her resistance clung to his memory and made his blood burn. He'd kissed many lasses, but he never felt as if he'd go mad if he didn't kiss them again. Was it the curve of that arrogant mouth that made him want to conquer her? The spark of resistance when she looked at him that made him hunger for her surrender? He was enjoying the fight, as any experienced warrior would. There was naught more invigorating than a worthy adversary, something he had found little of in his journeys. Aye, Claire Stuart was bonny indeed. The sight of her drove him to distraction, but it was her courage and conviction that sparked a desire for more than a victory with her.

A bit beyond the dying flames, the even rhythm of

Robert's breath ruptured into a snore, shifting Graham's languid thoughts back to those more pressing. Connor Stuart was dead. Or was he? According to those he and Robert had questioned during their search for him, Stuart was not only alive and well but had taken up a vicious campaign against General Monck's men, as well as Lambert's. Who was this James Claire had spoken of? The way her tone turned soft when she admitted her relief that he was not dead had pricked Graham's temper. What was it about this James that she liked so well? He had to be a member of the resistance, for Graham was certain Claire would not give her heart to a man who did not support her cause. Most likely James was a recruit of Connor's, mayhap even a commander if he had spent enough time with Connor to have been "duped" along with him.

A movement caught Graham's attention. His gaze slipped to Claire's fingers closing slowly around the hilt resting on her belly. She lifted her head, looking first at Robert sleeping across from the fire. As her face tilted upward to find Graham, he closed his eyes and remained still.

She moved like a wraith along the violet shadows. Each footfall fell with the stealth and silence of a predatory cat as she moved away from the firelight. She gave a tug to the cap under her belt, then lifted it to her head and stuffed her thick braid beneath it.

Sword in hand, she made her way to her horse. Graham smiled. What was this pleasure she caused in him that led him to pursue her? He would let her run for a little while before catching her. Their agreement, he would be forced to remind her, was that she remain until the morn, and it was not morn just yet.

The sound of a man's laughter from beyond the trees snapped Graham to his feet, careless if she heard him. She did, and to his disbelief and horror, she pointed in the direction from which the sound had erupted, and then charged toward it.

Without pausing to curse her haste, Graham sprang after her. She broke through the trees instants before him and crouched within the tall grass so fast, Graham tumbled right over her. He rolled back to his rump, then leaped at her.

"What the hell d'ye think ye're doing, lass?" Shackling her wrists above her head, he covered her from foot to crown with his body.

"Can you not tell by their direction that their route will take them straight through the camp?" Her reply was a low hiss in the fading darkness. Graham could feel her eyes burning into him. She struggled beneath him and then stopped abruptly when he lifted himself off her shoulders, shifting his weight to his hips.

"And ye thought to save me and Robert by rushing headlong into their path knowing not if there was one man or fifty?"

"I stopped to count, but you crashed into me, you lumbering oaf. Now take yourself off me before I—"

"How many, Claire?"

"What?" She tugged on her wrists.

"How many men are there?" He held her still.

"I did not have a chance—"

"There are twelve." He lowered his face to hers and whispered over her cheek. "And ye would have had nae chance against them."

His warm breath caressed her earlobe and she found she could not protest. She could barely form a thought.

"They are MacGregors, and if they hear us skulking around in the brush, our death will be swift. Will ye remain silent and let me try to prevent that from happening?"

He took her silence to mean aye and raised himself slowly off her. "Angus MacGregor, 'tis Graham Grant," he called out, facing the traveling men, and stood to his feet.

One of the men, a huge figure upon a chestnut behemoth, lifted his hand and halted the approaching troop. "Graham? Is it ye, ye bastard? Step closer so we can see ye." An instant later, he hauled his great sword from its sheath and raised it over his head. "'Tis no' Graham!" he shouted to the others.

"Hold! 'Tis me!" Graham held up his hands to ward them off.

"Graham Grant doesna bed lads by day or by night!" another man to the leader's left called out.

Graham followed the tip of Brodie MacGregor's claymore and turned to see Claire standing beside him. He looked at the cap tilted atop her head, frowned at it, then plucked it off. Her long braid unraveled and swung to her waist, revealing her true sex to the onlookers.

"Aye, 'tis Graham," Brodie announced to all, with a sigh of great relief. "'Tis a lass he tumbles 'neath the moon." He sheathed his blade and grinned openly at Claire.

"I have not been tumbled," Claire corrected and snatched her cap from Graham's fingers. "Save for when he tripped over me."

"How the hell have ye been, Graham?" Ignoring her outburst, Angus dismounted with a heavy grunt. "'Tis been near a pair o' years since we've seen ye at Camlochlin. Does Robert ride wi' ye?"

"Aye, he sleeps in a nearby glade," Graham said,

leaving Claire's side to be hauled into Angus's crushing embrace. "What brings ye so far south?" he asked when his giant friend released him.

"We travel to Edinburgh," Angus told him. "Callum was invited there by the governor, but he refuses to leave Kate or their babe. He sent us to—"

"General Monck sent fer Callum?" Graham's jaw was rigid when he turned to Claire. "Fetch Rob."

"Nae need. I'm here." Robert sprinted forward from the trees. After a brief but friendly reunion with his friends, and assurance that his sister and her son were well, he repeated Graham's query, asking what the MacGregors were doing near Edinburgh.

"Monck has asked to speak with Callum," Graham filled Robert in while Angus slipped his hand into his plaid to retrieve a pouch of brew.

"For what purpose?" Robert asked, looking at Angus at the same time Graham did.

Angus swiped his knuckles across his mouth, then returned the pouch to its hiding place. "The general needed Callum's aid." Before saying anything more, he turned his head left, then right. "Might we get off the road and discuss this? There could be enemies afoot."

Nodding, Graham led the entire troop back to the campsite. After refusing Robert's offer to break fast with the roots he'd collected, Angus and the others sat around the dying embers of the campfire.

Now, with the veil of darkness fully behind them, Claire studied the Highlanders before her. So, these were the Mac-Gregors. Seldom seen after the proscription, save for when a handful of their rebel warriors were butchering English and Scottish nobles alike, their propensity for violence made them a legend to be feared in the Midlands. Claire wasn't afraid of them, though. No, she felt a kinship with the outlawed clansmen. They had fought back when all had been taken from them. Just as Connor had taught her to do. She was sizing up the dark-haired one called Brodie when his cool gaze met hers. He gave her a slight nod, as if recognizing the belligerence in the tilt of her chin.

"Now tell us what Monck wanted with Callum," Graham asked the men.

"Who is Callum?"

Every eye turned to her, and for a moment Claire felt utterly exposed, acutely aware of the attention the men finally gave her.

"Who is the wench, Graham?" Angus's eyes narrowed on her, taking in every inch, including the sword resting at her side. His deep auburn hair hung past shoulders a yard wide. His hard expression was made more dangerous by the long scar marring the left side of his face. Claire fought the temptation to look away from his piercing appraisal.

"She is King Charles's cousin, Claire Stuart."

Claire shot Graham a look of murderous intentions, which he answered by winking at her.

"Och, is she kin to the Lady Anne Stuart?"

Claire blinked and turned to him slowly. "What do you know of my sister?"

"We've come to fetch her," Angus explained. "Callum . . . he is our laird," he added for Claire's clarification, "received a missive from Monck requestin' that he come to Edinburgh to retrieve the lady and bring—"

"He gave my sister to your laird?" Claire bolted to her feet, and for the first time since Graham met her, panic marked her features. She looked around as if not knowing which direction to take when she fled. Then her lips tightened and her hands balled into fists. "I will kill him slowly for this."

"Does she speak o' Callum?" Angus leaned closer to Graham and whispered. "Because if she does—"

"She speaks of Monck," Graham explained, lifting his hand to touch hers. "Claire," he spoke softly, his eyes warming on hers when she looked down at him. "Yer brother did not teach ye to be so rash, aye? We'll find out what this is about, and then ye and I need to speak." She had planned on killing Monck all along. Hell, the wee fool was going to get herself killed.

"I'll tell ye what 'tis aboot if ye can keep the lass from interruptin' me."

Graham nodded at Angus and closed his fingers around Claire's hand. His tender pull brought her back down to sit beside him.

"The governor," Angus finally got on to it, "told Callum that the Stuarts were in his care."

Claire made a huffing sound, and Graham tugged her hand again.

"His missive said that he feared Parliament would soon be dissolved."

"It has been," Robert told him, then motioned for him to continue.

"He believes there is treachery among his allies. And that the lives o' Ladies Anne and Claire might be in jeopardy. He wrote that they were to be wed immediately in his court, to men o' his choosin' as per his agreement wi' their guardian."

"I knew it!" Claire exclaimed, casting back her head at the stars.

Graham slid his gaze to her. So, she was to be married. Oddly, the thought of it did not sit well with him, but he said nothing.

"But," Angus continued, "until he discovers who the traitors are, he will give them to nae one, save the MacGregors."

"Did his missive mention what sort of treachery?" Robert asked him.

"Nae, but he did write that he's awaitin' yer arrival with the lady's brother, Connor Stuart."

"He believes Stuart can be found, then." Robert cut a satisfied glance to Claire, and then to Graham. He knew Monck had no idea of Connor's death. The general had not betrayed him.

"Is he missin'?" Angus retrieved his pouch and took another swig.

"He is dead," Claire told him.

"Then," Brodie said over the cooling embers of the campfire, "Monck has a reason to fear fer the life o' yer sister, and yers as well, I'd imagine."

"Aye," Angus agreed. "Ye'll come back to Skye wi' us, Lady Stuart. Dinna fret aboot yer safety any longer. Ye'll be safe now." He swept a menacing glance to Graham. "Ye have no defiled her, have ye, ye bastard?"

"Your reputation certainly does precede you, rogue," Claire threw at Graham before turning back to Angus. "If Skye is where you'll be returning, I can assure you, you will be returning to it without me or my sister. The danger to our lives comes from the man your chieftain so easily trusts. Callum MacGregor is either a traitor to the king, or he is being lied to as my brother was. I tell you, Monck cannot be trusted!"

The sound of Brodie's blade swooshing out of its sheath turned Graham's attention to him. He gave Brodie a hard look that warned the warrior to back down.

"I've killed men fer callin' Callum a traitor fer less than what she suggests," Brodie replied in a low growl. "I'll warn her once to watch her tongue."

"Aye, ye warned her then. I'm still yer commander. Put away yer sword," Graham demanded just as menacingly. When Brodie obeyed, Graham turned to Claire. "And ye'll not speak so carelessly about The MacGregor. He is not a traitor. If Monck is a threat to him, I vow I will help ye kill him."

"Monck is no threat," Robert said, still convinced. "He wants Anne sent to Skye because no one will think to look for her there, and even if they did, they would have a hard time reaching her. I've been to Camlochlin, my lady. Its stronghold is the land that surrounds it. If Anne is in danger, she should be with the MacGregors."

"'Tis true," Graham told her. "Only a few noblemen from Cromwell's rule know of Camlochlin. 'Tis hidden beyond the cliffs of Elgol."

Claire still wasn't convinced that Anne would be safe anywhere but with James. None of the generals knew about Ravenglade. Though Connor trusted Monck, he hadn't given him the location of his army. Still, her brother had trusted him enough, and it had cost him his life. She would not make the same error.

Getting out of Edinburgh alive and with Anne was going to be difficult enough. How the hell was she going to rescue her sister from these brutes? She looked down at her hand, still coiled within Graham Grant's. Those fingers closing around hers had near shaken her to her core. She was used to the feel of a hilt in her hand, not the warm, calloused strength of a man's fingers. She didn't like how his touch affected her. It made her feel defenseless. She could handle herself on a battlefield, but a mere smile from this man made her limbs go weak. She couldn't think with him holding her so intimately. But she had to, for Anne's sake.

She smiled as a way of delivering her sister out of the hands of the MacGregors hatched in her mind. She did not have to trust them. She simply had to make them trust her. And the best place to begin was with their commander. She would give him what he wanted. What he had wanted since he'd come upon her in the hands of Lambert's men; time to try to seduce her. She simply had to stay focused on her task, ignoring what he did to her insides.

"Let us travel to Edinburgh together, then," Claire offered, lifting a veiled gaze to Graham's. Her plans had changed, and she made the adjustment as needed. Grant was a man, and growing up around men who tried to deny her every wish had taught her how to get what she wanted using tactics other than force. "I will do as you say until we discover where the true treachery lies."

A hint of amusement crossed his features at her unexpected compliance. He rubbed the pad of his thumb over her knuckles, sending a sizzling lick of flame to her belly. "Ye have naught to fear from these men. Once ye return to Skye with them, ye'll be convinced." He turned to two of the men sitting near Angus. "Andrew, Donel, ye'll leave with the lady now. The rest of us will continue to the city and get Anne."

Claire yanked her hand free of his. What had just happened? He'd been eager to follow her since they'd met, but now that she agreed to spend days with him, he was casting her off? He was daft if he thought . . . "I'm not going anywhere without my sister."

His eyes met the stark, raw determination in hers and she blinked as his gaze seemed to penetrate her garments, her flesh, her very thoughts. Her eyes darted to Andrew and Donel rising to their feet, readying to leave and take her with them. God's fury, a fight with these men could possibly injure her, leave her helpless to save Anne. She remembered the first time James had refused to let her join an ambush on a group of English soldiers. He'd even fought with Connor about it, but in the end she was victorious. A simple kiss and a few softly spoken words to stroke his male pride was all it had cost her. Biting back a scathing oath, because she had a feeling Graham might cost her more, she placed her palm on his thigh. "I would prefer to remain with you. I feel . . . safer."

The wry curve of his mouth made her doubt her own words.

"Hell, that had to be difficult."

Not as difficult as it is maintaining the control not to punch you in the nose right now, Claire thought. "On the contrary," she said, softening her voice to a rich murmur and moving an inch closer to him. "Is it difficult to concede to a man who is clearly stronger, quicker, and more intelligent than I?" His eyes narrowed, but och, she could tell by the elusive spark of satisfaction in them that this was what he wanted to hear. "I have no other choice but to place myself entirely in your hands." His green eyes grew dark with intensity. She had the rogue. "But *only* in yours," she added to clinch his agreement.

His sensual lips pursed, contemplating her newly

docile demeanor. Then he shrugged as if he didn't care what purpose lay behind it. "Verra well, in my hands ye shall be."

She had prevailed. Victory was once again hers. Why then did she feel as if she'd just stepped into the devil's lair?

Chapter Nine

By means of deception, I myself have been deceived.

Two hours into her journey toward Edinburgh, Claire Stuart realized that trying to think about anyone or anything other than Graham Grant was useless.

He kept his mount at an even pace just ahead and to the right of her, granting her full view of the flare of his back, the billowy spray of burnished locks flowing from beneath his cap, glimpses of a lean, gold-dusted thigh pressed against his horse. Hell, it was all making her daft.

Of course, Anne remained a constant concern, but there was naught she could do for her sister at present. At least the general had decided to wait before he married Anne off to a Roundhead. But what if he planned on giving her to a MacGregor? Claire looked at the men surrounding her and felt a cold tremor pass though her. Her sister would never survive a night with one of these hard mountain men. Claire had to find a way to get to Perth after Anne was freed from Monck. There, she could take up arms with James and the men of Ravenglade's garrison and rid herself of her unwanted companions once and for all. She simply needed to figure out a way to get them there.

She tried to concentrate on Connor, and the way he used to sound when he laughed with James. She thought of his voice and remembered the pitch and depth of it while he tirelessly taught her how to fight. He was thoughtful and trustworthy, and always optimistic. He'd trusted General Monck and agreed to a meeting of truce with Charles Fleetwood. Aye, there was a way to kill a warrior without engaging in battle with him. It was betrayal, and it was cowardly. And worse, it robbed the warrior of his glory in death.

She would find a way to kill her brother's betrayer. Of that, the saints in heaven could be sure. But for now, naught could be done. Naught but keeping her senses alert to danger while they traveled, and her eyes off a certain golden-haired Highland warrior. The trouble was, Graham Grant was excruciatingly handsome and insufferably vain. She was certain he was fully aware of the devastating power in even his most casual smile, which he felt compelled to aim at her several times during their journey.

What in blazes was wrong with her? He was simply a man! A rogue used to women swooning at his feet. *Enough!* she chastised herself, slapping her thigh. She would not spare him another thought, save to relish the idea of what a blow it was going to be to him when he finally realized she was immune to his wiles. She did not like him, and she would never . . .

"D'ye need to stop fer a rest?"

. . . lie with him.

His honeyed burr drew her eyes to him. He'd slowed his mount and was keeping an even pace with hers. His gaze lingered leisurely on her lips, then rose to meet her eyes without a trace of guilt over his blatant perusal.

"Ye look weary and uncomfortable in yer saddle," he

said, after a moment passed with no response from her but a heated glare.

So far he'd told her she looked ragged and dusty and weary. How often did he intend to insult her? "The longer I know you," she said in a voice she reserved for her most scathing sarcasm, "the more convinced I am that your mouth is not the deadliest weapon in your arsenal against women."

He shrugged his powerful shoulders, a lazy ripple of muscle. "There are many lasses who would disagree with that assessment."

Damn him to Hades, but he was probably correct. Every blasted time she looked at him she remembered the way he'd kissed her, so rough and so . . . acutely arousing. Such an uninvited kiss should have enraged her, but instead she had near melted all over him.

"Yer mouth, on the other hand," he said with an irrepressible smile, "is deadly, indeed."

Claire felt her cheeks burn and looked away so that he wouldn't see. This effect he had on her was completely foreign and entirely unwelcome. Few men had ever praised her for the skill of her arm; none, for the power of her kiss. She had no idea how to respond, save to blush to her roots and warn him to never dare kiss her again.

"Yer tongue," he continued mercilessly, "is as swift as a viper's, and as cunning as one."

Her face grew even hotter. The lout wasn't speaking of her kiss at all, but of her . . . "Cunning?" She tossed him an anxious glance. "I've no idea what you—"

"Ye're proficient at deception, Claire Stuart." His eyes sparkled watching her, as if enjoying the unease he provoked in her. "Did ye think a man as *quick and intelligent* as I could be so easily fooled?"

Her lips tightened into a rigid line at hearing her words thrown back at her. "Bastard."

He wrapped his fingers around his reins and steered his horse closer, until his knee rubbed against hers. Leaning in, he closed the distance between them further, his breath mingling with hers when he said, "If I was truly a bastard, I would have made ye prove yer promise to do as I say by demanding another kiss from ye before agreeing to let ye ride with us."

Claire did not draw back, though part of her warned that she should. No matter the danger he presented to her sound mind, she would not show him his effect on her. "And would I have swooned at your forceful seduction?"

"Aye, I think ye would have if ye thought it would aid yer purpose." He lifted his fingers to the curve of her jaw. His touch was tender, delicate, his thoughts intent on examining every inch of her face. He withdrew, leaving her with the lingering warmth of his breath upon her flesh. " 'Tis a resolve I find quite commendable."

Dear God, that was a charming thing to say. Och, but he was infinitely more dangerous than she had thought. What perfect cunning to seduce her with compliments, not on her appearance, but with the kind only one other man had thought her worthy to receive.

She watched him ride away from her, feeling as if he were taking her common sense with him. God help her, she wanted to kiss him again.

Graham called a halt several hours later. He sat with Robert while he ate and laughed with Angus and Brodie, but his eyes often found Claire's during their meal.

"Why is Jamie not with ye?" he asked Angus, and

refused the pouch the burly Highlander offered him. "I would know if my brother fares well."

Brodie snorted and shoved a piece of stale black bread into his mouth. "Maggie conspires wi' Kate to turn him into a pansy."

Robert laughed, and Brodie's scowl deepened. "His sister," he complained to Graham, "keeps the reins tight around Callum's heart, and she need but ask the laird to prohibit Jamie from comin', fer Maggie's sake, and 'tis done."

Graham looked as disturbed as Brodie when he shook his head. "'Tis what marriage does to a man."

"I'm sure there are women in Skye who have surrendered their dignity to their husbands." Claire met Graham's pointed look with an insolent arch in her brow.

"I am corrected then," Graham acknowledged. "'Tis what marriage does to everyone."

Oddly, Claire found no satisfaction in his concession. She did not care if she ever wed. Swelling with child and spending her days keeping a home tidy were not things she hoped to accomplish someday. But for some reason, the discovery of Graham's aversion to holy wedlock displeased her.

"Mayhap not everyone," she countered before she could stop herself. "My sister believes that love can make a marriage bearable, though she has no way of knowing if it's true."

"Mayhap 'tis true" Graham allowed. "My brother believes he has found love. I'm certain Callum does also, and they seem happy enough."

Beside him, Robert gave Graham a stunned look. Graham chose to ignore him. "Some are born to love, while others are not." He shrugged, dismissing the conversation.

"All are born to love," Robert argued. "It is the master design."

Graham laughed, making Claire's belly flip.

"What are the others born to do?" she asked, fully expecting him to reply with a crude comment about bedding wenches.

He looked at her, his mirth fading into a slightly menacing smile. "They are born to set things aright. With this." He set his fingers to the hilt at his side and watched her while she nodded. His cheerful grin returned an instant later when Angus agreed with a hearty belch, then raised his pouch to toast comrades old and new who found their death on the battlefield.

Claire studied Graham in the fading light of the day. When the men built a fire, she grew mesmerized by the way the shimmering light danced over the finely carved angle of his gold dusted jaw, his nimbus of angelic curls. She watched his mouth as he spoke, drawn to its tantalizing curves and achingly sensual movements. He smiled at something Robert said and Claire drew her bottom lip between her teeth. For the love of God, he possessed a glorious smile. She imagined him in battle with the promise of death hardening his features, his sleek muscles pulsing with strength and purpose. She looked away quickly when he lifted his emerald gaze over the flames and found her. Her shoulders grew tense when he rose to his feet a moment later and came to sit beside her.

"We will reach Edinburgh on the morrow. Ye will not try to run again while I pretend to sleep, will ye, Claire?"

The hopeful crook of his mouth made her smile against

her better judgment. "You do not care how obvious you are, do you? Why, any moment now I expect you to beg."

"Fer what?" His gaze on her was warm and teasing, yet intense.

She knew exactly for what. He stared at her mouth as often as she stared at his. She was surprised that he might want to kiss her again, since her reaction to him the first time had been so cold. But mayhap this could give her the advantage over him that she needed. She had judged him too quickly. He was not simply a foolish scoundrel with no other thought in his head but which woman to bed next, he was a commander, a leader on the battlefield. By his own words, he'd admitted to being born to battle. She understood him, for she was born for the same purpose, and she would do whatever it took to win. She looked out over the flames at the others conversing among themselves. Drawing her knees to her chest, she finally turned to him. "For a kiss, mayhap?"

He puckered his mouth and narrowed his gaze on her, as if considering it, then he shook his head. "Nae, when I kiss ye again, ye will be willing."

Now it was Claire's turn to laugh. What a pompous knave he was. Well, she had just as much confidence as he. She was no muddleheaded maiden ready to fall at his boots, and it was high time he understood it.

"There are many things I would do willingly for my king and kin. Kissing you is not among them."

He pouted, giving her an instant to doubt her declaration. "'Tis a pity. Ye could use the practice—fer James, mayhap."

She would have found his suggestion about James a curious one if she didn't want to wrap her fingers around his throat and squeeze the life out him for insulting her yet again. "Lord Buchanan made no complaint when last he kissed me," she retorted haughtily, noting with immense satisfaction the fading arrogance in his expression.

"Ah, he's a gentleman then," he said with a bit of an edge in his voice, then stood up and bade her good eve.

By the time Claire had absorbed the full meaning of his words, he was halfway across the small campsite, heading for Robert. Still, she was tempted to fling her dagger at his back.

"James Buchanan."

"What?" Robert looked up when Graham reached him.

"Her James. Have ye heard the name before?"

Shaking his head, Robert studied his friend's brooding countenance, then looked across the fire at Claire. *Her* James? "What has she told you of him?"

"Only his name."

Robert eyed him warily, then smiled. "And his name alone is enough to cause you to look like you're ready to remove some heads? Be vigilant, Graham, or you might find your claymore traded for a sprig of heather clutched in your fist."

Graham stared down at him with a warning glint in his eyes that said Robert's head might be the first to roll. Then without another word, he turned on his heel and stalked over to a nearby tree, sat beneath it, and closed his eyes.

Chapter Ten

Forgive me, for I cannot save her.

Just beyond the outskirts of Edinburgh early the next day, Graham called a halt to those riding behind him. All obeyed the commander and prepared to listen as he pranced his snorting mount around. His gaze fell first on Claire, then passed over the rest. "Robert, ye are expected by Monck. Angus, ye were invited. Ye'll enter the city together. If there are dangers within, I want nae one alone." Without waiting for acknowledgment from either man, his eyes turned to Claire. "Fer now, ye present the greatest danger to us all. If ye attempt to harm the general in any way, we will be forced to fight an army, and we are not enough men." His voice was unyielding and decisive, despite his disarming burr. It didn't matter how he knew of her plans to kill Monck, the fact was he knew of them, and he was going to stop her.

Gritting her teeth, Claire gave her reins a firm yank. She was intercepted almost instantly by his horse's shoulders and teeth chomping at the bridle, and then by an even firmer hold on her bare upper arm.

"If Monck is guilty of betraying yer brother and causing

his death, he is yers and I will stop anyone who hinders ye in yer quest to see him dead."

"Graham," Robert interrupted now. "If Monck is murdered, the army will go to war with Scotland."

"Ye have no faith in yer man, then, Rob?" Graham asked him without releasing Claire's arm. "If he's innocent nae harm shall come to him. But let us know with certainty which course we follow before we disagree upon it." He turned to Claire again, his gaze a bit less obstinate. "I will stand by what I promised. And in the meanwhile, ye will do as I say, as ye have promised."

She had no choice but to trust him. She hated that he'd turned her own game on her, but she had to admit it was a wise tactic. She had vowed to obey him until they discovered the truth. She would keep her word.

When Robert and the others broke ranks and veered left toward the city a few moments later, she regretted her easy concession. She turned to Graham as an instant of sheer panic engulfed her. She did not know these men, or if they would be able to save her sister should this be another trap. "If there is danger, we should be with them! Robert cannot even fight!" Somewhere among the men, Brodie snickered. "And these others could be struck down!"

Robert cut a path between her and the now-offended MacGregors, all moving in to shout their disapproval of her words. "Lady Stuart," he said, not caring anymore if she believed he couldn't fight. His strength at arms was not what made him a man. "I will bring your sister back to you. Whatever happens once we arrive, you will see her again. On this, you have my pledge."

Claire believed that he meant it, this knight who sought

to surpass the noble Sir Galahad where honor was concerned. She just wasn't sure if he could carry out his vow.

She felt someone tug on her reins and saw that it was Graham when he pulled her horse back and stationed his in front of her.

"Off with ye, now." The threat in his command was unmistakable, and Claire realized why when she looked at the other Highlanders still grumbling at her.

When they finally rode away, and she was alone with Graham, she glared at his back. "Why can't you keep your eye on me in the castle? Why must we wait here?"

"Because I do not trust ye so close to the man ye want dead." He wheeled his mount around and passed her, bending close to her as he went. "And I don't trust myself if I have to chase ye down in the castle."

She bit down on her tongue to halt the tremor he caused along her spine at the thought of what he didn't trust himself not to do. What was this effect his virility had on her senses? What power did he possess to make her forget every blasted thing but the promise of complete seduction in his sultry green gaze? His rank among his men pleased her, for she could never envision herself with a man stationed any lower than commander. Dear God, she was mad for entertaining such thoughts of him! And madder still because she was so tempted to discover if she could match him on this kind of battlefield.

"What makes you so certain you could catch me?" she challenged him while he dismounted and began rummaging through his saddlebag.

"I'm not." He barely turned to answer her. "And that is what makes ye so satisfying to pursue." Finding what he was looking for, he sank his teeth into a bruised apple, and then tossed it to her. "Ye're a strong, stubborn wench, Claire Stuart. But ye should know now," he added, letting his potent gaze drift over her features. "I plan on having ye."

Despite the silky lilt in his warning that stilled her breath and set her nerves aflame, Claire smiled at him almost pityingly. "I promise you, it may cost more than a rogue is willing to part with."

Built upon the throne of an ancient volcanic crag, Edinburgh Castle dominated the skyline from miles away. Robert had visited the capital twice before, when his uncle was hanged for the murder of Liam Campbell, Robert's grandfather, and then again when Robert was named eleventh Earl of Argyll. When he'd first come here, Robert believed the marvelous fortress a symbol of Scotland herself, strong, ancient, impregnable. Strange how he saw things differently now. For the English had invaded both. Gazing at the grand military structure protected by sheer cliffs to the south, west, and north, Robert wondered just how clever the military was to have secured either.

The only accessible route to the fortress was from the east, along a herringbone pattern of long sloping streets, which he traveled now with Angus and the others close behind him.

They remained alert and cautious as they passed large squares where the people gathered in markets, and around the law courts. Robert still refused to believe the governor had had Connor Stuart killed and then planned on killing the Earl of Argyll by getting him to Edinburgh on the pretext of hunting a man the general knew was dead. Monck had no reason to wish Robert dead, and if he did, he had had two prior opportunities to kill him.

"The traitors must be within," Angus grumbled, pushing his weary horse up the long trek. "The garrison can see an enemy approachin' fer bloody leagues."

Robert looked up at the high battlements surrounding the Crown Square and David's Tower. He squinted at the hundreds of tiny figures on patrol. Were he and the others in the range of archers? His heart quickened in his chest; then he swore an oath at his cowardice and trotted on.

They reached the outer gate without getting shot and continued beyond the garrison to the mammoth portcullis, where they were welcomed by fifty guardsmen stationed around Monck's steward, Edward. Clearly every moment of their approach had been observed.

As Robert's group slowed to a halt, Edward turned to the Highlanders, eyeing their slightly tattered plaids with a somewhat distasteful look. "You must be the MacGregors."

Brodie growled at him in response, and the steward took two steps back and cleared his throat. "Lord Campbell." Edward bowed low, knowing the young earl from his previous visits. "The governor has been expecting you."

To come alone? Or with Connor Stuart in my custody? Robert wanted to ask him.

"I hear some o' the finest whisky can be found here in Edinburgh," Angus said, looking around and scratching his belly. "Might we sample a bit o' yer brew?"

"Of course, I will have some brought to each of your chambers if you will just follow—"

"We'll follow ye to the great hall and naewhere else," Brodie cut him off sharply. "We'll no' be separated."

After a bob of his head and a quick glance at Robert,

the steward snapped an order to one of the guards. "Clear the great hall." He turned back to his guests and swept his arm across his waist. "This way." He led them over a broad cobbled road and then up a steep stone stairway and around a small chapel before they came to the Crown Square. Finally, they were led into the cavernous great hall, once used for meetings of the Parliament. Now the hall was empty save for a massive oak table at its center, wreathed by forty ornately carved chairs. Enormous tapestries lined the walls, and a massive hearth alcoved the north wall, adding warmth and soft light to the hall.

"Please, have a seat, my lords," the steward offered, his voice echoing off the high hammer-beamed ceiling. "I will inform the governor that you await him, and then see to your drinks."

"Good man." Angus gave him a hearty pat on the back, nearly catapulting the steward into the hearth.

"He'd line up the members o' Parliament and kiss every one o' their bloody arses fer a drink," Brodie complained to Robert when they were alone and the others had taken their seats around the table.

His burly cousin cast him a wounded look before he joined them. "We are here on goodwill," he said as he sat. "I was tryin' to be gracious to the poor sot. He looked frightened when he saw us, and I—"

"He should be frightened," Brodie said sourly. "If there's treachery here, they should all know well what they're comin' up against."

"Monck has no reason to come against the Mac-Gregors," Robert asserted. "He isn't that foolish."

"The law has always been against us," Brodie reminded him. "Mayhap he wants to show the other generals his strength and cunnin' by killin' outlaws far more deadly than Connor Stuart." Hearing him, the rest of the Mac-Gregors began whispering among themselves.

"Nae," Robert insisted quietly. He had to stay their growing concern, or Claire would not be the only threat to General Monck's safety. "Parliament accepted my pardon of your kin's crimes when I became earl. The Mac-Gregors have been left alone."

"We're still proscribed," Brodie sneered. "Our heads are still worth much, and there is nae more Parliament. Mayhap, Claire Stuart is correct in her thinkin' and the governor is no' to be trusted."

Robert stared at him across the table. "Callum would not have sent any of you if he believed that."

"Callum doesna know what became o' Connor Stuart."

"Nor do I." A voice at the entrance pulled their attention there. The man standing in the doorframe was tall, a full two heads taller than the woman beside him, her arm loosely coiled around the crook of his elbow. His eyes, slightly darker than his curly, shoulder-length hair, were a piercing shade of gray, like twin blades forged from the finest steel. He set them on Brodie first, and then on Robert.

"You have found Claire Stuart then?"

The woman with him lifted her face to the men. Her creamy complexion was slightly flushed. Her storm-colored eyes were wide and as fathomless as the sea as she settled them on Robert.

Robert came slowly to his feet, though later, he did not remember moving, nor even breathing looking at her. It was Anne, for Claire had described her to perfection. She wore a flowing gown of pale coral, adding to the delicacy of her appearance. A thin circlet of beaten bronze wreathed her brow. Beneath it, a gossamer veil of white draped her long, loose-flowing hair, like a mist over a summer sunset. Her beauty was timeless, and he felt transported into another age when Scotland was young and maidens were fair and gentle beings who loved men for their honor.

Unable to take his gaze from her, he bowed before her. "I . . . ehm . . . I am Lord Robert Campbell." He did not let himself forget his name, for he wanted her to know it. To come to know him.

"Have you found my sister, Lord Robert Campbell?" Her voice fell sweetly upon his ears. Her eyes did not blink while she waited for his reply.

"Aye, I've found her." He was glad to tell her. But there was more, and for this he looked away and addressed the governor of Scotland as he led her into the hall. "But I have not found her brother. I fear he has perished in England."

"Alas, we feared as much." Monck rested his hand on Anne's shoulder when she dipped her head to hide her tears.

Robert's gaze hardened on the general as he took a step toward him. "Then . . . you knew?"

"He disappeared some months ago," Monck said, offering Anne her seat. "Why do you think I sent you to find him and made haste bringing his sister here where I thought it safe?"

"I didn't know why," Robert answered truthfully.

"Now you do." The general pulled out his chair and waited until Robert had returned to his own before he sat. "We have prepared for the worst news, but we did not expect you to bring it. My representatives are already in

London engaged in other business. I have advised them to look into Stuart's disappearance. I've dispatched three dozen others to search for Lady Stuart, but she is much like her brother. When she does not want to be found—"

"They are twins," Anne said, turning to Robert.

"That explains much." He smiled at the glistening warmth in her eyes when she spoke of her brother and sister.

"Is she well?"

"Aye, my lady. She waits anxiously to see you again." He was rewarded with the faintest trace of a smile hovering about her mouth. When his gaze lingered on her, she looked away, veiling her eyes beneath a lush spray of russet lashes. He could smell her. Like the heather moors in the stillness of dawn, her scent washed over his senses, leaving him helpless to say or do anything but look at her. His gaze dipped to her lips, full and wide above a deeply cleft chin.

"How did you find her?" the general asked, hauling Robert's attention to him once again.

"Quite by chance," Robert answered. "We came upon her just before two of General Lambert's men were about to . . ."

Monck bolted upright in his chair. His gray eyes sparked like lightning across a charcoal sky. "Lambert's men are here in Scotland?" When Robert nodded, the general leaned back and rubbed his jaw, coming to some conclusion that drew his hand into a fist.

"And where is Lady Stuart now?" he asked, fixing his gaze on Robert.

"She's safe," Brodie informed him, shooting Robert a warning look to mind his mouth.

"I would see her."

"There's nae need," Angus said, looking around for a server with their drinks. "If ye changed yer mind aboot trustin' us with her safety, then we'll leave now, withoot either o' them."

Monck sized up the beefy, auburn-haired Highlander with a penetrating, somewhat surprised look. "You are the one they call the Devil?"

"Nae," Brodie answered again, "our laird had other matters to attend. We are here in his stead."

When the general looked about to protest, Robert interjected. "My lord, I can vouch that these men are every bit as lethal as their chieftain. The sisters will be well protected with them until they reach Skye. I will escort them also, along with The MacGregor's first in command, who waits with Lady Stuart while we speak."

The general turned to Anne, then drew in a long breath before he returned his steady gaze to the others. "Your caution, even with me, is wise, though unnecessary."

"That remains to be established," Brodie murmured as two servers entered the hall with their refreshments.

Monck's eyes drifted slowly back to the lethal-looking Highlander. Though his spine went stiff in his chair, his voice remained calm. "A legion of my own men were attacked outside Stirling; two were killed. Lambert and Fleetwood, who I might remind you all now practically rule the country, have made open accusations that I stand with the Royalists."

"Do you?" Robert asked him after the drinks were served and the servers left.

"I stand alone, Argyll."

"But it is true then, you were allied with Stuart?" Saying it gave Robert a sense of disquiet. So far, Claire had spoken the truth.

Monck lifted his flagon to his lips and sipped slowly, looking into its claret depths while he spoke. "He had my respect, and I his. That is all any of you need to know."

"I need more than that," Robert said, the determination to see that he got it burning in his eyes as he leaned over the table.

"Very well then. I will tell you only this, young man. Peace is more grievous to men in subjection, than war is to those who enjoy their liberties."*

Robert nodded, and a ghost of a smile curved his lips. He understood, but there was one more thing he had to ask. "Is there any reason one might believe that you had something to do with Connor Stuart's demise?"

Immediately, Anne's face paled, and Robert was sorry to be discussing this in front of her.

"Absolutely not!" Anger passed over the general's features, leaving them taut and hard. "Connor was my friend." He turned to Anne and took her hand in his. "I will discover what happened to your brother, my dear, and justice will be done."

While the general's face was difficult to read, Anne's was not. She wanted to believe him. She had no reason not to. She had no idea what her sister suspected. Claire had to be wrong. Robert just could not accept that the governor had had anything to do with Connor's death. But he could not be absolutely certain, and for that reason, he found himself eager and impatient to protect her from whoever might do her harm. Delicate and quiet, she was nothing like her sister. He looked at her hand, alabaster smooth and elegant. This one had never wielded a sword. Her gaze was not bold, but rather shy and modest. Yet, there was strength in her, as well. She had controlled her sorrow and faced what her heart did not want to accept—her brother's death. She did not recoil at the sight of twelve of the most feared Highlanders in Scotland, with whom she would soon be traveling, but sat among them unfazed. That is, until Angus, who had given only half his attention to the conversation from the moment the drinks were served, and the other half to the large cup clutched in his fingers, looked up.

"Ye said yer own men were attacked outside Stirling. This occurred after Stuart's death, nae?" When Monck nodded, Angus shrugged his massive shoulders. "It sounds to me like whoever attacked yer men had somethin' more personal against ye than the possibility of ye bein' a Royalist. As Campbell said, there might be more than one who believe ye responsible fer Stuart's death. Some of his followers, mayhap."

Only because Robert was giving Anne his rapt attention did he notice the sudden flare of panic in her eyes. Every muscle in her body went tight, and she looked around the hall as if on the verge of fleeing.

She knew something. Why did she remain silent, Robert wondered, eyeing her? Was she protecting someone? A man, mayhap? Suddenly he understood Graham's sour mood when Claire spoke of . . . "James Buchanan."

Robert didn't realize he had spoken the name aloud until Monck and Anne turned to him in unison. "What about him?" It was the general who spoke.

"How well do you know him, General?"

"Well enough for him to trust that I had naught to do with Connor's death. He—" the governor paused suddenly, then said, "Is James dead, as well? I have neither seen nor heard from him in quite some time."

"Lady Stuart told us that Buchanan lives," Robert said and did not miss the gentle squeeze Monck gave to Anne's hand.

"That is pleasing news. Lord Buchanan is a good man," the general said, then turned to Angus. "This is not about revenge. Buchanan would never attack my men. My enemies and Stuart's are the same. Does Claire know where to find Buchanan?" Monck asked Robert next.

"I presume she does," Robert said.

"Good. I would have you deliver a message to him. Tell him I wish to see him and hear what happened to Connor from his own lips."

"Of course," Robert agreed. "But if I might ask, why have you not sent him a missive to question him sooner?"

"Because I do not know where the rebel army resides. And even if I did, I would not send a written missive to a known Royalist rebel. It is safer that way for all involved. That is why I must call on your service yet again. I need someone who is trustworthy. Will you aid me in this and deliver the message?"

Robert squared his shoulders. "Consider it done."

The general nodded, then sighed, as if with great relief. Though his eyes remained somber, he smiled at the young earl. "Connor made it his duty to learn all about the lords of the realm. In the event of his demise, he wanted his sisters married to trustworthy men. He learned much about you." He continued despite Robert's look of disbelief. "He learned that you have remained unsoiled by the politics of the land. And that you are a man set apart from your grandfather and your uncle. He told me you have proven yourself to be fair and unprejudiced, and that those whom he questioned regarding you all agreed that you hold honor and integrity above all else."

"That he does," Angus agreed with a muffled belch.

"That is why I chose you to find him," General Monck went on. "And why he asked that when I chose husbands for his sisters, it would be you whom Lady Claire Stuart weds—when this matter is settled, of course."

Robert remained utterly still in his seat. Somewhere beyond his range of awareness, he heard Brodie snicker and swear an oath not fit for Lady Anne's ears. He heard the general continue mercilessly about fate, and how God in His great wisdom had brought Claire to Robert when no one else could find her. He felt his gaze shift to Anne. Her eyes grew large and tender on him, her lips spread into a kind smile, almost sympathetic. Would she pat his hand next and try to assure him that he would not be miserable married to her warrior sister?

"Nae!" Robert sprang from his chair.

"Pardon?" Monck looked up at him, puzzlement marring his dark brow.

"Lady Stuart is not—" Robert's eyes fell to Anne. Her displeasure at his harsh refusal was clearly visible in her unshielded expression. He was about to cause her great insult, and it sickened him. "She is violently opposed to Roundheads, my lord. She will refuse me, and I—"

"You will win her heart, I've no doubt," Monck finished for him firmly but gently. "Lady Stuart needs a husband who is patient and open-minded. You once told me that you taught your sister to fight, so you are familiar with women who choose to wield a blade, rather than a broom. You can teach Claire that though you value her sword, it is not needed."

"Save to use it on me," Robert muttered, more to himself than to Monck.

The general laughed. "I know she is headstrong. Her father complained of it many times. That is why she needs a man who can guide her with a firm yet fair hand."

No. Robert raked his hand through his hair. He did not want to wed a woman he had to tame, and who would hate him every day of her life for trying to do so. And damnation, but he swore Graham had taken a fancy to her. How the hell was he going to explain to his best friend that he needn't trouble his thoughts with James Buchanan any longer because Claire was his? God help him, he didn't want her. "My lord, I fear that man is not me."

"Does my sister displease you?"

He blinked at Anne's furrowed brow; flicked his gaze to the dour tilt of her lips. Damnation, how was he to answer that?

"Nae, my lady, I displease her."

Her mouth, as well as her voice, went soft on him. Her eyes grazed his face, his shoulders, and the rest of him standing before her until she looked away, a slight blush coloring her cheeks. "Whatever would she find displeasing about you, my lord?"

Before Robert had a chance to reply, though he was quite certain the only words that would have left his mouth were words of devotion to *her*, General Monck rose from his chair. "I will put my decisions to Parliament once it has been restored, and it will be, and I know you will all be safe." He stepped around the table and laid his hand on Robert's shoulder. "You do this for Scotland, Lord Campbell. Trust me, if not in anything else, then in this; it is for her good, as well as the kingdom's, that you wed her."

Robert couldn't bring himself to answer, or to ask what the governor's words meant. There was only one thing he wanted to know at the moment. Monck had said he would put his decisions to Parliament. More than one. What else would he put to them?

With a heaviness in his heart he hadn't felt since he discovered that his grandfather was a torturous madman, he set his reluctant gaze on Monck's. "And Lady Anne? Who is to be her husband?"

Turning to her, the general reached for her hand. "Why, this fair gem will only be given to Connor's first in command and most loyal friend, of course."

Robert ground his teeth, and for the first time in his life, he felt like killing someone.

James Buchanan.

*Portions of this passage are taken from *Observations upon Military & Political Affairs,* written by General George Monck, 1644–46. Published 1671.

Chapter Eleven

Just as I could not save you.

As night began to fall, Claire rubbed the chill out of her bare arms and gazed out over the city in the distance. From her position—indeed, from almost any position in every direction—one could see Edinburgh's ancient fortress, illuminated by thousands of torches, butted up against the heavens, as if it held dominion over all the earth and everyone on it. Almost everyone.

For the hundredth time, she cursed herself for not going with Robert and the MacGregors to bring Anne back. What if they were all dead, killed by General Monck and his mighty garrison? What if Robert had betrayed her and was sitting with Monck right now, drinking and laughing at her while she waited in the dark, freezing to death? He was a Roundhead, after all. And what if Monck, grateful for Robert's loyalty, wed him to Anne this very night? Och, God, there would not be a rock big enough in Scotland to hide them from her fury.

"They'll be along soon."

The deep melodious voice over her shoulder startled her, but she did not turn around, lest he see the fear in her

eyes. And what about Graham Grant? Did he truly trust
Robert and the MacGregors to see this through? Why had
she listened to him and let him keep her from her task?
And why the hell shouldn't she cut his blasted throat for
ripping off her sleeves?

"What if they are all dead?"

His soft chuckle along her collarbone sent a quaver of
heat through her body. "Monck is not so foolish as to start
a war with Callum MacGregor fer killing his men and his
wife's beloved brother."

He was too close. The velvety warmth of his breath
drifted over her skin, and she closed her eyes at the odd
comfort it brought her. She could feel the contours of his
hard body framing her own. The scent of wood smoke,
and an alluring hint of something undeniably male, made
her ache to turn to him, or run the other way.

"Come, Claire." He touched her arm, letting his fingers graze her bare flesh. "Ye're cold. Come to the fire.
All will be well. Come sit with me."

She might have refused if he hadn't closed his fingers
around hers and drawn her gently along. In truth, she welcomed the reprieve from her worries. Still, when she sat,
she found herself turning to watch the road for any sign
of her sister's approach. She jumped at the sound of some
creature rushing through the bushes.

"Did ye fight at Connor's side?"

"Many times," she answered, craning her neck to look
behind her.

"And he did not worry fer ye?"

Now she turned to him, her lips quirked with indignation. "Why should he have worried? Because I am a
woman?"

One corner of his mouth hooked into a smile that made Claire's pulse race, while his eyes poured over her features. "Because he might lose ye. Though it gladdens me to know that ye haven't fergotten what ye are."

How could she when he made her acutely aware of it every time he set his eyes on her? When she faced an enemy, she knew exactly what to do. But here, alone with Graham, she was unsure of the simplest things, such as where to put her hands. She severed her gaze from his and peered into the fire. "Nor have I forgotten what you are."

"A man?" His voice was low, teasing, as he bent his knees to his chest and rested his elbows atop them. "A rogue . . ."

"A careless rogue," she murmured into the flames, too aware of his closeness. She was beginning to perspire.

"I am not so careless, Claire."

She shrugged, but cut her glance to his. "You think women are here solely for your pleasure."

He laughed, and she found it astounding how guileless he looked doing it. "Do you deny it then?" she asked.

"Nae, I don't. Nor am I sorry fer it. I was bred to fight. My father stood by Dougal MacGregor's side during the atrocities his clan suffered at the whim of King James. I grew to manhood around bloodshed and battle. I've seen things that haunt me. I will not deny that I seek the pleasures of women to help me ferget."

"I will not be one of those women."

"Not true, Claire." The deep pulse of his voice dragged her eyes to his. "Ye give me pleasure just looking at ye."

Hell, why did he have to say that? It tempted her to smile at him like a besotted fool. Blast him, but he would say anything a woman wanted to hear to get her to his bed. "I'd wager you have left a trail of weeping wenches from Skye to Edinburgh."

"And I'd wager that many of yer brother's men lost a limb or two in battle with ye there to distract them."

"You're insufferable." She resigned with a sigh.

"Ye're pigheaded."

She flashed him an angry look, and then she laughed in spite of herself. Och, he was right. She was pigheaded. Connor and Anne had told her enough times. But, damn him, the Highlander was just as stubborn as she. They could go on like this all night without either giving an inch!

Her laughter faded when she remembered Anne. She cast another anxious look over her shoulder.

"How about ye, Claire? What d'ye do fer pleasure?"

He was clever, the way he distracted her from worrying. She looked at him, expecting to see that devilish quirk of his lips, dimples fashioned for beguiling the senses right out of a woman. Instead, she found him staring at her with hypnotic intensity. His breath was a bit short, as if he'd just finished running a distance.

She thought about his question and shrugged one shoulder. "I practice."

"Is that all?" He sounded surprised, and . . . relieved. When she nodded, he shook his head. "Pity, ye should laugh more."

Satan's arse, she was blushing! And she felt like giggling! His eyes glittered against the firelight, touching her, caressing her. She looked away in an effort to quell her pounding heart. She picked up a long twig and poked it into the fire.

"Tell me how a lass of royal lineage came to be a warrior. Does yer cousin the king approve of yer unconventional ways?"

Claire looked up. "He is aware that I fight for his restoration."

"Still . . ."

She went back to poking, avoiding his gaze. "I have been frowned upon by everyone in my family, save Connor. It has been a struggle, but I am committed to restoring the king to his rightful place and bringing an end to Charles's enemies in Scotland."

"A noble cause," he said. Claire could feel his eyes on her while moments of silence stretched between them. Then, "Is there nae man in yer life to help unravel yer nerves?"

The twig snapped in her fingers. "My nerves are not raveled."

He moved closer and, reaching out, he smoothed a lock of her hair away from her cheek. When she angled her face, he did not move his hand away and she found her cheek nestled in his rough palm.

"And even if they were . . ." Her voice was wispy low, her lips, suddenly as dry as the broken twig in her hand. She licked them and his gaze fell to her mouth. "A man could not help me unravel them."

"Then ye haven't met the right man." He leaned in, and slipping his hand behind her nape, he kissed her. Exquisitely. Masterfully. His lips caressed her, molded hers with such tender care, she sighed into his mouth and went weak against him. His tongue did not maraud, but he ravished her nonetheless with a silken lick across the seam of her mouth. He smiled against her when she lifted her hand to his chest and clutched a fistful of his plaid; then he opened his mouth to take her more fully as passion's talons gripped them both.

"Ah, shyt. I knew we couldna trust the bastard wi' her."

Claire jerked away at the sound of Brodie's voice above her. Behind him, her sister sat perched upon a horse of pale gray, but instead of returning Claire's joyful smile at their reunion, she turned to Robert, flanked at her right, and looked about to weep.

"Anne!" Claire rushed to her, but Robert was already there to help her sister dismount. The instant Anne's feet touched the ground, Claire took her in her arms. "Are you well?" She withdrew to sweep Anne's hair off her shoulders and touch her cheek. "Have you been harmed in any way? Did Monck treat you poorly?" Before her sister could answer her queries, Claire pulled her into her arms again. "Thank God you are here with me." She looked at Robert over Anne's shoulder, broke away, and flung her arms around him. "Thank you, Robert. Are you hurt?" She pulled away to examine him next.

When he assured her that they were all well, she grasped Anne's hand and kissed it. "I was so worried about you."

"As I was over you, Claire," Anne replied, but looked past her at Graham. "Who is he?"

Suddenly, Claire felt like a child caught playing in the pigpen. Without looking at him, for she knew he must look as disheveled as she, she told Anne his name. She was vaguely aware of Graham's gentle greeting, and it seemed, Anne was even less interested.

"Claire," she said softly. "Lord Campbell . . ."

"Gave her the sorrowful news of your brother," Robert cut her off. He placed his hand over both of theirs, but when he spoke again, it was to Anne alone. "I pray that I should not be the cause of any more sadness this night."

Looking up at him, Anne nodded, then turned to Claire with heavy tears gathering at the rims of her eyes. "Come, tell me what happened to our brother."

As they walked together to the fire and sat, Graham smiled at Robert and started for him. Brodie cut across his path first, scowled at him, muttered something unintelligible, then wandered off into the shadows.

Arms spread, Graham tossed Angus a puzzled look. "What was that about?"

"Graham." It was Robert who answered. "There is something I must discuss with you."

Graham frowned at the mildly ill look on his friend's face and the somber tone of his voice, then strode forward. "What's happened?"

Robert waited for the others to disperse, and when they were finally alone, he pulled Graham closer. "I . . ." He looked toward the women and began again. "Do you care for her?"

"Who?"

"Hell." Now Robert glared at him. "Claire. Do you care for Claire? You were kissing her. I would know if she means anything to you."

"Why?" Graham asked, casting him a narrowed look. He knew Robert wanted him to find a woman, one woman, to give his heart to. He'd badgered him about it enough, but this was different. Robert was agitated, angry . . . forlorn. Graham's eye caught the shimmering lights of Edinburgh Castle in the distance and suddenly his expression hardened. "Why d'ye want to know? Has Monck promised her to someone?"

"Aye." His friend raked at his hair as if he meant to pull out every strand. "He has promised them both, with their brother's approval. Anne is to wed James Buchanan."

Graham looked over his shoulder at where Claire was sitting, her long pale braid gathered at her rump. He tightened his jaw remembering the softness of her hair when he swept it from her face to better gaze at her profile. The taste of her still lingered on his mouth, his tongue. The memory of her laughter invaded his thoughts like a warning that he would never forget the sound of it.

"And Claire. Who has she been promised to?" Mayhap he could find the bastard and shove a dagger in his throat.

"Do you care for her?"

Grabbing Robert's tunic, Graham hauled him close. "Rob, I've never struck ye, but I vow before God that I will if ye do not answer me. Who has he promised her to?"

"Me!" Robert pushed off him. Then, sounding more defeated than Graham had ever heard him sound before, he repeated. "He's promised her to me."

For a few moments, Graham simply stood in his spot, not believing what he'd just heard. "Ye will refuse him."

"I tried. Graham, he is the governor. His word is law." Robert's gaze drifted toward Anne. He had to make her understand that not wanting her sister was no insult to her, and then he would . . . "I will—"

"Ye trust him then and will do as he commands?" Graham's eyes shone like flames. His expression grew so dark and hard that for an instant, Robert was certain this man, who had saved his life many times, would strike him dead now.

"Aye, I do trust him, but if you care for her I will go back to Monck right now and refuse her. I don't care—"

"Ye do care." Graham cut him off. The rigid angles of his face dissolved into resignation. "Ye ferget I know ye well, brother. The law means much to ye."

"Aye, it does. But your happiness means more."

Graham smiled, though he felt as if he'd just been kicked in the chest. She was promised to Robert. She could never be his. And hell, did he want her to be? No! She enthralled him. He was curious about what she'd be like in his bed. That was all. Nothing more. He would not have his friend go back to the castle and lose his integrity, mayhap even more than that, by fighting the governor on this. Why should he care whom she married? He didn't want a woman weeping over him every time a battle needed to be fought. Although Claire would likely want to join him. Now there was a frightening thought, watching the woman he loved bleed on the field. He shook his head to clear it. Damnation! why was he even thinking in terms of love?

"Of course I don't care fer her. You will do as the law says." He knew, for Robert, there was no other choice. "She means naught to me."

"Are you certain?" Robert worried.

"Aye," Graham assured him, hooking his mouth into a roguish grin. "Ye saved her from me, Rob."

"Very well then." Robert didn't look relieved. "I don't want her to know yet. She will never believe her brother promised her to a Roundhead. It will only convince her that Monck lies. She might take Anne and flee."

"There is the possibility that Monck deceives ye."

Robert nodded, but looked even worse than before when he said, "It is best if we do not tell her of Anne's betrothal either. At least until we meet with Buchanan. I have a message to deliver to him from the general. Monck trusts him, but I do not know if I do. Why would Connor Stuart agree to hand his sister and his lands over to a Roundhead, and not his close friend?"

They spoke for a little while longer about the meeting with Monck, and then with nothing else to say, Graham walked away. He did not return to the fire, to her. He had to get Claire Stuart out of his thoughts. She was betrothed to a man he considered his brother, and Graham would never betray him.

He had to put her out of his thoughts.

It would not be difficult. She meant naught to him. Naught at all.

Chapter Twelve

Who has seen the great warrior arrayed in the frost of winter? Alas, he has perished. And yet, he lives.

When he returned to the camp later that night, Graham knew he was doomed. He could not stop thinking about her. He could not stop looking at her, watching her every movement, listening to each word she uttered to her sister—to Robert. She seemed a bit softer, less guarded now that Anne was returned to her. When she smiled, he felt as if someone had taken a hook to his guts. What had come over him? Never in all his life had he let a lass affect him this way. He'd promised himself long ago that he never would. How could he ever give his heart to a lass knowing that each time he rode into battle he might not return? He knew the pain it caused. He'd seen it, lived it when his father was killed and his mother wept until there was little left of her.

He did not care for Claire Stuart. He wanted her. Aye, that was all. He wanted her and she was the one woman he could never have. Hell, why Robert? If she'd been promised to someone else, Graham would have taken her and to hell with the law. But she was to be *Robert's* wife!

He scrubbed his hand down his face, looking at her across the flames, wanting to kiss her, touch her, caress her, hold her to his body and feel the slow yielding of her surrender, her soft curves molding to his hard ones. He wanted to hear her laughter again, taste her, take her, and . . . And what? What then? What would he have done once he had a true taste of her? Likely, the same thing he'd done to countless other women; walk away. She was better off with Robert, a man who believed that everyone was born to love, that there was more to life than fighting and rutting. Graham knew better. He always had. War was all that was certain and lasting in his world. Life was short and love was fleeting. He was better off free of anyone who caused him to worry about dying. He was better off without her.

"Graham." Robert dragged his attention away from the sweet contours of Claire's face. "Monck knew of Connor's disappearance, but not of his death."

"How can you be certain of that?" Claire asked him, looking up over the flames. "He could have been deceiving you as he did to my brother."

Aye, Graham thought. And what would Robert do if he'd been tricked by the general? Would he stand with Claire when she sought the governor's life as payment for his betrayal?

"Claire," Anne said quietly, dragging her sister's attention to her. "I have spent these many weeks in General Monck's care. I do not believe he betrayed Connor. There must be more to this than you have been told."

Grateful that someone else among them believed in Monck's innocence, Robert spread his warmest smile on Anne and then flicked his gaze guiltily back to Claire.

"Anne, our brother was killed on his way to London

after he received word from the governor telling him to go there!" Claire exclaimed when every eye turned to her, awaiting her answer. "Is that not enough to prove Monck's guilt? Our parents were sent to London, never to return. Think you Connor would have gone there if not commissioned to go by someone he trusted? You know I speak true," she added when Anne lowered her gaze to her hands folded in her lap. "Knowing the price on his head, Connor used every precaution."

"Then Angus was correct."

Claire cut her glance to Robert. "About what?"

"There have been attacks on the general's men since your brother vanished. If you're correct and the general sent Connor to London to die, someone besides you knows it. Someone who wants him dead because of it."

"And who do you think is behind these attacks?" Claire angled her head at Anne's soft touch to her hand.

Graham caught the subtle communication between them. Instantly, his eyes swept to the bonnet tucked in Claire's belt. Could it have been her? She had meant to kill Monck when she reached Edinburgh. Would she be so foolish as to attack a regiment of the governor's men?

"There is only one I can think of," Robert said.

"Aye," Graham agreed quickly. If it had been Claire, he would protect her at all cost. "Connor's dear friend."

"James?" Anne asked, stunned, and then shook her head. But it was Claire, Graham noted with a sting of pure jealousy, who immediately shot to his defense.

"James is not behind any attacks on Monck's men."

"How d'ye know?" Angus asked.

"I simply do. You will all just have to trust me on that. Lambert's men are here in Scotland. You both saw them that morn." She turned to Robert. "Did you tell Monck they were here?"

"Aye," he admitted quietly. "And he did not look pleased."

"There, then, you see?" Claire insisted. "It was Lambert's men who attacked."

"Aye, Lambert's men," Anne added hastily, casting her sister a nervous glance.

"I do not know what to believe anymore," Robert told them with weariness deepening his voice. "Mayhap all will be made clear when I meet Buchanan. You mentioned Ravenglade. Where is it?"

Claire's entire demeanor changed, and Graham couldn't help but frown at the hope that made her eyes spark like sapphires. Did she love the bastard? Somehow, that particular thought was more distressing to him than her wedding his best friend. She didn't love Robert and she probably never would. They were too different. But if her heart belonged to Buchanan . . .

"If I tell you, will you give me your word, and the word of all your company, that you will tell no one else?" She had no choice. This was the only way to get Anne to James.

When Robert made his vow, she told him and said a silent prayer that her brother would forgive her.

Claire rode in silence beside Anne as they neared Stirling. Her backside ached and she vowed if she didn't eat something other than berries, roots, and rock-hard bread soon, she was going to take a bite out of someone's arm. She was used to being in the saddle for days at a time, but it had been weeks since she'd felt a bed beneath her, or even a blasted chair! With each league they traveled, her mood grew blacker. Robert wasn't helping matters by taking a sudden and intense interest in her and Anne's well-being. He rode at their shoulder by day and at their heels by night. Claire was sure he didn't mean to rankle her nerves by asking her endless questions about everything from her childhood, to what colors she liked best. She was relieved when Anne, clearly more interested in chatting than she was, began answering for her. Soon the two were laughing and left her alone.

Angus and Brodie MacGregor's constant bickering did not disturb her as much as the fists they pummeled each other with at every chance offered them. She appreciated fighting men, but these two were hellions to be reckoned with! As the hours wore on and their faces grew more swollen and purple, she began to worry about how James's men would fare against them.

Her plans to seek refuge at Ravenglade hadn't changed. Indeed, she was more determined than ever to be away from the true cause of her petulance; the man currently riding in front of her.

Since the day they'd left Edinburgh, Graham had barely spoken a word to her, and when he did, it was more of a grumble. Gone were his irritatingly sensual smiles. Gone, in fact, were all traces of humor toward anyone. When she caught his eye, he looked away, though many times during the day she felt his eyes on her. He did not seek her out when they rested their horses or camped for the night. Why had he changed, and why was it driving her mad?

When they finally stopped at an inn, she thought she might have a chance to speak to him, though she hated herself for wanting to.

"What think you of him?"

Claire blinked her gaze away from Graham dismounting and glanced at her sister. "I'd like to take my sword to him."

"Not Graham." Anne tugged her wrist when Claire's gaze found him again. "But I would know why he fires your temper without having to speak a word."

"Who then?" Claire asked before her sister delved any deeper.

Anne motioned with her dimpled chin toward Robert leaning over his saddle to retrieve something on the other side. "Lord Campbell." Her gaze, lingering on his snug-fitting trews stretching across his thighs and backside, darkened from misty gray to stormy blue. She began to smile, but burped instead.

"Anne," Claire snapped at her, breaking the dreamy trance the view had on her sister. "He's a Roundhead."

When Anne met her gaze, Claire scrutinized her a bit more carefully. "Are you drunk, sister? You look drunk!"

"I shared a taste of dear Angus's brew." Anne shrugged, casting off her sister's worried look. Her wistful gaze wandered back to the Earl of Argyll offering the stable boy a smile as he handed over his reins. "Look at him, Claire. He is not our enemy." Her avowal was tempered with a somber urgency that piqued Claire's interest. "He is kind, and gently mannered. Thoughtful and intelligent. And do you not find him terribly handsome? Why, look at his form, so fine and well toned. And his eyes—have you ever seen a more radiant combination of gold and brown, ringed by such long black lashes?" Anne blinked her own luminously wide eyes at her. "Well, have you?"

"Satan's balls, you fancy him," Claire breathed, not

really so opposed as she thought she would be. After all, Robert was extremely likable—for a Roundhead.

Her sister sat back in her saddle, aghast. "Nae! I would never think to take him . . ." She snapped her mouth shut and lowered her gaze. "I simply want you to be happy," she said more quietly.

"I am happy," Claire assured her while she dismounted.

"You are not! And it is Graham Grant's fault. You should not have kissed him, Claire." She darted a sympathetic glance in Lord Campbell's direction, then back to her sister. "I see the way you look at him. Are you angry that he has not kissed you again?"

"Don't be ridiculous, Anne. And do not question me about him again. I hate him. I loathe him. I wish I'd never—"

She walked straight into him. She looked up as his hands came around her upper arms to keep her from tumbling backward. He stared at her with unblinking intensity that set her head reeling.

"Watch where ye're going."

He stepped around her and was gone, leaving Claire a bit stunned, a little hurt, and spitting mad. She thought about shouting a curse at his back, but Anne was watching her with a knowing tilt of her brow. "Robert!" she shouted instead and stormed toward the inn. "Help my sister dismount!"

She stepped inside the small tavern with Brodie just in front of her and craned her neck around the brute's arm to see where that bastard had gone. She found Graham almost immediately, for he was difficult to miss, with a giggling group of wenches already surrounding him. Claire gaped at them for a moment, wondering what the other patrons would do if she pulled out her dagger and flung it at him. Someone behind her gave her a gentle push and she spun around and glowered up at Angus.

"Dinna lose yer heart to him, lass. There's nae point in it now anyway."

Her fists curled at her sides. "Thank you, Angus, but my heart is lost to no one."

He gave her a sympathetic look, and then he, too, left her. Robert and Anne entered the inn next, laughing as they usually did when they were together, which at the moment, made Claire want to scream. When Robert saw her glaring at them, he jerked away from Anne and looked more repentant than if she'd just discovered he'd killed her brother.

"I will get us rooms," he said, practically running away from her. What the hell was wrong with him? Claire wondered. Had they all gone mad?

"I think he is afraid of me," Claire told Anne, watching Robert's swift departure.

"That's absurd," Anne huffed. "He doesn't know you well enough yet." Her sister looked around, then cut her gaze to Claire. "Are you not worried someone here might recognize you?"

Claire was too angry to play ignorant, so she shrugged her shoulders instead. "No one will recognize me, and if they do, they will not live long enough to make the accusation."

Anne shook her head at her, her eyes pleading when she spoke. "I knew it was you when I heard of the attack on the governor's men. Connor would not want you to do this."

"Connor is dead, and I will avenge him." Claire left her sister's side and joined Brodie and Angus at a nearby table. After ordering a cup of mead, she went back to glar-

ing at Graham. She tried several times to give her attention to the conversation around her, but every time one
of the wenches attached to his arm laughed, it drew her
flashing eyes back to him.

Why had she let him kiss her again? Did her inexperi-
ence in the art disappoint him so much that he decided she
wasn't worth any more of his attention? He'd warned her
of his wickedness, and she was certain, so certain, that
he could not affect her. But he did, blast him to Hades.
He took advantage of her moment of weakness when she
was so worried over Anne and he kissed her, then tossed
her aside. Well, Anne was safe now, and Graham Grant
would never see weakness in her again.

From the corner of her eye, she saw him coming toward
the table with a cup clutched in one hand and a serving wench
in the other. She watched him in seething silence as he threw
himself into a chair and pulled the wench into his lap.

The woman's pale blue eyes settled instantly on Claire,
and then on her thick flaxen braid and bare arms. Her gaze
narrowed, coming upon the sheathed sword at Claire's
hips. "Have we met before?"

Claire smiled dryly and dipped her glacial gaze to
the woman's ample cleavage jiggling beneath her chin.
"It's difficult to say. I've met many wenches, and all your
bosoms look the same."

Brodie chuckled and Angus coughed into his cup, but
Graham's eyes pinned her. She stared right back at him,
hoping he could read her thoughts so he would know what
a witless pig she considered him to be.

"Lianne will be serving our table tonight," Graham
said, and turned his dimpled grin back to the lusty wench
perched upon him.

Serving indeed, Claire fumed. She ripped her eyes away from them when Anne and Robert reached the table. She watched as Robert waited for her sister to sit and then, looking a bit torn, he picked up the empty chair beside her and carried it to Claire's side, where he promptly sat. Claire cast him a befuddled look and moved her chair an inch closer to Brodie's to give Robert more room. Graham wolfed down the remainder of his drink and pushed the empty cup at Lianne.

"And bring some food," he told her, giving her a gentle nudge off his knee. "Something hot."

"I've somethin' that's been cookin' fer ye," she promised with a suggestive wink before she left. On her way around the table, she bent over Robert's shoulder. "And I've somethin' fer ye, as well, angel."

Robert shifted uncomfortably and looked up from beneath his lashes at Anne.

"You've been here before, then?" Anne asked him, trying to sound blasé about it. Her sister knew better. The tight smile Anne offered the earl gave her away.

Claire wanted to kick Robert in the kneecaps. While she might not look favorably on Anne's obvious fondness for a Campbell, if he bedded that wench tonight, he would answer to her in the morning.

"I haven't been . . . ehm . . . *there*, nae," Robert made haste to assure her.

"Still savin' yerself fer love, are ye, Rob?" Brodie laughed, taking no mercy on the chaste earl.

Claire elbowed him in the ribs. "It's a noble aspiration that others here should strive for." She slipped her gaze to Graham. "Do not chide him for it."

Graham threw her an indulgent smile that blatantly

mocked her own innocence. "Some might consider it a noble aspiration to please a lass in bed."

The fight that had been brewing for days was unmistakable in the upward tilt of her brow, the slight flare of her nostrils. "And there are others who consider it a failure that a rogue must continually practice at becoming better at it."

He laughed, as if he knew better and her words did not disturb him at all. But he did not speak to her, and barely to anyone else, until they all rose to retire some time later.

On his way toward the stairs, he stopped a buxom redhead server as she passed him. "Send Lianne to me."

Claire glanced over her shoulder at him as she climbed the stairs behind Anne. Let him go with the wench. As soon as they reached Ravenglade she would be free of him. Satan's balls, she thought, tripping over a step, she could not wait.

Chapter Thirteen

Betrayed. Betrayed by his friend. There is no greater offense. There is no greater sorrow.

Claire lay wide awake thinking about Graham an hour later, and another hour after that. Every time she closed her eyes, she saw him smiling at the women in the tavern—at Lianne. What was wrong with her? She didn't even like him! He was an arrogant, unrefined, conceited knave. He called himself friend to Royalists and Roundheads alike, with no other passion firing his heart than that for his own pleasure. His pleasure . . . Was he kissing Lianne right now the way he had kissed her? Claire sat up in her bed and pounded the thin mattress with her fist. She swept her long hair away from her face, and, careful not to wake Anne, she slipped from the bed. What was the sense in lying here all night plagued with images that made her angry? She wanted a drink. Aye, a cup of warm mead would help her sleep. Most of the patrons were likely either gone for the night, or in bed—having their way with lusty wenches. She was certain she wouldn't meet any of them, but slipped her dagger into her trews, just in case.

She tiptoed out of the room and trod silently down the stairs to the tavern. The hearth fire still glowed, illuminating the tables, most of them empty. Two patrons remained, slumped over their chairs in a drunken stupor. A swarthy serving girl rested in a chair by the hearth, rubbing her feet while the innkeeper sat across from her counting the coins he'd made for the day. They both looked up when she entered.

"If ye're lookin' fer a drink, come back in the morn," the innkeeper called out. The girl gave him a slight kick with her foot and motioned to another table hidden in the corner, where the light did not reach.

Claire followed her gaze and stopped in her tracks when Graham rose from the shadows, his gaze fastened upon her. "What's wrong? What are ye doing down here?"

She shrugged her shoulders and moved toward him. "I had trouble sleeping and thought a cup of mead might help."

He took his time looking her over, from her bare feet to the loose mane of buttery tresses falling over her arms. In the dim light, she noted the tightening of his jaw. She tilted her chin. Let him be angry that she'd interrupted his . . . She looked around for Lianne.

"Finished already?" She made certain he heard the mocking contempt in her voice.

If he did, he made no show of it, but went back to his seat. "Go back to bed, Claire."

"What are you doing here alone?" She ignored his rigid command and pulled out a chair beside him.

"Praying."

She made a small sound like a laugh and picked up his cup, bringing her nose to it. Ale. She took a sip and felt his eyes on her; burning, brooding, and something else that made her nerve endings sizzle.

"Tell me," she asked without looking at him. "What does a man like you pray for?"

"A woman like ye."

She raised her gaze to his shadowy silhouette. She wished she could see his features, his eyes, his mouth. Was he smiling, mocking her? No, his voice was low and thick, with none of the teasing arrogance she was used to from him.

"Like me?" Her own voice sounded ragged and anxious against her ears.

He leaned toward her, his handsome face leaving the dimness to fill her vision. His cap rested on the table, leaving his spray of bronze curls free to dangle over his brows. Saints, but he was dangerous to be near. His eyes gleamed with hunger that made her fear for her virtue, or want to hand it to him to do with it as he pleased. "Aye, like ye. Ye fire up my passions like none . . ."

"You're drunk," she said as his warm breath fell against her cheek.

His jaw clenched and he drew back. "Aye, and in danger of betraying a good friend."

"What are you talking about?"

Instead of answering her query, he finished off the ale in his cup and slammed it back to the table. "Why are ye wandering the inn at this time of night looking like that?"

"Like what?" she demanded, not liking the change in his tone.

"Like ye're in search of a good tumble?"

If she had had a clear view of his face, she would have slapped it.

"I warn ye now," he practically growled at her. "Go back to yer bed or ye might find what ye seek."

She looked around, then settled her gleaming blue eyes back on him. "There is no one here who poses a threat to my virtue, Grant. Least of all, you."

Without warning, he sprang from his chair and yanked her from hers. She pummeled his shoulders with her fists as he swooped down, slipped one arm around her waist and the other behind her knees, and lifted her off her feet.

"Put me down this instant!" she shrieked as he headed for the stairs, barely straining a muscle against her struggle to be free of him.

Claire went still. Would he force himself on her? "Graham," she warned, tight-lipped, as he carried her up the stairs. "I've a dagger with me. Do not force me to use it on you."

"Aim fer my heart first, lass," he said, his gaze fixed and hard on hers. "Fer I think it has turned traitor on me."

His heart? Dear God, she did not want to kill him! And why would he say such a thing to her? What the hell did he mean? Did it have something to do with his being here alone instead of off somewhere rutting with a serving wench? She stared up at him and for an instant his expression went soft all over her before he turned away, gritting his teeth.

He wanted to kiss her. She saw it in his eyes, along with the strength he called upon to keep himself from doing it. Her heart leaped in her chest and she feared she'd gone completely mad. She wanted him to kiss her, to *want* to kiss her! He had stopped deliberately trying to seduce her. But his assault on her senses, on her every waking thought, had become even more dangerous than before. For it was quiet, brooding, and, she understood now, fully restrained. But why? Why did he force himself to resist her? And why did it make him so damned irresistible?

When he reached the upper landing, he set her on her feet, not knowing which was her room, and turned to leave. "Go back to yer bed."

"Is that it?" she blurted before she could stop herself.

He paused then, his wide shoulders stiff with tension as he slowly pivoted to face her. "What else would ye have me do?"

Do? She was thinking more in terms of him *saying* something, but suddenly myriad images flooded her thoughts of things she might like him to *do*. She had never cared much for the way a "proper" lady ought to think, and it was a good thing, because the images were lewd indeed. Instead of giving him an answer, she simply stared at him, wondering when she had begun to think on such a basely primitive level.

"Claire." He spoke her name as if the feel of it on his lips was torturous, then closed the distance between them in one long stride. Clutching her by the arms, he hauled her up against his iron frame and dipped his face to hers, but only his warm breath touched her flesh. "Ye fight against losing yer country, when yer life is not even yer own." A muscle in his jaw flexed as he battled within himself. "I would fight to gain it back fer ye, if it were against anyone but him."

He moved away in silence, leaving Claire with an aching need to go after him. What was it about his angry touch, the hoarse pitch of his voice that made her believe every word he spoke? And what in the hell was he talking about?

Graham stormed through the front door of the inn and entered the night without pause and without concern for what could be awaiting in the shadows. Neither man nor beast would survive if they came upon him now. He cursed when he lifted his hand to push back his cap and found it wasn't there. He tore his fingers through his hair and kicked at a bug that flew into his path. Panic rose like a tide, smashing against his lungs. He couldn't care for her. It was not possible. He enjoyed his life just the way it was; rough and sometimes bloody, and with a warm wench beneath him now and then to remind him of something softer. It was all he needed. All he wanted. Or was it?

He crashed into the forest with a curse on his lips. What he felt for her was simply lust. Aye. No, it was more than that. He was fond of her. That was all. He liked the way she looked, the way she spoke, the way she thought, the way she kissed.

Hell!

He should have taken Lianne tonight. It would have proven that his heart wasn't betraying him after all these years. Now he was left trembling like . . . like a lass! Ah, God, why did it have to be Robert? If she were promised to Buchanan he would bed her and get her out of his blood. No, he knew if he had her, he would want her again, and again. And then he would be doomed on the battlefield.

Finding a thick oak, he unbelted his plaid and lay beneath it. He looked toward the dimly lit windows of the inn. He did not trust himself in the same place with her. Aye, he thought pitifully, he'd already lost control of his willpower. What would she take from him next?

She will take naught. The same I would surrender to any opponent in battle. I will not be betrayed, he told his slowing heart as he closed his eyes. *Nor will I betray my friend.*

Chapter Fourteen

And no enemy more deadly than the one who avoids the battlefield, yet covets the prize.

Graham decided that battling with his opponent only tempted him to kiss the insolence right off her mouth. So he continued to stay away from her. That didn't mean he didn't watch her. She'd only caught him twice, and both times he vowed not to look at her again. But his eyes were drawn to her whether she spoke to anyone or remained silent. Nights were the most agonizing, when she sat with Anne, her bonny face faintly illuminated by firelight. It required every ounce of strength he possessed not to fall, mesmerized by the perfect sublimity of her smiles. Sometimes, though, he found it impossible not to let his gaze linger on her, even after she found him watching.

But even depriving himself of all the pleasures he could find in her was not as difficult as seeing Robert staring at her across the same fire.

Since leaving Edinburgh, Robert had often tried to make conversation with the woman he was going to take as his wife. And for the first part of their journey, it was apparent by Rob's sullen demeanor that they shared naught.

This changed on their way to Perth. They found one thing for which they both had a fondness. Claire's sister drew them together with laughter and whispers that made Anne giggle, knowing they were about her.

It was enough to make Graham want to crack a few heads. Would he have to watch this budding romance between Claire and Robert bloom before his eyes? No, he would leave their company first. Better to see them off without him than to feel a prick of anger toward Robert. And better that Graham did his best to avoid her until then.

But Claire Stuart was not a lass easily ignored.

"This way," Graham whispered as he crept low against the forest floor, his dagger in one hand and Donel's lance in the other. Claire huddled close to him, straining to see through the overgrowth of bushes. She'd insisted on hunting with him this morning. He'd refused emphatically, but he was learning that Claire Stuart did what she wanted.

They had spotted a large gray hare moments earlier but then lost it again, when its long ears shot upright at the sound of their advance.

It was the second hare that had escaped, along with a number of grouse. How the hell was he supposed to concentrate on stealth with her here alone with him?

A twig snapped beneath Claire's boot, echoing through the woods like a clap of thunder. Graham scowled, hearing the rustle of leaves as the hare escaped them once again. He flashed her a cool stare.

"A dozen apologies." She gifted him with a cheeky smile. "I should have swept the ground before treading upon it."

"Just watch where ye're going. Can ye manage that?"

Her nostrils flared. She nodded, saying nothing—until he caught the hare again out of the corner of his eye.

"I thought you said you knew what you were doing."

His shoulders stiffened and he pivoted. For a brief moment he seriously considered throttling her senseless. He drew in a deep breath, gathering his patience. "If ye would shut up fer five breaths, we might enjoy a hot meal this night."

She arched her pale brow at him, always ready for a fight. "My, but you Highlanders certainly are temperamental. Might I make a suggestion?"

His jaw tightened. "Nae."

"Why not let *me* do the hunting?" she said anyway. "I did not come with you to watch you waste away the day."

He wouldn't let her bait him. Engaging in battle with her would only ignite his desire for her. "Stay here," he said woodenly and turned his back on her.

He spotted the hare nibbling an acorn a few feet away and lifted his lance, taking great care not to make a sound. The hare lifted itself on its powerful hind legs and wiggled its whiskers as it sniffed the air. Graham aimed, and then was nearly knocked unconscious when a rock the size of his fist bounced off the back of his head. His legs wobbled and the lance dropped harmlessly to the ground.

Behind him, Claire's muffled gasp drew his lethal, somewhat dazed glare to her.

"Forgive me," she called out. The flicker of a smile belied her apology. "You were taking so long to throw the lance I feared our supper was going to escape you yet again."

His green eyes darkened and he took a step toward

her. "Ye find it humorous that ye nearly cracked open my skull?"

"Only a little," she replied, backing away. "You deserved it." She bent swiftly, snatched up another rock, and held it aloft. His steps halted, but the slow curl of his lips dared her to throw it. "You think I won't?" she challenged him with a menacing sneer of her own. "This time I will aim for something lower, since you scarcely felt the first one, what with that thick head of yours."

He sprang at her so fast she barely had time to turn and run. His outstretched hand grabbed for her shirt and just missed. Claire shrieked at his closeness and dropped her rock as she bolted over fallen branches and gnarled tree roots protruding from the leafy ground. She risked a glance over her shoulder and would have crashed headlong into the tree in front of her if his arms hadn't closed around her waist, stopping her at the last instant.

Ignoring her heedless struggle to be free, he bent over her spine and pressed his mouth against her ear. "Ye don't seem to realize the danger of me chasing ye, Claire. Ye tempt me beyond reason to end my misery and take ye in every way possible." He pushed her forward against the tree until the rough bark brushed her cheek. One arm tightened around her, holding her still, while his other hand slipped below her belt, pressing the curve of her buttocks deeper against his hardening arousal. "Starting from behind," he growled low in her ear. "But nae, I will not be bested."

Releasing her, he turned away, his muscles trembling with the effort it took to let her go. He bent to retrieve Donel's lance just as her dagger sailed over his head. He straightened slowly, his eyes fixed on the dead hare a few feet away.

Cocking his head, Graham tossed her an incredulous look at how close her dagger had come to his back.

Claire's eyes gleamed a startling blue against her flushed cheeks and the long, stray tendrils of pale blonde that fluttered around them. "Supper," she said simply, glaring at him as if she wished her dagger was sticking out of his guts instead of the hare's.

Hell, he *had* to smile at her.

Claire stomped over the carpet of leaves and twigs snapping beneath her boots, careless of whatever the hell she frightened away. She wanted to run, but she knew Graham was behind her, and damn him to Hades, she *would not* let him see what he'd done to her. Besides that, she doubted her knees would continue to support her should she move at a faster pace. Her breath still came so hard it was making her dizzy. Her nerve endings still sizzled from his savage touch. Dear God, what kind of sinful beast was he that he could wreak such havoc on her body, her thoughts? If she was a bit more devout, she would have let her knees give out and offered up a prayer of forgiveness for the thoroughly wicked desires he ignited in her. His body, so hard and ready to fulfill his heated promise to take her in every way possible, roused images so perverse she was certain she'd never be able to look at him again without blushing. Naked, sweating, panting beasts locked in a primitively sexual embrace while the other forest creatures looked on. That she had been so tempted to rub her buttocks over the full, unrelenting length of him while he pressed her so intimately close mortified her. That he made her want to submit to such raw male dominance frightened her witless. That he'd won the battle over his lust should have pleased her. He could have easily taken her with force, plunged himself deep inside her while she clung help-lessly to a tree. But he had resisted her yet again, as he had at the inn. He would not be bested. This was a game to him; a challenge, a chase he exhilarated in. He wanted her to give in, to surrender as his other conquests had. To swoon at his feet, claw at his garments and feast upon the full glory of his battle-hardened body. God's mercy, she'd come close to doing it, too! Never in her life had she been so tempted to stroke her palms over a man's hard curves, to feel the pleasure pulsing through all those muscles. But it was she who would not be bested by any opponent, no matter how daft he made her.

Chapter Fifteen

How shall I keep the prize from him when his hands have so skillfully subdued me?

"Lord Buchanan does not know any of you." Claire reined in on her mount a few leagues into Perth. "He might order his men to shoot at you from the battlements." She looked around at the others. "It's best if I ride on ahead and warn him of your approach."

Breaking formation, Graham cantered his horse toward her. If she thought he was going to let her go on alone, she was truly daft. "Does he always shoot at men approaching his holding?"

"When the men look like they've come for a good day's raiding"—she skimmed her gaze over the MacGregors—"aye, he does."

Graham couldn't argue against that bit of logic. Still, she wasn't going anywhere without him. Someone had killed her brother, who, though she would most likely deny it, was more skilled with a weapon than she. That someone could be waiting for her next at Ravenglade.

"I will go with ye."

"Nae. I don't need—"

"I did not ask ye what ye needed." His voice overrode hers. His unblinking, steady gaze promised that arguing would be fruitless.

Claire scalded him with a venomous look before she turned to Anne. "You will be safe here with Robert and the others until James's men come for you. Do not fear."

When her sister smiled, assuring her that she trusted the men in her company, Claire nodded and turned to leave. "And Angus, do not give her any of that poison you call brew."

Angus turned to Anne with a sheepish grin. "'Twasn't that bad, was it, lass?"

"On the contrary, kind sir," she said with the most delicate of smiles. "It was quite soothing."

Angus's grin widened with worshipful appreciation, and then he turned to Brodie. "The Stuart lass is blessed with an iron fortitude, eh, cousin?"

"Aye," Brodie agreed, watching Claire as she grew smaller in the distance. "A good quality, that."

"Will my sister be safe with him alone?"

Every eye turned to Anne after she spoke. The men all knew who she meant, and Donel, for one, took offense. "Commander Grant is unmatched in battle. Dinna let his smile fool ye."

"I wouldn't," Anne declared in mild defense, "should I ever see it. The man does naught but brood."

Hearing her, Robert realized she was correct. Even Brodie had to agree. Graham was behaving strangely indeed. They discussed it among themselves while they dismounted and began setting up a temporary camp.

"You did tell him of your betrothal to Claire, did you not, Lord Campbell?"

"Robert, please, my lady." He smiled at her while he struggled to untie a small sack hanging from his saddle. "Aye, I told him."

"Mayhap he fancies her." Anne stepped toward him to help him with the knot. "It would explain why he is not the dashing, devilish rogue you all speak of."

"Lass," Angus uncorked the lid of his pouch of brew and offered it to her, "Graham Grant would stab himself in the innards before he handed his heart to any maiden. I have known him fer many a year. He is exactly what he appears to be, an angel wi' horns."

Hearing this, Robert nodded in agreement. Graham was a likable fellow, even while he took down his opponent's castle. The taking of Kildun's entire garrison with the MacGregors two years past was proof enough for Robert. He set his eyes on the narrow path Graham had taken with Claire. What if Anne was right? What if his best friend had not been honest with him, and he did indeed care for Claire? Could that be the cause of Graham's morose mood? And would Robert stand in his way if Graham had finally found the woman who could tame his heart? He glanced at Anne. What of her? Would he be able to hand her over to James Buchanan when the time came, knowing that his heart would remain with her in Perth for the remainder of his days? He'd vowed to himself to always do the right thing. To take not the easy path, but the right one. How could making Graham's, Claire's, and his own life miserable be the right thing to do, even if the law demanded it? He would speak to General Monck. But first, he had to make Anne understand how necessary love was to him. He would not be seen as dishonorable, especially not in her eyes.

"My lady." He turned to her after spreading out his blanket for her use and offered her his arm. "May I have a word with you alone?"

"Of course." She accepted his arm and let him lead her away from the others.

"Your sister told me that you are familiar with Sir Thomas Malory's tales of Arthur Pendragon and his noble knights," he began slowly, thoughtfully, keeping his eyes on the ground ahead.

"Aye, I know them well." The wistful pitch of her voice was enough to set his heart racing.

"You pretended to be Guinevere when you were a child." He smiled at his boots and then raised his eyes to her to bask in her soft laughter.

"I drove my poor father daft, but I so wanted to be her."

"Why?"

She sighed and tilted her face up at him to ponder his question. "Because she was loved by such an honorable man. She would have had to have been quite an extraordinary woman, do you not agree?"

Robert simply stared into her wide, haunting eyes and nodded. He wanted to touch her so badly it near doubled him over. What else was there to do but tell her? He knew now that she would understand.

"Your sister is very beautiful," he said earnestly. "She's very brave. Her devotion to you and to her cause is an exceptional quality." Anne smiled at him, then looked away. "But," he added, drawing her gaze back. "I do not love her."

"Are you certain?" she asked him quietly, without a trace of anger in her honeyed voice.

Robert's relief was evident in his smile when he nodded. "Aye, for my heart has been claimed by a queen."

They were alone. Finally. Of all the things Claire wanted to say to him, shout at him, over the past sennight, she could remember none now. She glanced at Graham riding at her left. He'd changed her plans once again. She'd wanted a chance to speak to James alone. To tell him what she wanted him to do to help her and Anne escape the MacGregors and their two friends. Now she would not get that chance. She had to think clearly and not let Graham get in the way.

"D'ye love him?"

His question was so unexpected, Claire narrowly avoided getting struck by a branch in her path.

"What? Who?"

"Buchanan."

She slowed her mount, and Graham slowed his. "What does that matter to you?" When his eyes hardened on her, her nostrils flared. "I have a question of my own, since we are asking. Why do you take such great care in avoiding me?"

For a moment, he looked as if he wouldn't answer her. She let him know with a deliberate tilt of her chin that she would be just as stubborn.

"I'm ill," he conceded vaguely.

"Och, I did not know. Is it something . . ." She paused, her concern turning to suspicion. "You converse with everyone else. This affliction is only a danger to me, then?"

"Ye are the cause of it."

Anger sparked her eyes. "Is it the lack of anything truly important to you that makes you so cold, so uncaring toward the women who have shared with you something precious? You use all to gain for yourself alone." He parted his lips to speak but Claire would not have it. She'd wanted to tell him this since the morning they left the inn. He had deliberately made her like him, and then treated her like the plague. He had kissed her, but each time only to prove that he could best her, if he so desired. Which, he made most evident, he had no desire to do. And the worst part? He did not care about any of it!

"Even warriors care about something," she accused. "Where does your loyalty flow? To the Royalist Mac-Gregors, or to the Roundhead Campbells? They call you commander, but you are truly just a rogue."

His expression darkened. His lips tightened with anger, and his mount bucked and snorted forward at the pressure applied to its ribcage. Sensing the sudden danger to her well-being tempted Claire to reach for her sword.

"D'ye love him?" he asked again, refusing to be pulled into her fight, and proving to Claire once again the resolute command he held over his emotions.

"Aye, I love him!" she shouted at him, frustrated by his silly question. "I am considering wedding him because I want a husband to obey and a dozen babes at my breasts!"

The dark furrow of Graham's brow vanished, and he smiled at her so suddenly, every moment but this one fled from her memory.

"What d'ye know of babes?"

She shrugged and quirked her mouth at him, liking the fact that he knew her enough already to appreciate the sheer absurdity of her declaration. "I know they need to eat."

"And, one hopes, not all at the same time." Graham

laughed, and Claire joined him. She didn't ask him again about the days that had passed between them. She wanted to put the past behind her and let her guard down a little with him. She wanted to laugh with him more often and not worry about who was besting whom. His mirth made her feel ridiculously lighthearted, a condition that was sorely lacking in her life since Connor died.

"So tell me about James Buchanan," he said as his laughter faded.

"What do you want to know?"

"How long has he been a friend of your brother's?"

"Since we were eight. Connor and I are . . . were twins."

Graham studied her face, a smile hovering at the corners of his mouth. "Do twins fight as often as other siblings do?"

"Connor and I had fights aplenty," she laughed softly. "But he fought with James more. They were like true brothers."

"I did not fight with my brother much. But my sisters bickered endlessly."

Claire narrowed her eyes and snaked a grin at him. "Mayhap that explains your aversion to living with a woman."

"Mayhap," Graham agreed. "There were eleven of them."

Claire let out a little gasp of surprise and repulsion. "Dear God, you poor man. Connor would have hanged himself if there had been eleven of us."

"I spent much time with Callum as a boy. We fought all the time, but 'twas never serious. Who usually won?"

When Claire cast him a puzzled look, he clarified, "When Connor and James fought, who usually won?"

"Och, Connor did. All the time."

They talked the entire way to Ravenglade, and Claire was glad they did. She saw a more open and genuine side of Graham. She had been wrong about his not caring for anyone. He cared deeply about his kin and his friends, and Claire found herself a bit envious of them. She was sorry she had said all those terrible things to him, but he seemed to have forgotten them, and that was fine with her.

"Do as I say," she said in a low voice as they waited for the drawbridge to descend in front of them. "Give the others a chance to get accustomed to you and all will be fine."

Graham didn't answer, but scanned the entire inner bailey when it came into view. It was deserted but for a few bothies, a smith, and at least fifty men waiting on horseback on the other side of the drawbridge. Another fifty stood watching them from the battlements, alert to the visitors below.

"Impressive," Graham muttered to Claire as the horsemen approached. "All Buchanans?"

"Hardly any Buchanans," Claire told him. "These are mostly men who follow my brother. The Buchanans hold this land in fief for my cousin Charles, but Connor ruled here. All are outlaws, and don't care who they kill." She cut him a teasing glance. "So make sure they like you.

"Captain," she called out, and a rider took the lead, reaching her first. The man looked happy enough to see her, but spared her only a brief look before his eyes settled on Graham.

"Steven, there is a group of men waiting beyond the forest. Anne is with them. They are Royalists, save one, and he is a friend. You will ride out now and bring them here while I inform James."

The captain did not hesitate to do her bidding, even as another man, riding out from the rest, ordered him to make haste.

He sat tall in the saddle, his raven hair slicked back into a tight queue tied at his nape. His eyes were a deep shade of cobalt lit from within when he looked at Claire. Graham watched him closely as he offered Claire a loving smile and raised her hand to his lips.

"I should throttle your neck for leaving here without a word. I feared you dead."

"Monck took Anne," Claire informed him. "She has been safely returned to us," she hastened to add when his expression went black. Graham eyed her, noting her use of the word "us." "James, this is Commander Graham Grant. He and his companion . . ."

James finally turned to Graham. "Commander of the clan Grant?"

Graham shook his head. "The clan MacGregor."

Looking rather impressed himself, James held his hand out to him. "Have you come to fight on our side? We certainly could use you."

"James," Claire drew his attention back to her. "Commander Grant and the MacGregors aided me in rescuing Anne. The rest of his men await safe approach."

"They have it!" Buchanan ordered without hesitation. "They are welcome to stay for as long as they wish."

"One night is sufficient," Graham thanked him.

"James, they saved Anne with the invaluable aid of Lord Campbell of Argyll."

"A Campbell?" James turned back to her, a deep frown marking his brow. "They are Roundheads, Claire."

"Aye, I know that," Claire agreed with a wry smile. She

loved James dearly, but he had a way of speaking down to her, as if she could not possibly understand the ways of war, her being a woman and all. "I trust him."

James lifted a doubtful brow at her, then offered her an indulgent smile. "There is much you need to tell me, I think."

Claire nodded, then looked at Graham. How would she get James alone before the morning? Did she even want to anymore? Aye, she had no choice. James had to help her now. Once she and her sister reached Skye there would be no escaping the fearsome protection of the chieftain whose name his own men whispered. And all to be brought right back to Monck when he sent for them.

Chapter Sixteen

If only we could see what is truly written on a man's heart.

Robert sat with Graham and the others in Ravenglade's great hall. They'd been here for over an hour now discussing the social unrest of the country and Monck's reasoning for requesting the MacGregors' aid in keeping Connor Stuart's sisters safe until he found them trustworthy husbands. When Buchanan asked if the governor had chosen who those husbands might be, Robert answered with a resounding no before Graham or anyone else had a chance to reply. He worried that Buchanan might claim his bride now that she was here. Robert was not opposed to fighting, but four and ten men would have no chance against Ravenglade's garrison should Buchanan refuse to let Anne leave.

"Claire said that her brother was killed in London?" Robert heard Graham ask.

"That is correct," Buchanan replied somberly. "We were ambushed on our way to meet with General Fleetwood. I feel responsible for Connor's death."

And mayhap you are, Robert thought before his mind wandered back to Anne. Where had she been carted off to? It was the first time she'd been out of his sight since they left Edinburgh. He hoped Claire was with her. There were too many unruly looking men here for him to feel comfortable with Anne anywhere but at his side.

"And how did Connor receive word that Fleetwood had agreed to a meeting?" Graham asked. "Did Monck send a missive?"

Robert perked his ear to Buchanan's reply. If he answered aye, they would have him. General Monck said he put nothing in writing when communicating with Royalists.

"There was no missive," Buchanan said, dashing Robert's hopes. "One of the agreements Monck had with Connor was that there could never exist any proof of the governor's associations with the rebel Royalists."

"Then who delivered the message about the meeting?" Robert asked, tapping his fingers on the table.

"I did," Buchanan said. "After it was delivered to me by one of Monck's captains."

Robert turned his full attention to Anne's betrothed. "Why was it not delivered to Stuart directly?"

"I do not know," Buchanan replied, meeting the suspicion in Robert's eyes with a rapier-sharp sneer. "Tell me, Roundhead, how it is that you succeeded in gaining the trust of Connor Stuart's sister?"

Robert explained how they had come upon her being held captive by Lambert's men outside Stirling.

"Ah, so you saved her." Buchanan guessed the rest.

"Don't tell her that." Graham's easy laughter filled the hall. "Six men were already dead by the time we arrived on the scene. Lady Stuart is a bit overzealous, aye?"

"A bit?" Buchanan leaned back in his chair and drew

out a long-suffering sigh. "God protect the poor fool who takes her as a wife."

Graham agreed, and the two men burst into hearty laughter.

Robert was surprised that Graham was finding such amusement in his predicament. It seemed his friend's humor had been fully restored. Robert glowered at him, then went back to frowning at the comely bastard Anne was to marry. "General Monck's men were attacked outside Stirling. Do you know anything about that?"

"Are you suggesting that I do, Campbell?" Buchanan's laughter faded as he pushed forward slowly in his seat.

"Of course not," Graham intervened jovially before Robert opened his mouth again. "We've been in the saddle longer than any of us cares to recall. Mayhap another drink will help restore our normally agreeable natures."

"A fine idea!" Angus nearly stood up and cheered Graham's suggestion.

Agreeable natures? Why in damnation was Graham insinuating that they might be willing to accept whatever Buchanan told them? Robert certainly would not be swayed so easily. Graham knew that.

Sparing Robert one last warning look, Buchanan motioned for more drinks to be served before turning his attention back to Graham. "General Monck is now my mortal enemy, it is true," he amended with a casual shrug of his broad shoulders. "But I would be a fool to attack him or his men. Surely you realize that, Commander. When the king is restored, the governor will be brought to justice."

"I respect yer restraint, Buchanan." Graham accepted his cup and raised it to Claire's "dear James." Beside him,

Robert's chair screeched against the floorboards as he left it. "If 'twere my best friend that had been slain," Graham continued as if no interruption had occurred, "I fear my rash emotions would get the best of me."

Robert stewed, gazing out the window at the bailey below. How much longer was Graham going to kiss Buchanan's arse? He'd delivered his message to Buchanan. Monck wanted to see him. Buchanan refused, citing his mistrust for the man he claimed had betrayed his friend. There was naught more to discuss. They were no closer to knowing the truth than they were yesterday. Robert wanted to leave, to take Anne to Skye, where he could . . .

"'Tis the mark of a great leader when his men show such ferbearance," Graham went on, further irritating Robert.

The hall grew uncomfortably silent for the space of a breath. Robert tapped his foot on the floor.

"Aye," Buchanan finally said. "A great leader, indeed."

"Claire told me ye were good friends."

"Aye, we were."

"Like brothers."

"I loved him, I am not ashamed to say."

Robert prayed for patience when Graham began talking about Callum. When Angus and Brodie joined in the praising of *their* great laird and leader, Robert swore under his breath. How much more time would they waste here? Why the hell was Graham so talkative, so damned affable? God's blood, Graham could befriend all of Parliament if he set his mind to it.

Robert's eyes widened suddenly as understanding dawned on him and he realized what Graham was doing.

"Let us drink to Connor Stuart." Graham's voice was

downright reverent. "Tell us about this man who was like a brother to ye, and that fateful day of his death. Ye were with him. It must have been painful fer ye, indeed."

Robert finally smiled when Buchanan began to talk, lured by the warm smile and the "agreeable nature" of his guest.

Clever bastard.

Claire closed the heavy wooden door behind her, looked around to ensure that no one in Graham's company had seen her, and stole down the torchlit hall of the upper landing. James had agreed to aid her, and promised to do so without bloodshed. Now she only had to convince Anne to go along with their plan.

She came to an abrupt halt when she saw Graham turning the corner with Mary, the wife of Iain MacDonald, one of Connor's most faithful followers. It was clear by Mary's low, inviting laughter that Graham was in the process of seducing her right out of her marriage vows! Claire gritted her teeth. Did the rogue's decadence know no bounds?

He looked up from Mary's dreamy gaze, bringing his slow, salacious smile with him. It faded an instant later when he looked over Claire's shoulder at James leaving the chamber a few feet behind her. When his potent emerald gaze fell back to her, Claire recoiled at the betrayal and fury she saw in them. Och, dear God, he knew! How could he know?

"Lady Stuart, I was looking fer ye." Graham left Mary and reached her five breaths before James did. "A clandestine meeting with yer dear friend?" he bent to her and murmured low to her ear while cupping her elbow in his palm.

"Grant," Buchanan slapped Graham's shoulder. "I was hoping you'd share a drink with me tonight. It's been a long time since I've enjoyed my wine."

Graham spared him the briefest glance. "Ye have my thanks fer the offer, but right now I intend to have a word with Claire." He smiled, just in case Buchanan thought to take offense, and if he did, let him draw his sword and do something about it. Graham almost wished he would. He did not trust the bastard, and knowing now that Claire had just left his private chambers scalded his veins with rage. His dismissal of Buchanan was abrupt, and turning his attention to Claire once more, he ground out, "This will take but a moment."

She tried to free her elbow from his hard fingers, but he pulled her along to the other end of the hall. When he reached the chambers he'd been given to use for the night, he shoved open the door, looked over his shoulder, and pushed her inside.

"Are you mad?" Claire turned on him the moment he shut the door. "He barely trusts any of you. A Campbell and a bunch of barbaric Highlanders have a secret meeting with Monck—"

"Secret meeting?" Graham asked incredulously. "Is that what he has ye believing now?"

"Nae, Graham, he does not know what to believe, just as you and Robert don't. He does nothing because he is still undecided about you. Do not give him reason to decide against you."

Graham almost laughed in her face, but he was too angry with her. "I don't like secret meetings either, Claire." He took a step toward her, and when she didn't back up, he gave her a slight push. Her legs hit the bed and she fell back on her rump. "What were ye doing in his chamber if 'twasn't to grow fat with a dozen of his babes?"

She sprang back to her feet, and when he pushed her back a second time, she swung her fist at his face. He caught her wrist seconds before it hit his jaw. He advanced, forcing her onto the mattress. He swooped over her, pinning one wrist above her head and the other behind her back. "I'll subdue ye, Claire. Nae matter how skilled ye are, ye will not win, nor will Buchanan. Now, tell me. What were ye doing in his chamber?"

"You have ten breaths to get off me before I start screaming."

Poised above her, he stared down into her eyes, so damn tempted to kiss her. God, just to taste her again. "Och, Claire, I beg ye don't, fer then I'll be forced to quiet ye."

Something in his raspy plea convinced her not to scream. "Graham," she said his name softly instead, not wanting to fight with him. "Anne and I cannot go to Skye with you. Would you have us go there to await our fate with no way of escape? Monck will try to wed us to Roundheads."

Only one of you. Graham felt anguish looking at her. Ah, God's mercy! He pushed himself off her and sank back on his haunches. "Hell, Claire," he said looking as if she'd just struck him with a fatal blow.

She rose on her elbows and faced him. "I must stay here where I'm safe."

"And how d'ye intend to do that, lass?" he asked her quietly.

Before she could stop herself, she lifted her hand to his jaw and ran her fingers along its bristly edge. He did not move away. His gaze on her warmed, proving her touch affected him. She had to tell him the truth. If he was injured . . . killed because he thought the attack was real and fought harder. . . . She had betrayed him, and she needed to tell him the truth, even if he hated her for it. "I asked James to dispatch a legion of his men toward Killiecrankie." Now he pulled his face away, his eyes burning her. "No one would be harmed," she hastened to explain, trying to smooth the harsh steel of her betrayal. "James gave me his word on it. It is a strategy we have used many times with Lambert's troops. James's men are to lie in wait and come upon us in the night. None of your men will be harmed, just restrained . . . mayhap knocked unconscious. Anne and I will be brought back here, where James will hide us."

"And no one will suspect 'twas James since we were attacked far from Ravenglade."

"Aye," she spoke as softly as he. "This is where Anne and I will be safest, Graham. Not with the MacGregors, whom I do not even know."

"Nae, Claire." He shook his head. "This is where you are the most unsafe. Here, with the man who killed Connor."

Claire sprang from the bed and glared at him. "James did not kill my brother! How dare you speak such a horrible thing?"

"He did," Graham said, following her off the bed. "But I cannot prove it to ye."

"Of course you can't, because it is not true!"

"I believe James hated yer brother."

Claire tried to laugh at him, but she was too angry, too stunned by his accusation. "Nae, Graham. You are wrong."

"James was jealous of him," he continued even while

she shook her head. He had to make her see the truth. She was in danger here. "It began as lads. Connor always won. James leads an entire army of men who are not his and who would likely kill him if they knew the truth. Think, Claire. Do not let yer heart cloud yer judgment."

"It is too late for that." Her eyes flashed at him. "You truly are a devil-tongued viper!" When he cast her a puzzled look, she gritted her teeth at him. "You used me to gain information about James, and then used what I told you to aid you in your decision against him." She whirled on her heel and headed for the door.

"He accompanied yer brother to England, but returned completely unscathed without him." He spoke quickly, reaching her before she reached the door. "'Twas he who told Connor about the meeting, not Monck. They lost forty men, but Buchanan was fortunate enough to escape."

Claire paused, keeping her gaze averted from his, lest she be tempted to listen to any more of this . . . this blasphemy! "That means naught save James is better skilled than the rest."

"Better than Connor? Nae, Connor died because he trusted a friend who led him straight to Lambert's men."

Now she raised her gaze to his, uncertainty and fear clearly visible in her sapphire eyes. "You are right. You have no proof."

"I understand brotherhood, friendship." His words stopped her again when she would have pushed past him. "I know it well, and I would give my life's blood fer it. A man who grudgingly toasts his dead brother, or who boasts of his prowess in battle instead of boasting of his friend, is not a friend at all."

Claire squared her shoulders, took a deep breath,

and left the chamber. When she closed the door, she fell against it. Graham was mad! He had to be. She knew James, had grown up with him. He was incapable of such a devious deed. Never would he have betrayed Connor so. Graham was wrong! He had to be!

Chapter Seventeen

Is he ruled by honor, or by avarice? I fear I no longer know which is more powerful of the two.

The great hall was alive with the sound of merriment. Everywhere Claire looked men drank, laughed, and stumbled into chairs. Ravenglade had not changed since last she'd seen it. The men were never so rowdy when she used to visit with Connor. If she and her brother remained for a month, the men practiced every day of that month, almost without pause. Connor had built a strong army, but after he died, the men grew lax and fat. Why did James allow it?

She spotted the man she'd known since childhood reclining in the chair that had once been reserved for her brother, as leader. Was it so unusual that James should claim it now? He was the new head of the resistance, after all. Her eyes moved over the long table to Graham seated at James's left. At his right sat her sister, with Robert beside her. All looked happy enough, save for Robert, who appeared preoccupied with darker thoughts. Claire wondered what they were as she watched him. Anne was right about the young earl's eyes being radiant. It wasn't their extraordinary mixture of color, but his utter lack of guile that made them so. Did he share Graham's belief about James? And what would the noble knight try to do about it, if he did?

She should march straight to them and tell James everything. Her loyalty was to him, after all. But he would kill Graham and Robert for making such a heinous accusation, and mayhap go to war with the MacGregors. What was she to do? She thought about running from Ravenglade, from all of them. She knew many places to hide where they would never find her. She could forget them all and never think again about who had betrayed her brother, or who she betrayed. But that would be cowardly, and she could not leave Anne alone.

Her eyes settled again on Graham reclining comfortably in his chair, his cap pushed over his forehead. Why did she tell him of her and James's plans? She thought he would understand her plight, mayhap even agree to help her. If he fought James, one of them would surely die.

She watched James throw his head back with laughter at something Graham said to him. She met the Highlander's sober gaze and realized what he was doing. He was making James like him, trust him, as he had done to her. It was the commander's most effective weapon.

"Ah, Claire, come join us." James beckoned her to their table.

She did not want to go, but Graham's potent gaze drew her toward him. She had changed into fresh trews and a clean, blouse-sleeved shirt. Her thick, pale braid dangled over her breast. His eyes took in every inch of her, touching her like a heated caress. God help her, she knew the true reason she'd told him all. She wanted to trust him with her life, with her heart. She wanted to believe that he was not so uncaring toward her. That his kisses, his warm smiles were real. Hell have her for wanting it, but she did.

When she reached the table, he stood and offered her his seat beside James. She severed her gaze from him and fought to keep her breath at an even pace when she stepped around him and her body brushed his.

She offered her smile to James as she sat. In return, he took her hand, and then her sister's, and set his rather proud gaze on the inhabitants of the hall. Everything that was Connor's was his now, and a moment of terror and fury passed through Claire at seeing him revel in it.

She closed her eyes, refusing to entertain such horrible notions. She had the urge to kick Graham under the table for putting them in her head.

"Lord Buchanan has informed me that when the monarchy is restored, he will ask fer yer hand."

Claire opened her eyes on Graham, certain that her ears had just deceived her. Slowly, she pulled her hand out of James's grasp. "Is this true?" She turned to him.

Releasing Anne, James leaned forward in his chair and cast a dark glare at Graham. "I told you that in confidence."

"Fergive me." Graham's daring smirk looked anything but repentant. "I wanted to see the joy in her eyes ye told me she'd feel when she learned of yer plans fer her."

"James?" Claire backed away from him, almost landing in Graham's lap. "You know I will not marry you. Why would you tell him such a thing?"

"Why will you not marry me, Claire?" He shifted in her brother's chair and reached for her hand again with both of his. "I know Connor and I used to talk of my wedding Anne, but you are the elder. Now that Connor is gone everything has changed. There is much to consider."

"Mayhap Connor chose another man for Lady Stuart?"

All eyes turned on Robert, sitting quietly up to that moment. He did not look up right away, but continued drawing small circles on the table with his finger. "Did he not discuss his twin sister's future with you, or the lands that came with her, should he perish?" He lifted his eyes to Buchanan. "Surely, a man who lived such a perilous life would make arrangements for both his sisters. And surely, he would share his decisions with his closest friend."

"Surely he would," Graham intoned, and smiled at Claire when she turned to stare at him.

"As a matter of fact," James told them both, "Connor never made any arrangements for Claire. She fought with us as a man, and he—"

"As a man?" Graham asked curiously, staring at her.

"He means that I fight like one," Claire hastened to explain. "Isn't that correct, James."

"Aye," James corrected, reaching under the table for his shin. "She fights like a man, and in truth, her brother doubted she would live long enough to wed."

Claire went still in her seat. She felt as if a bolt of lightning had just coursed through her. Connor did not doubt she would live. He had never put that fear into her. Aye, he worried for her, as any brother would, but he was confident in the skill he taught her. And he had made certain to teach her everything he knew, so that she would live.

She wiped her brow. Suddenly, nothing made sense anymore. Connor was the only man in her life who had truly accepted who she was, the life she chose. And James knew it. Why would he say such a cruel thing?

She could not breathe. She had to get away from them and try to sort this all out. Her family loved James, and he loved them. She simply could not accept that he hated Connor and had betrayed him out of jealousy. No. She shook her head, but tears welled up in her eyes, and she bolted to her feet before anyone took notice.

"Excuse me. I need air."

James and Graham stood at the same time, both men ready to follow her. "Angus," Graham called his bulky friend over while he placed a hand on Buchanan's shoulder to stop him from moving. "What sort of ill-mannered ruffian are ye, MacGregor, to dine in a man's home and not offer him some of yer brew?" He patted Buchanan's arm and winked at him. "I'll see to the lass. Ye stay and have a drink with Angus, lest ye insult his cousin, Brodie." He leaned in and added in a whisper, "That one isn't right in the head."

Before turning away from the table, Graham caught Robert's eye. Here was the one who should follow her, damn it. Graham would respect it. He would take his seat and try for the thousandth time to keep her from his thoughts. But hell, he had seen her tears and he wanted to go to her.

Seeming to read his thoughts, or mayhap seeing the torn look of his best friend, Robert motioned for him to hurry.

Chapter Eighteen

Would that I had learned to better discern the truth in a man's eyes.

Graham found her in the lists. It was the second place he looked after finding her horse in the stable. Beneath the light of the pale full moon, Claire found comfort in what she did best. He approached slowly, his eyes fastened on the beauty of her form while she swung her blade at an unseen opponent, her flaxen braid whipping around her waist. Softly defined against the golden incandescence of torchlight along the castle walls, she appeared like some warrior princess of old; fair, fervent, and agile. She was so bonny he found it almost painful to look at her for too long. Still he could not take his eyes off her. When she'd fought at his side against the thieves, he barely had time to watch her movements. Now, he stood in silence noting each impeccably timed execution, every seamless combination of parry, sweep, retreat, and jab. Her blade played the air in a flawlessly savage arrangement of skill, focus, and purpose.

"Claire," he whispered, moving toward her as if pulled by an iron chain he was helpless to resist. She stopped and turned to him with a look of such despair, he almost ran the rest of the way.

With a twist of her wrist, she sheathed her blade and tried to blink away the tears misting her eyes. "Graham, my brother did not doubt my skill."

"I can see why."

A smile gently touched her lips, but it faded when she spoke again. "I refuse to believe that James betrayed Connor."

"It matters not, Claire. I will not leave Ravenglade without ye."

She stepped closer to him and caught her breath as yearning flooded through her. Never in her life had she felt so alone, so vulnerable. She wanted him to hold her, tell her that all would be well, and that he was wrong about James.

"I did not think chivalry was in your nature, rogue." She stopped a hair's breadth away from him and tilted her face up to meet his gaze.

"Nor did I." He stared into her eyes, wanting her, needing her more than anything in his life. But he did not touch her.

He drove Claire mad with excruciating awareness of every inch of his body. The way his shoulders rose and fell with a deep inhalation of breath, a chest rigid, save for his thrashing heartbeat, with an extravagant expanse of warm muscle. He did not move when she reached for him, but simply watched her with dark, hooded, hungry eyes. Emboldened by his silence, or her madness, she smoothed her palms over his chest and up his shoulders. Driven by a need she barely understood, she coiled her arms around his neck and pulled him down.

"Do not be chivalrous now, I beg you."

No longer able to resist her, Graham's arm snaked around her waist, snatching her clear off the floor. He took her mouth with savage intensity, absolute possession, until she felt as if she was drowning in his kiss, dying in his arms.

"Graham?"

Robert's voice in the night shattered their embrace and pulled a wretched groan from Graham. He turned, already knowing there was nothing he could say; still a dozen words battered against his lips. "Rob, I . . . I'm . . ." God, he was sorry. Why could he not he say it?

Robert simply looked at Claire, then at him, then at his boots. "There's a brawl going on inside. Brodie broke Steven's nose. You're needed."

Pushing Graham out of her way, Claire stepped around him. "Why did Brodie break his nose?" she demanded. She liked her brother's captain. He was a brave warrior and a friend of hers.

"The captain made a jest about the MacGregors," Robert told her quietly, calmly for one who had just stepped out of a brawl. "Too much drink."

"The damn fools." Sensing Graham still behind her, she wheeled around. "Well? Are you going to stop them?"

His eyes fell from Robert's to hers. "Aye. Gather yer sister in the meantime. We are leaving." He turned on his heel and strode away before she could protest.

Left alone with Robert, Claire angled her glance at him and gave her hair a prim pat. "I know what you must be thinking."

"And what is that?" He clasped his hands behind his back and looked down at her.

"That I'm a fool." She sighed and closed her eyes. "He cares for no one."

"That is not true, my lady."

She opened her eyes and nodded, her frustration clearly evident. "Aye, he cares for you, and he cares for Callum MacGregor. I can hear it in his voice. But you know exactly what I mean."

"I don't think you're a fool." His eyes softened on her and Claire realized once again how incredibly handsome and kind he was. Anne would be happy with this man.

"Come." He held out his arm for her. "Let's go inside before Angus brings down the castle."

Taking his arm, Claire smiled and pressed into him as they walked. "You have become a friend to me, Roundhead."

"That pleases me."

She looked up at his strong jaw, his soft, dark hair curling slightly at his neck, and those lashes—hell, Anne was right—they were long. "What think you of Anne?" She smiled, feeling his body stiffen. "I see. I used to think James would make a good husband for her, but I see the way she looks at you, and I must admit—"

He stopped walking and turned her around to face him fully. "There is something you need to know, Claire."

She dipped her gaze. Why did they have to speak of this? "Graham has already told me."

He blinked. "He has?"

"Aye, he believes James is behind Connor's death. You believe it too, then?"

"I do, but that is—"

"Nae, you are both wrong. There is an explanation for

all of this. I will speak to James about it and he shall prove his innocence to you."

"Prove my innocence?"

Claire and Robert both started when James stepped out of the shadows and right up to them. "In what matter?" His sapphire eyes settled on Claire first, and then on Robert.

"James." Claire pulled his attention back to her gently. "May we speak for a moment in the solar?"

Catching Robert's wary look, James nodded and took her hand.

Robert sprang to the other side of her, refusing to leave her alone with Buchanan.

"We should pick up Commander Grant on the way," Claire suggested as they entered the castle. "These are things he should hear, as well."

"Of course," James agreed pleasantly. "But then I shall have to bring Steven, and mayhap a few others. Claire," he quieted her with a quelling stare when she tried to protest. "I do not know what these men have told you, but if they have made charges against me, should I sit with them alone and unprotected?"

"Nae," she amended softly. "Of course not." Someone would most definitely end up dead. "Lord Campbell can simply tell Grant what he heard."

"Very well, let us go then." Buchanan led her toward the stairs. Passing the great hall, Robert looked inside for Graham, but did not see him amid the crowd.

The small solar above was clearly a place Claire had spent much of her time with her brother. Her posture relaxed the moment she entered. She smiled, crossing the room to a high-backed chair of carved oak and velvet claret. She stood before it and gave it a thoughtful look before she turned and sat in it.

"James," she began without waiting, while Robert pulled a less ornate chair up to hers. James chose to stand, and Claire had to crane her neck to look at him. "Your guests mean you no harm. Like you, they are eager to discover who the man is who betrayed Connor."

"Then why are they not in Edinburgh accusing him?"

"Because," Robert answered for Claire. When he looked up, his disdain for Buchanan shone clearly in his eyes. "We hold no suspicion of General Monck."

James's lips tightened across his teeth and his hand slipped toward his sword. Claire bolted to her feet, but Robert remained still.

"You accuse me then of betraying my brother?"

Robert met Buchanan's murderous glare with equal measure. "I have made no such accusation."

Just when Claire began to relax her shoulders, relieved that the confrontation had been averted, Robert rose slowly to his feet.

"Connor Stuart was not your brother."

Claire closed her eyes and ground her teeth. How could he say such a thing? And what the hell was wrong with the fool? Robert Campbell did not know how to fight, yet here he was, roaring like a lion. A dead lion, if she did nothing.

Stepping between them, she laid her hand on James's chest. "I know you did not do this terrible thing." She looked up into her dear friend's eyes and saw the deep insult Robert and Graham had cut him with. "But they do not know you as I do. Explain to Lord Campbell how Connor died, as you told me."

His gaze cut like glass, slicing her to the quick. "You doubt my word, and before a Campbell, Claire?"

"Nae, it is not that . . ." she shook her head.

"You ask me to explain. To him!"

"I would request that you not shout at her," Robert warned from over her head.

A snarl curled one end of James's mouth as he swept his sword free of its sheath with one hand and pushed Claire out of his way with the other.

His blade sang while Claire fell against her brother's chair, slicing her lip on the wood. She could do naught but close her eyes as James swung at poor Robert. His blade, though, did not meet flesh, but steel. The clang made her teeth itch. She leaped to her feet, prepared to block Robert from another swing. Someone had to save him. Instead, her eyes widened as they followed the young earl's claymore moving in a blinding flash of speed against the hearth's firelight. He met James's next assault with a well-timed step to the left, and a combination block, arc, and swing.

Satan's balls, Claire would have smiled if she wasn't so terrified for them both. The lad *could* fight! When Robert lifted his sword over his head and brought down a blow that drove James back toward the door, she rethought her first opinion of who would not survive this altercation.

She had made a move to intervene when the door opened and James spilled into Graham's arms.

Immediately, Robert sheathed his blade and smiled at his friend, thankful that Graham had saved him from having to kill Buchanan.

Graham did not smile back, but fastened his eyes on the blood staining Claire's lips. His face went hard as he hauled James upright, clutched him by the back of the throat, and hurled him face-first into the wall.

When he turned to check on Claire, letting James's limp body slip from his grasp, she was right behind him and in midswing. Her fist caught him square in the mouth, tilting his head back. Grasping his jaw, he looked down at her with something akin to stunned disbelief widening his eyes. He reached for her and she swung at him again. This time, he caught her, spun her around, and tucked her under his arm.

"Let's get the hell out of here." He cut Robert a look of annoyance on his way to the door. "Ye'll tell me what happened later."

"Are you bloody mad?" Claire screeched at both of them as she dug her nails into her captor's arm and tried to kick him. "I'm not going anywhere with you!" She twisted her arm to punch Graham in his chest, but her swing could gain no momentum. "Why did you do that to him? I think you must have broken his nose!"

"Claire, unless ye want to get us killed, be silent."

She peered up at Graham while her long braid swept the floor. Damn him, he was right. If Steven saw her being carted down the stairs like a sack of wheat, he would alert the guard. Graham and Robert would never get out of Ravenglade alive. Damn them to Hades, why did she care? "Put me down, you son of a dog," she ground out at Graham. "Though you do not deserve it, I will do what I can to save your lives, but Anne and I are not leaving Ravenglade with you."

When her feet hit the floor, she smoothed the wrinkles out of her sleeves and took a step forward. Graham's chest stopped her from taking another.

"I'm not leaving ye here with him, Claire." He spoke quickly, his jaw rigid, his gaze impaling her. "If ye insist on staying, I'll have nae choice but to return to Buchanan right now and make certain he will never be a threat to ye."

Claire went pale. Dear God, he was serious. He would kill James. "I hate you," she whispered on a shaky breath.

He swallowed, and for an instant she thought she saw his resolve falter, but then his eyes hardened on her, ruthless, merciless. "Decide."

"What choice do I have?" she bit out acidly.

He nodded, proving that he gave her no choice at all. "Ye will do as I say and obey my commands. If we are forced to fight our way out, many lives will be lost on both sides."

Claire conceded with a tight nod and let him and Robert lead her down the stairs. What else could she do? If she screamed, Steven would come running. A battle would ensue, and Claire would have to choose a side on which to fight. She was angry with Graham, but she knew she couldn't fight against him.

When they reached the bottom step, Graham surveyed the great hall with sharp eyes. He found Steven first, seated now, his face wiped clean of blood. He moved on until he found the man he sought.

A subtle nod from his longtime commander pulled Brodie to his feet. Within an instant, the silent order passed throughout the hall and every MacGregor followed. They were leaving—and they might need to fight to get out. Being warriors, they knew that ofttimes hasty retreats could not be avoided. There was no cowardice in it. They would fight another day.

Angus led the group across the crowded floor, his bulk carving a straight path to Graham. Robert dashed to their table and escorted Anne back to his group.

"To the stables," Graham commanded. "Angus and Donel will hold the rear while Robert and I lower the drawbridge." He looked up at his burly friend. "Angus, if anyone goes after them, take off their heads."

"Nae!" Claire whispered hotly. She would not stand by while the MacGregors slaughtered Connor's men.

Graham cut his gaze to her and then withdrew his order and told Angus to make them sleep instead.

"Claire, what is going on?" Anne's eyes were wide with fear as she clutched her sister's wrist.

"Where is the drawbridge room, Claire?" Graham demanded, cutting off her reply to Anne.

Casting him a reproachful look, she told him and then gave her sister a slight shove forward, following the others out the doors.

When they reached the stables, Brodie pushed her into the darkness. "Ye know where the stalls are. They need to be opened, now."

Claire sprinted to the stalls and released the horses as Angus and Donel joined them, unimpeded. Brodie was the first to mount and the first one out. Claire took last position with Anne between herself and Angus. They sped across the moonlit bailey, halting at the drawbridge and waiting for it to descend.

Satan's balls, what should I do? Claire looked behind her. Her instincts told her to go back. She could not abandon James. He would never forgive her. But if she returned, Graham would kill him. She was certain of it. Why? Why did he suspect James of such a terrible thing? Would he and Robert go to Monck with their suspicions? No, they had no proof. They could do nothing. *Nothing but kill him themselves.* Dear God, were they doing that now?

"Claire, please tell me what is going on?" Her sister's terrified voice pulled her attention back. "Why are we fleeing like this? What has happened?"

"A misunderstanding," Claire promised lightly. "I will explain it to you later, but there is naught to fret over."

When the massive chains of the drawbridge screeched and rolled through Claire's ears, she closed her eyes and tried to quiet her pounding heart. They'd gone directly to the drawbridge room as Graham had said. Relief flooded through her. James was still alive.

The thick planks were going down fast. Too fast. She pulled her shoulders around her ears as the drawbridge smashed down, sending dirt and splinters flying.

"Let's go!" she heard Brodie order, and joined him as he flew across.

When they reached the other side, Claire wheeled her horse around. The men of Ravenglade had to have heard that! She was right. The captain was the first one out, followed by a charge of others. To her right, Claire caught a flash of metal beneath the moonlight as Brodie unsheathed his long claymore.

"Steven, stop! Do not come across!" Claire shouted at him, and was not surprised when he obeyed, calling a halt to the rest.

"My lady, what is the meaning of this?" He motioned to the drawbridge, having no idea why she, her sister, and the MacGregors were on the other side.

"I am afraid we must leave. We have a long journey ahead, you know." She prayed with all her heart for some miracle that would make the captain simply smile and wave them farewell. She groaned when Steven began to advance again.

"Why are there only fourteen horses with you?" He peered across the bridge at them, straining to see who was missing, but it was too dark and too far. "Where are the other two riders?"

Claire glanced at the castle gate. Aye, where the hell were Graham and Robert? How were they going to get past Steven and the small army behind him? Her fingers tightened on her reins, but she managed to keep her voice steady as she called out, "They are receiving rations from Amish, the cook. They should be along any moment now. Ah," she smiled past Steven's shoulder at Graham and Robert rounding the lists, their horses tearing up the earth behind them. "Here they are now." She swung her gaze back to Steven when he reached for his sword. "Captain, you shall let them pass."

To her chagrin and distress, Steven did not obey her this time. With a commander's shout, he ordered his men into battle formation. Fortunately, most of them were too drunk to know their direction.

With a curse that bit at the wind, Claire ripped her cap from her belt, yanked her braid up into it, and charged her mount over the drawbridge. She had to stop Steven before he lifted his blade to Graham and the twelve strapping Highlanders behind her rushed into the fray. She meant to stop the captain, not kill him. So when she came upon him, she whipped her sword across her chest and brought it back hard against his, knocking it from his hand.

"Captain, you will call a halt!" she commanded with the same force her brother would have used, and looking much like him, wearing his cap. Her blade flashed beneath the moonlight as its tip came to rest against Steven's throat. "Do not make me tell you a third time."

Steven stared up at her with muted fury, but he did nothing while Robert sped past them and onward to Anne. Graham slowed his mount to a halt when he reached Claire.

"This was all a terrible misunderstanding, Steven," Claire promised the captain, with regret softening her voice. "I will return and give a full account. But for now, you must do as I say." She sheathed her blade and snapped her reins, taking off with Graham over the drawbridge without another word.

Chapter Nineteen

What is there to trust, save what we have been taught?

They were not followed into the black woods. Still, they rode on through the labyrinth of thick oak and birch for leagues, until the next morn. They traveled west, avoiding Killiekrankie and James's waiting men, and did not stop until they reached the banks of Loch Tay.

In silence, Claire helped her sister dismount. Anne's legs buckled beneath her from being in the saddle so long, but as she led her away, Claire praised her for not issuing a word of complaint. Graham watched them as they reached the center of the small, sunlit clearing and Claire laid out her sister's pallet. His eyes followed her a moment later when Claire cut across the campsite and squatted at the edge of the loch to dip her hands in the water. He wanted to go to her, to take her in his arms and make certain that nothing more than her lip had been injured. Hell, he'd never forget how she looked when she told him she hated him. She was angry with him for making her leave Ravenglade and for pounding Buchanan's face into the wall when she should be grateful that he did not skewer the bastard after seeing her bloody mouth. How was he to know that her injury was accidental? While they rode, Robert had told him what happened in Ravenglade's solar. She believed in Buchanan's innocence, and Graham could not fault her for it. Such betrayal from a friend was difficult to accept. He would not force her to listen to any more of his charges against the man she considered her friend. She was safe, for now, away from her brother's killer. They had to tell General Monck, of course, but that could wait until after they reached Skye. What happened after that, Graham did not want to ponder. Monck would go forward with his marriage arrangement for Claire and Rob. But what of Anne, now that her betrothed was sure to hang?

Rob had said naught of the passionate kiss he'd witnessed between his best friend and his betrothed in the lists, and Graham almost wished he had. He had had many lasses—could have his pick of dozens more. Was he so black-hearted that he sought to take his friend's woman? What was this madness that made him desire Claire Stuart more than any other?

He cursed fate for bringing him to her. How the hell could his life change so profoundly in so short a time? He could not think clearly on anything but her. Not battle. Not women. Just her. Her mouth. Her eyes. Her hair. Her scent. He knew how she walked, talked, ate, breathed. It was driving him mad. Hell, even when she punched him in the mouth he wanted to drag her into his arms and kiss her senseless. His gaze settled on her again. She snatched his breath away, even looking like a lad . . .

He moved toward her as if his legs had a mind of their own. His eyes were fastened to the bonnet on her head. Hell, he'd been right. Fear gripped him as never before when he thought of her fighting the governor's men alone.

When he reached her, he bent his knees beside her and looked out over the water. "'Twas ye who had attacked Monck's men."

She nodded without looking at him. "Monck betrayed Connor."

"I do not believe he did," he said quietly, turning to look at her. "Hell, Claire, ye could have been killed."

"I wasn't."

He studied her profile while she kept her gaze on the loch. He didn't know whether to shake her for being so foolish, or admire her courage and skill. How in blazes had Connor lived each day without being sick with fear for her safety? He taught her to fight like a man, Graham answered himself. More than that, her brother had trained her to be a warrior. And yet, here she was, a lass, more bonny than any other, setting his heart aflame with a need that rattled him to his core.

"You and Robert are wrong," she said quietly. "James loved Connor. He did not betray him, and I shall never forgive you for striking him."

"I struck him because I thought he struck ye," he corrected her. When she finally tilted her face to look at him, the curious quirk of her flaxen brow, the vivid bonny blue of her eyes hit him like a kick in the guts. He turned away, knowing that if she looked into his eyes she would perceive a weakness in him that scared the hell out of him. A weakness for her, and her alone. He was a Highland warrior, willing to fight any war, but even he knew enough to flee when defeat was imminent. He stood up and left her, and did not look back. When he passed Robert, he guiltily avoided his friend's gaze. Snapping up Angus's pouch as it came to the big man's lips, Graham pushed through the dense forest growth until it swallowed him up.

Claire watched him go, wishing, for the first time in her life, that she possessed the candid abandon of her sister. Anne would have called him back, casting discipline and pride to the wind. Claire wanted to know what it was about her that had changed an arrogant rogue into a brooding bear. He'd practically taken off James's head because of her, not because of Connor. But he'd threatened to kill her dearest friend, she reminded herself. He'd forced her to leave Ravenglade in a way that would convince poor James that she, too, believed in his guilt. Och, how could Graham suspect him? She understood that Graham didn't know James the way she did, but what reason could he possibly have for believing the one man who loved her brother as much as she did had led him to his death? Was there another reason for his accusation? Graham had demanded to know if she loved James. Could he be jealous? She was trained to trust her instincts, and her instincts were telling her that Graham had softened to her. It was in the way he kissed her, with both possession and surrender. It was in his eyes, always on her, and in the way he looked at her, as if she delighted him and tortured him but a moment later. Did he care for her? No, he was a self-professed rogue of the worst sort. Besides, she didn't truly believe that Graham was the kind of man who would kill another out of jealousy.

This was all her fault. She had allowed Graham to trick her into telling him things about James that could be incriminating. Graham Grant was a warrior who knew how to wield his devastating charm as well as he wielded his fists in order to get what he wanted.

Aye, she remembered his promise not to be bested by her, how effortlessly he had smiled at James's side in the great hall while he conspired against him. She wanted to believe the aching need in Graham's kiss in Ravenglade's lists was real. But how could it be when the instant it was over, he had the look of a man who hated himself? She glared in the direction he'd gone. She wanted to know why he accused James, and what he planned on doing about it. She was also damned good and tired of being the source of his sour mood. Did he find her so unappealing that trying to win her favor, whatever his rogue heart wanted it for, repulsed him? Determined to get some answers, she straightened, dusted off her trews, and took off after him.

Claire elbowed her way through prickly branches, climbed over rocks, and fought swarms of gnats, cursing all the way. Where in blazes was he? Satan's balls, if he was drunk and fell into the hands of thieves, she'd kill him. Why the hell was she even looking for him when she could have just waited for his return to put her questions to him? She fought vehemently to convince herself that she was not some addlebrained wench chasing after him the way Lianne had at the inn. She would let him know that, as well!

She almost walked straight into the loch. The forest ended abruptly, with a three-foot fall directly in front of her. She would have tumbled over a few rocks before she sank into the water face-first. When she looked up, she saw him and almost stumbled head over heels anyway.

Soaking up the sun like one of Poseidon's lazy princes, Graham stretched his back over a large boulder along the bank's edge, his clothes and weapons resting close behind him. His golden hair was slicked away from his face. Droplets glistened on his bare chest and dripped in sinuous rivulets over his rippled belly and down the beguiling crease above his hip, back into the water. One arm lay sprawled out at his side, his hand clutching Angus's pouch of whisky. His other hand was hidden from her sight beneath the murky surface. His muscles flexed as his grip tightened and he rode his arm up and then down again. Suddenly, Claire knew what he was holding. She knew about cocks, having seen and heard enough about them in the garrison. She'd found out by accident how men pleasured themselves when they were without a woman for too long. She knew by the tautness of the rest of him that his was probably swollen and stiff. She watched him, mesmerized by the pleasure on his face, growing hotter and wetter as his arm plunged and then pulled. She'd never seen a man climax before. Hell, it was sinful, but she couldn't look away. She didn't want to. Shockingly, she found herself wondering what it would be like to swim to him and climb up that hard body. Her eyes basked in his fine form as he bent into himself, his arm moving with an urgency that made him purse his mouth and grit his teeth. Finally, he tossed his head back and groaned with unabashed ecstasy. Claire didn't realize, until it was over, that she was panting with him. And then she fled.

She broke through the tangle of trees and into the campsite as if there were a horde of generals on her arse. Anne looked up, startled. Robert leaped to his feet.

"What is it?" he demanded, looking behind her.

Calling up every ounce of control she had left, Claire smiled and waved away his concern. "It is nothing. I thought I saw a wild boar. That is all."

He did not look convinced. "Were you looking for Graham?"

She shook her head and broke away from him. "Nae, and I would prefer not to speak of him." Or think of him ever again, she thought, blushing to her roots. She felt like a stranger in her own skin. A shameless trollop who spied on men while they . . . Her cheeks flamed hotter and she turned her back on the others, fearful that they might see and recognize the depth of her depravity.

Anne would never have watched. And she certainly would not have become aroused by it. Her sister was pure, modest, with feminine thoughts filling her head, not immoral ones. Anne was soft and delicate; the kind of woman men preferred. Why couldn't she be more like Anne? Connor had never asked that question of her. He had been the only man in her life who accepted fully that she would rather fight than stitch. She closed her eyes, missing him. She wanted to speak to him about these unfamiliar, unchaste stirrings, the way she spoke to him about everything.

She heard Graham enter the camp. Her face burned all over again as he strode past her, filling her lungs with the fragrance of forest and fresh water. Unable to stop herself, she lifted her gaze to look at him as he handed Angus back his pouch, and then wished she hadn't. He looked as maddeningly virile half clothed as he did naked. His tunic dangled from his hand. His plaid was draped low around his hips, enthralling her senses with the splendid view of his broad back and lean waist. Damnation, even the sight of his booted calves made her breath stall. He turned and she looked up mortified to find him staring at her. She blushed from her neck to her scalp.

"We should leave now. We could cross the mountain range by tomorrow," she blurted out, not wanting to spend another instant here with nothing to do but gawk at him.

"We'll nap first," he replied, tossing the extra wool of his plaid over his shoulder for comfort. He said nothing else as he sat against the rough bark of an old oak and closed his eyes.

"Claire," her sister called out behind her. "Take off that Godawful cap and come here by me."

Claire reached up and yanked off the cap she had forgotten she was wearing. Hell, not only did she think like a man, but she looked like one. No wonder Graham scowled every damn time he looked at her. She went to Anne and dropped down beside her.

"You remind me of Connor," Anne sighed sadly, pulling Claire closer. "You and he always looked so much alike."

Normally, Claire would have delighted in such a sentiment, but now it only served as a reminder that she possessed such manly attributes.

"Let me work on this hair a bit," Anne said, positioning herself behind her. "Goodness, it looks like it hasn't been out of this plait in ages." Without waiting for her sister's consent, Anne tugged at the string binding the long braid and began unraveling Claire's pale tresses.

"Robert told me all that happened. You are distressed about James."

"Aren't you?" Claire turned slightly to ask her. "You don't give any credence to this madness about him betraying Connor, do you?"

"Of course not. But they are only trying to protect us. *Someone* is responsible for Connor's death."

"Aye. General Monck."

"I do not believe that either."

Now Claire turned to face her sister fully. "How could you not? What lies did he feed you, Anne?"

Her sister merely shrugged, pushing Claire's shoulders forward again. "Contrary to what you believe, I am not so gullible as to believe whatever is told me."

"That is not what I meant."

"That I did not spend my days wielding a sword with Connor doesn't mean he did not tell me things."

"I know that, Anne."

"He spoke very highly of General Monck, and after spending time with the governor, I understood why."

Claire said nothing as her sister stroked her fingers through her hair.

"I also understand why Robert and Graham think James is guilty." She held Claire's shoulders still when her sister tried to whirl around again. "Claire, I am not saying that I agree, only that I understand. James was the one who gave Connor the alleged message from the general. Our brother trusted Monck, aye, but he trusted James, as well. He would have done as either of them asked."

Claire shook her head. It made no sense. "Why would James want Connor dead, Anne? He loved him."

Behind her, her sister sighed. "I don't know, and I don't know how we shall discover the truth in this."

"I already know the truth. James is innocent. We have known him our whole lives. We must have faith in him."

Anne nodded and continued working the thick strands of Claire's hair.

"Robert assured me that as long as we continue onward toward Skye, where he knows we will be safe, neither he nor Graham will leave us to go back to Edinburgh. So we needn't worry over James at present. Robert has also guessed that it has been you fighting General Monck's men. Do not fear, though. He has promised not to tell the governor."

"That is kind of him," Claire muttered, letting herself relax a little now that she knew James was safe from the noose—for now.

"Aye, he is kind. He told me of his sister Katherine in Skye. He said she is a combination of you and me. She can wield a sword, but is as finely fashioned as a rose."

Anne being the rose, of course, Claire thought despairingly, and hugged her knees to her chest.

"Och, now I see why you wear your hair so tightly braided. There is so much of it!" Anne pulled and twisted Claire's long locks but soon gave up whatever she was trying to do. "I think a pair of braids will suit you better. I need another string."

They both looked around, then, realizing there was nothing in the grass that would work, Anne tapped her sister on the shoulder. "Go and ask your Highlander for a thread from his plaid. It looks tattered enough. There should be plenty of threads hanging loose."

"He is not my Highlander, Anne," Claire corrected her with an audible frown in her voice. "And besides, he is asleep and I do not want to disturb him."

"Nonsense. He is awake and looking right at you. Now, just go ask." Anne gave her a push to get her on her feet.

Claire slipped her gaze to him from beneath her lashes. Hell, he *was* awake, and he did not look away this time when their gazes met. He barely blinked as she reluctantly rose to her feet and swept her mane off her shoulders. The short journey to him was a torturous one. His penetrating gaze unnerved her. His naturally pouty mouth made it difficult to focus on what she wanted from him. A kiss. A smile. A flattering word. An apology.

"I need a thread from your plaid." Saints in heaven, was that her voice that sounded so shaky and unsure? She wanted to kick him for making her so muddleheaded. "For my hair," she added tersely when he continued to do nothing but stare up at her. Finally, he lowered his head and lifted his hand to the wool draping his chest. Without looking up again, he broke off one of the loose fibers and offered it to her.

Claire took it and backed away, fearful of the mad urge coursing through her to drop to her knees, clasp his face firmly in her hands and kiss him . . . or slap him for being such a brute at Ravenglade. *They are only trying to protect us.* Was it truly this noble cause that made him force her to leave Ravenglade? Dear God, she was mad, all right. Why wouldn't he look at her? Just a short while ago she had been angry with him for charming her to get what he wanted. Now, she was angry that he obviously wanted nothing. He was a rogue, for hell's sake! A careless seducer of women. Why was he holding back with *her*? Was it displeasure that darkened his gaze, or something else? Something that made her legs weak, her mouth dry: desire, emotion, and the resolve to resist both. *He would kill to protect her.* Did he resist her because he knew Monck was going to choose her husband? Rogues did not care about husbands, did they? Was he angry at her for being angry at him? Was it simply that she was not womanly enough for him? She felt dizzy from all the uncertainties floating around in her head. Satan's balls, fighting the English was easier than this!

With a muttered curse she stomped off and flung herself down in front of her sister. "He is not what I want in a man anyway." She handed Anne the thread over her shoulder.

Parting Claire's hair down the middle, Anne glanced at the object of her sister's contempt. Graham Grant, commander at war to the MacGregors, of all people. A man from the misty north where warriors were born, not taught. Even without his halo of sun-kissed hair and glittering green eyes, Commander Grant would be a difficult man for Claire to resist. Why, Anne believed him to be everything her warrior sister wanted in a man. Claire would never be happy with Robert. The poor earl had known it all along and had tried to tell General Monck. As perfect a man as Robert Campbell was, Claire was not meant for him. Connor had chosen the wrong sister.

"Then your heart remains free to love another?"

"Love!" Claire scoffed at her sister's hesitant question. Och, God, what did she even know of it? "I was not born to love, but to fight."

"But what about a husband? General Monck said that . . ."

"I don't care what he said! If he tries to force me into marriage, I will breach Edinburgh's walls and do what I had intended to do a sennight ago." Ignoring her sister's sharp gasp as Anne concluded what her sister's intentions had been, Claire crossed her legs and folded her arms across her chest. "Now, I have something to ask you."

"What is it?" Anne asked, fumbling with Claire's braids.

"Do you think I could fight in a skirt?"

Chapter Twenty

We are the same. Split apart in our mother's womb, though secretly, and because I love you, I have wished it were not so.

General George Monck rested his feather quill on the table and blew his breath onto the missive, drying the ink. He read and reread his words. He knew that if this parchment fell into any hands save those of the one to whom it was written, all his plans would come to naught. It was a chance he had to take. The time was approaching. He could feel it in the marrow of his bones. Decades of battles hard won had honed his senses to know when his enemies were about to make a move. His men had sent him word that since the expulsion of Parliament, London had fallen into chaos. To quell the uprising, the military Committee of Safety was reinstated to act as an interim government and Lambert was restored to the rank of major general over all the forces in England and Scotland. Now, Lambert's men were in Scotland, which could only mean that Lambert's arrival would be next. He would come to seek Monck's support against Parliament. Support he would never receive.

With careful fingers, Monck folded the letter and melted his wax over a flickering candle flame. Fate would dictate his course of action from this night hence.

With nothing more to do than see it delivered, he rose from his chair and beckoned to the man waiting beyond the shadows of his private solar.

"Edward, guard it with your very life. Deliver it into his hands yourself."

"I vow I shall do both, my lord." The steward took the parchment, bowed slightly, and left to perform his task.

Rubbing his hands down his face, the general went to the window. His eyes turned toward an unseen ocean. It would be many months until he saw Edward again if the messenger proved successful.

There came a knock at the door, and without turning, Monck called, "Come." The hinges creaked, reminding the general to have them oiled.

"My lord, you have received two missives from London."

"London?" Monck turned, his dark brow furrowed with surprise. "Here, give them to me." Reaching out, he snatched the missives from the vassal's hand, then waved him out.

London? he thought, breaking both seals. The first message he opened appeared to be written by a bloodied hand, the words barely distinguishable. He turned to the second, this written by John Murray, one of the two captains he had sent to London. His eyes scanned the words, then shot once again to the first parchment, which, according to Murray, belonged to Connor Stuart. It had been given to the captain by a servant in Wallingford

House, the home of Charles Fleetwood. After reading it, the captain had felt it warranted further examination.

Monck agreed and held it up closer to the candle flame. Much of it was difficult to decipher, but what he read turned his blood cold.

My dearest C,

It has all gone terribly ——. —— feared has come to pass. —— all been betrayed. I had known ——. Now —— naught I can do but think on his death. Would that I were with you, ——. —— fox's snare. I am pla—d by the flower of Scotland crying —— Save me from the kiss of the devil! —— escape that —— keeps me from my utmost duty ——? —— I myself have been deceived. Forgive me, for I —— save her. Just as I could not ——. Who has —— the —— warrior arrayed in the frost of ——? —— has perished. And yet, he lives.

He lives? Mother Mary, was it possible? The governor rushed through the rest.

Betrayed. —— by his friend. No greater sorrow. —— enemy —— the one —— covets the prize. General Monck read on until he came to the end.

Your lo—— brother, Conno—Stuart.

He lowered the parchment and set his eyes toward the window again. Dear God, was Stuart still alive? His stomach churned knowing the matter was out of his hands. He could not deviate from his plans, nor could he chance the truth being discovered. Not now when his armies were gathering from the four winds. Not after he had just set every plan he'd held secret for so long into motion.

He could do nothing, but there was someone who could. With no time to spare, the general picked up his quill, scribbled a few lines at the top of Connor's letter, then sealed it with his stamp. When he was done, he pulled open his door and stuck his head out. "Send for Captain Fraser," he commanded a passing servant, then shut the door again and paced while he waited for his second in command.

When the captain arrived, Monck shoved the parchment into his hand and told him where to deliver it. To this messenger, he gave the same orders as he'd given the first.

Claire was so happy when they stopped at a warm inn nestled within the hills of Glen Nevis, she was tempted to push a giggling serving wench out of her way so that she could get to Graham first and thank him. But Anne had taken so much pleasure in teaching her how to behave like a lady, she did not want to disappoint. Och, a bath, a warm supper, a bed! She could not wait to enjoy all three. Determined to be polite, she grinned at a swarthy lass when she offered, with a bit more welcome in her dark eyes for Graham than for anyone else, to bring them to their room. Her new manners and docile demeanor had naught to do with Graham, despite Anne's teasing to the contrary. She simply wanted to see what she was missing, if anything. As it turned out, she was not missing much. Graham still avoided being alone with her, and instead of brooding, he looked at her with something akin to pure confoundedness animating his features. Still, she did not let that stop her from practicing her lessons in femininity, even though, by God, she hated them.

She practically raced Anne up the stairs, pausing only when Brodie, Angus, and Robert stopped at the top of the second landing. What was the bloody hold-up? Her thigh muscles were screaming for the blessed comfort of warm water. She had days of dirt to scrub off. Satan's balls, she was itching everywhere! Mumbling an oath she almost did not care if her sister heard or not, she reached behind her and gave her backside a scratch, then peered around Anne's back to glare at the men.

"Why have you stopped?"

"We dinna know which way to go," Angus told her, then looked around her shoulder at Graham at the bottom of the stairs.

Claire turned her head and found Graham still conversing with the swarthy wench. That is to say, the swarthy wench was the one doing all the talking. Graham's eyes were fastened on Claire's hand. Her scratching came to an abrupt halt, but it was the intimately sweet smile he gifted her with that made her blush three shades of scarlet. It galled her how swiftly this man could jolt every nerve ending in her body to life. When the wench—who should have been turning down their blasted bed by now—tossed Claire's trews a distasteful look before turning her lustful grin back on Graham, Claire struggled to remember her lessons. Ladies did not leap down the stairs and strangle other ladies, even if they were trollops with heaving bosoms twice the size of her own.

"Commander," Claire called down serenely. "If you would be so kind as to pry yourself free of your admirer's fingers and allow her to move her arse before I move it for her, I would be in your debt."

His smile on her widened before he turned it on the wench blocking his path. "Ye best go, lass. Her blade is as sharp as her tongue."

"My tongue is not sharp," Claire said through her teeth

when Graham took up his steps behind the girl. Anne shot her sister a now-what-have-I-taught-you look, and Claire feigned a more pleasant smile when he reached her. "Forgive me for frightening you both. I . . ." She glared at Anne for digging her heel into her boot. "What I mean to say is . . ." Her voice trailed off while Graham passed her without another look. Son of a . . .

"Do you smell the stew?" Anne closed her eyes and inhaled the glorious aroma wafting from the kitchen. "Heavenly."

"Aye," Claire breathed, forgetting about Graham for the moment. "Mutton,"

"And freshly baked bread."

"Och, let there be honey to go with it," Claire sighed, following the now-cleared path up the stairs. So preoccupied was she with the thought of a hot, delicious meal, she did not notice the serving wench's brooding expression when Graham closed his door with nothing but a muttered note of thanks before sending her on her way.

As Claire had hoped, supper was delicious. She did not even mind that it was cold. The mutton was tender, the bread was soft and sweetened with churned butter, and the ale was plentiful. She did her best not to wolf everything down as fast as Brodie did. Ladies ate slowly, with delicate bites, and—as Anne reminded her before they left their room—they did not chew with their mouths open.

But hell, she was hungry! And was it not enough that her hair was flowing freely around her demure face—and in her mouth more times than her spoon? She thought about what a pity it was that in this tavern of at least three dozen wenches, there was not a single extra gown to be worn, but she was in too good a mood to let that bother her. In truth, she did not look forward to wearing one. How women breathed with the laces of their bodices drawn so tight was beyond her.

The best part of the meal, though, was the company. The MacGregors' laughter was as boisterous as their reputation was lethal. Anne seemed to get along particularly well with Angus, which Claire suspected had something to do with their shared fondness for the Highlander's potent brew. Did ladies get soused? Claire would have to remember to ask her later.

"Enjoy the meat now, ladies," Robert said. The earl looked especially handsome tonight with his deep sable hair slicked neatly away from his cleanly shaven face. "There'll be none at Camlochlin."

"Why not?" Anne asked.

"Callum's sister has an aversion to killing animals for food."

"Truly?" Anne cast him a suspicious smile that warmed Robert's eyes to a rich hazel green. When he nodded, her wide eyes opened wider. "And the chieftain indulges his sister's wishes?"

"Near all o' them," Angus said, swiping the back of his hand over his mouth after a long guzzle of ale. "'Tis why Jamie Grant is home pickin' flowers instead o' bein' here wi' us."

"A pansy," Brodie reminded them all and brooded into his cup.

Claire smiled and looked up from her stew at Graham when Angus insisted he do something about it.

"I will speak to Callum," he promised, then continued chewing.

Claire watched him eat, then blinked away when he lifted his gaze to her.

"Does Jamie mind picking her flowers?" Anne asked all the men.

Angus shook his head and belched. "Been pickin' them fer years."

"Then why do you want him to stop? He sounds like a very devoted husband. I'm sure his wife is most happy with him."

"Must a lass's happiness be bought with a man's virility?" All eyes turned to Graham, washing down his bread with a swig of ale. He looked at Anne, and then at Claire, as he rested his cup back on the table. To his right, Brodie nodded in agreement.

"Love has no price, Commander," Anne pointed out gently, and smiled at him. He did not return the gesture, but shrugged and went back to his stew.

"It does when the man is afraid of being *bested* by a woman," Claire told her sister. Feeling Graham's hooded eyes on her, she turned and offered him a casual smile. "Do you not agree?"

He set down his spoon and gave her his full attention. "Nae, I do not. A true warrior should not fear being bested by anyone but himself."

Claire tilted her head and narrowed her gaze on his. What in blazes did *that* mean? And why was he looking at her as if she should know? Was he referring to her tiny outburst on the stairs earlier? Surely he had noticed the change in her over the last several days. She'd barely argued with anyone. Was he pointing out her inability to best her manly ways? Her hands balled into fists clutching her spoon and bread. Well, she would prove him wrong.

"You speak correctly, kind sir." With a short smile, she severed her gaze from his and spooned her stew into her mouth. Patience, decorum, modesty. She chomped on her mutton and almost choked upon swallowing, for it was accompanied by her pride.

Chapter Twenty-one

C,

The time has come to let the truth be known.

Kind sir? Graham would have laughed at Claire's strangled reply if he knew what the hell she was up to.

He had no idea what he'd said to spark those gloriously blue eyes, or why she fought so rigorously to douse the fire. Claire Stuart was many things, but docile was not among them. Since leaving Loch Tay she had done everything but curtsy when any of them addressed her. She was quiet, composed, and most disturbing, agreeable. He remembered her humble compliance when she wanted to accompany them to Edinburgh. She was a cunning little viper who would do whatever it took to get what she wanted.

And clearly, she wanted something.

What concerned Graham the most, though, was that he would likely grant her anything she wished. It was not the modest glances with which she graced him every time she caught him looking at her, or the way her lush mane of palest yellow tumbled about her shoulders, giving her the look of some wild-caught nymph, that tempted him to cast his loyalty to the four winds. No, it was the battle she fought with herself, rather than with him, that made her so irresistible.

It was what drove him to tease her.

"I want to tell ye, Claire—" He waited while her spoon paused at her mouth and she lifted her eyes to him again before he smiled. "—that I like this change in ye. It has been unusually pleasant as of late." He noted the challenge that flicked across her steady gaze, and his smile deepened. Ah, there was his she-devil.

"When there are no men about who pose a threat"— her brow dipped over her eyes, parrying his jab—"you'll find me quite serene and unruffled. I'm glad it pleases you." She smiled to prove it.

What pleased him was her vicious tongue, and the strength in her eyes that promised one hell of a fight—and delivered. "What pleases me even more," he countered coolly, "is yer confidence that I am here to protect ye, not to be a threat to ye." He almost grinned at how easy it was to bait her.

"Protect me?"

Hell, she was utterly and completely ravishing on the verge of leaping at him.

"Why you insuff—owww!" She howled and glared at her sister, who covered up her stinging pinch with a loving pat to Claire's arm. When Claire bolted to her feet, Anne shot her a warning look.

So, wee, innocent Anne was in on it, too, was she? Graham shook his head at the both of them. Lasses. One working against you to get what she wanted was bad enough. Two, and a man had no chance at all.

But Claire was done fighting this battle. Or was she? The daring tilt in her tight smile when she excused herself said otherwise.

Graham watched her go, enjoying the view. When she headed for the tavern doors instead of the stairs, he sprang from his chair and sprinted after her.

He entered the balmy twilight of dusk with the tip of a thin, sharp blade already at his throat. Looking over its shiny length, he met Claire's hard gaze.

"Protect yourself."

"Claire." Graham lifted his hand to swat away her sword. She gave his palm a stinging whack with the flat of her blade. His eyes blazed at her, but he did not move another muscle.

"Let us get one thing perfectly clear, Highlander," she said, bringing the razor edge of her sword back to his neck. "Cowering is not in my nature, and I refuse to do it for another instant just to please you. Now, protect yourself so that I do not kill you."

To please him? Why the hell . . . She allowed him no more time to ponder her words as she whirled her blade in a deadly dance before his eyes. Graham leaped back, his eyes wide with disbelief that she would actually strike him.

"Claire, put down yer sword before I . . .

She swung and nicked his forearm. Her mouth hooked into an unrepentant smirk. Eclipsed by a lock of flaxen hair, her blue eyes flashed. "Before you what? Run?"

He stared at her, fire leaping from his eyes, his blood pumping hard and fast. The thought of actually fighting her both worried and excited him. He knew he should concede whatever point she was trying to make. He did not want to hurt her—or Robert—but hell, she looked so damned alluring standing there, ready to take on his sword.

He dragged his powerful claymore from its sheath and

clipped her meager weapon away from his face. Instantly, her sword swooped over her shoulder, and grasping the hilt in both hands, she returned it once again to his throat. This time, he gave more force to his swing, and metal met metal in a grinding clash that sent her reeling back a few steps.

She smiled, igniting the blood in his veins to scalding. He advanced. She released one hand from her hilt, extending her arm for balance. His claymore sliced the air where she had been standing less than a moment ago.

"Ye were a good student," Graham remarked, cutting his sharp gaze to her when she came to a halt slightly to his right.

"Aye, Connor's best." She brought down a chopping blow, which he parried just before it cut through his shoulder.

Catching her sword beneath its edge, he swung wide and grinned when she held on to her weapon. But he'd pushed her off balance just enough to deliver another crushing blow that dropped her to one knee. Positioning the tip of his blade under her chin, he tilted her face up and flashed his dimples at her. "Surrender now, and I'll ferget ye lifted yer blade to me."

She quirked her brow as if he were the biggest dimwit in all of Scotland, blew her hair out of her mouth, and swept her leg cleanly across both his ankles.

Graham went down like a felled tree. Flat on his back, he looked up just in time to see her thin blade flash high over his head. He rolled to the side, astounded to think that she truly meant to whack off his head.

Luckily, she didn't, and backed up to give him a moment to gain his feet. Well now, he thought, pushing back his cap and facing her once again, if this was going to be a serious fight . . . She deflected two more mighty strokes that made her arms visibly tremble, but she did not back down. They both advanced, meeting face to face in a clash of sparks.

Graham stared deep into her eyes, his heavy breath sweeping tendrils of hair off her face. Hell, she excited him beyond endurance. He wanted to take her until she screamed her surrender.

Snatching her wrist with his free hand, he twisted her sword arm behind her back and hauled her body hard against his. His mouth descended without mercy; open, insatiable, devouring her with his plunging tongue. She struggled briefly, firing his passion even more. They dropped their swords at the same time. His arm snaked low around her waist to drag her closer, deeper against his stiffening erection. She gasped into his hungry mouth and pulled her wrist free to clutch his face in her palms. He knew she would answer his fervor with the same zeal once he had her, but when she rolled her hips to caress him more fully against her warm niche, his control snapped. Lifting her off her feet, he whirled her around and slammed her back up against the tavern's outer wall. Cupping her buttocks in his tight grip, he surged every throbbing inch of his arousal over her, cursing the fabric between them. He growled low in his throat with the need he suffered for her, and broke their kiss. Nothing needed to be said between them. They both wanted the same thing, though Claire did not understand what it was. He wanted to show her, to teach her—slowly and thoroughly. He wanted to forget Robert existed. His expression darkened as the thought crossed his mind,

"What is it?" The strain of Claire's breath pushed her

breasts up hard against his chest. "What is so terrible about me that it keeps such a devilish rogue away?"

His gaze warmed on her as he covered her fingers with his and kissed them. "There is naught terrible about ye, Claire. Ye are perfect."

She looked so surprised and pleased, he began to smile. Angus's gravelly voice stopped him.

"Fer hell's sake, no' again."

Still clutching Claire's hand between them, Graham turned his head to see his longtime friend shaking his head at him.

"Ye both do these lasses an injustice," Angus complained despite his commander's black look. "Rob's inside wi' another man's promised wife, and yer oot here wi' his."

"Angus!" Ready to haul the burly warrior back inside before he said another word, Graham broke away from Claire, but he paused and his heart stalled in his chest when he heard her voice.

"What are you talking about?" She passed Graham on her way to Angus, her footfalls light and cautionary. "I am not Robert's promised wife."

Angus lifted his pitying gaze from hers and shot Graham a repentant look for what he was about to do. What Graham and Robert should have done outside Edinburgh.

"Aye, lass, ye are. Yer brother wished it to be so, and it canna be undone."

She laughed, and Graham closed his eyes. He did not want her to find out this way. He should have told her. When he opened his eyes again, it was to aim his murderous glare at Angus. He did not notice that Claire had stopped laughing and was staring at him.

"Graham?" she asked quietly. "What is this nonsense he speaks?" When he did not answer her, she rushed to him and clasped his arm. Panic, disbelief, and rage all played across her fair expression. "This is not true. Tell me it is not true!"

"Claire . . ."

"Nae!" She pulled away from him as if touching him pained her. "My brother would *never* have promised me to a Roundhead! Monck told you this, did he not?" She spun around back to Angus. "He lies!"

"It does not matter, Claire," Graham spoke softly behind her. "Monck has decreed it, and Robert will not disobey the law."

Slowly, she pivoted on her heel to face him, her eyes aflame with defiance . . . and pain. "And you think I will obey it? I am but a woman who should do as she is told by the men who rule her. Men who would have me believe that my brother betrayed me."

"Nae." He reached for her, but she backed away.

"You knew this, and you did not tell me." Her eyes glistened with tears she refused to let fall. "Did you all laugh together at night while Anne and I slept?"

When Graham opened his mouth to answer her, she slapped him hard across his face. Without waiting for his reaction—or even caring what it was—she whirled around, snatched her sword from the ground, and stormed toward the tavern.

Graham shot Angus one last lethal glare and took off after her before she killed someone. Most likely, Robert.

Claire had no intention of killing the Earl of Argyll. Not yet anyway. She liked Robert. He just needed some convincing that if he obeyed the law in this, she would be forced to cut out his heart and feed it to a homeless dog. He was a reasonable, intelligent man. He would listen to her.

She pushed open the door, yanking her arm free when Graham appeared at her side and tried to stop her. She stepped into the tavern and looked toward the table where her sister sat with the smiling earl. Dear God, what would Anne think of all this? She would hate Robert for keeping this from her. He deserved it, Claire told herself. But poor Anne . . . Satan's arse, who was her sister promised to? She thought about asking Graham as she strode to the table, but she never wanted to speak to him again.

When Robert saw her coming, her sword clenched in her fist at her side, and Graham hot on her heels, he stood up.

"Roundhead," Claire spat when she reached him. "What spells do you weave for my sister with your pretty words and bewitching eyes?"

"Claire!" Anne sprang from her chair and stepped in front of him. "What is the matter? Put your sword away."

"Nae, I will not," Claire said, staring at Robert over Anne's head. "Tell her."

"Tell me what?" Anne insisted, dragging her sister's gaze back to her.

"That he intends to marry me while he woos you! He intends to, but it will not be. Do you understand me, Roundhead? I will kill you first."

"I do not intend . . ." Robert began, stepping around Anne. She stopped him and held her palm up to Claire, as if to stay her blade.

"Sister, Robert does not want this any more than you do,

but it was Connor who chose him. Our brother knew . . ." Her words trailed off as Claire's expression grew chillingly dark.

"How long have you known, Anne?"

"For some time now," Anne admitted, almost relieved to be finally telling her sister the truth. "General Monck told me when he brought me to Edinburgh. He was Connor's friend, Claire. He is our friend."

"I see." Claire's smile was strained to the point of being painful. "Well, that changes everything. Does it not? Now I agree to hand over all titles and lands to a Roundhead—whom my brother, a Royalist rebel, chose for me, according to a *Roundhead* governor who claims to be our friend. I was foolish to mistrust the general, despite this being a truly ingenious plan to put an end to the rebellion."

Behind her, Graham met Robert's gaze. It would have been an ingenious plan. What proof had Monck given them that he was an ally of Stuart's? His men were attacked. By Claire. Had they been wrong about Buchanan? Was this Monck's plan all along? Tie one sister to the new leader of the rebellion and the other to a Presbyterian Campbell?

"And to whom has the general promised you?" Claire asked her sister. When Anne told her of her betrothal to James, Claire aimed her scathing expression at Robert first, and then at Graham. "Now it becomes clear to me why you accused him of such treachery." Without giving either of them a chance to reply, she stepped forward and reached for her sister's hand. "General Monck lied to you, just as he did to Connor. Come, now. We are leaving." She stared wide-eyed when Anne pulled her hand away.

"Are you mad, Claire? Where shall we go? I cannot fight like you."

"No one's going anywhere." Graham stepped forward.

"Back to James." Claire ignored him. "To Connor's true friend."

Graham turned to her with a look of disbelief that quickly darkened into anger. "Ye're not going near Ravenglade."

"Why not?" Claire challenged, fisting her hands on her hips. "James is no more guilty of betraying Connor than you are. Now step aside and let us go."

"I am not going." Anne backed into Robert's chest. Her large, liquid eyes begged her sister not to go either. "Please, do not do this. We will not make it back to James alive."

Claire's spine went rigid. Pushing Graham out of her way, she glanced at her sister and then lowered her eyes as she passed her. "You insult me, Anne."

Silence fell over the table as they watched Claire climb the stairs and disappear silently around the corner.

When she was gone, Graham turned to Robert. "Walk with me. We need to talk."

Chapter Twenty-two

Everything you desire is in my hands, and I will give it to you freely.

Rob followed Graham across the rushes without hesitation. They had been through much together these past two years, strengthening their friendship. Despite the seriousness of what he wanted to speak to Robert about, Graham felt his expression warming as he thought of his friend. He'd been fond of this lad from the day he first met him. Robert Campbell had the heart of a knight and the courage of a thousand warriors. He did what he believed was right, no matter what the cost. A most noble trait, that—and one that he paid for with his hide more than once. All the more reason Graham had grown to admire him for it. Never would he ask Robert to abandon his ideals . . . to sacrifice what he believed was honorable. But Graham wanted to make certain his friend had all the facts before he chose the side on which he would stand.

Stopping at the hearth fire along the northern wall, Graham turned and looked Robert in the eyes—something he had been unable to do since they left Edinburgh. "What if Claire is correct about Monck?"

To Graham's surprise, Robert nodded. "I admit that such a devious scheme had not entered my mind. The determination to plan it, and see it through, would require an excellent pretender."

Graham agreed. "With Connor dead, who would contest him? Not the Campbells, who were gaining a royal Stuart in their clan. Not Buchanan, even if all he wants is Connor's lands. He cannot contest openly."

As Graham's points became obvious, Robert turned toward the hearth. His eyes lightened, capturing the searing golds and green-blues of the flames. "Our marriages would unite both parties."

"Aye." Graham looked across the hall, up the stairs. "A brilliant general's easy victory over the rebellion." Only Claire would never submit, and they would all pay the price.

Robert cut his gaze to Graham's. "Even if this is all true, there is a consideration of even more importance to me." He turned his head and met Graham's gaze fully. "Do you care for her?"

For a moment, Graham simply stared at him. His answer came immediately to his lips, yet he could not speak it. Robert should know the truth, but the truth was too terrifying to admit aloud.

"That . . ." Graham shifted his weight, and his gaze. "Well, that has naught to do with . . . I am . . . fond of her."

The more Graham stumbled over his words, the wider Robert's smile grew, until Graham scowled at him.

"I have not acted upon it."

Grinning, Robert slapped his friend's shoulder. "Aye, *that's* been painfully apparent to the rest of us who have suffered through your celibacy. Damnation, Graham," he said, growing serious again. "Why did you not tell me when I first asked? I would have returned straightaway to Edinburgh."

"I . . . well, I was not . . . I mean, I . . ."

Robert laughed. "You're scared to death, aren't you." It wasn't a question. "You haven't the slightest notion of how to cope with your own heart."

Graham offered him a sheepish look, pulled his cap off his head, and raked his hand through his hair. "My heart has never been involved before."

Robert patted him on the shoulder. "You'll do fine, warrior. She will make you happy."

"And the law?"

Robert shrugged. "That something is law does not mean it's right. The MacGregors have already proven that."

Aye, the heart of a knight, Graham thought, and smiled. "That they did, brother."

A flash of pale hair along the stairs caught his eye and he turned to see Claire heading straight for them. With a small sachet tossed over one shoulder and her freshly braided hair over the other, she looked ready for a journey.

"She is yours," Robert leaned in and whispered, giving up his claim on her.

Graham's mouth curved into a slow smile. *Not yet.*

"My sister has decided to put her trust in you." Claire's voice was as stiff as her spine when she stopped in front of Robert. "If she is harmed in your care before I return for her, I will hold you responsible. And you—" She swung her blazing blue eyes up at Graham next. "—If you come after me, I will kill you."

She did not linger long enough to see the feral spark that lit his eyes at such a challenge, but swept past him and headed for the door.

Of course, he was going to go after her. He'd been chasing her since the day he first clapped eyes on her. Now that she was free again, he intended to lay claim to her before anyone else did. He knew he had betrayed her, but he would earn back her trust. He would go slowly and win her heart, as a lady should be won. Hell, he knew enough about the courtly rules of wooing from Robert. *'Twouldn't be difficult at all,* he thought, pushing chairs out of his way and following her out the door.

Graham wanted to strangle her—and just as soon as he caught her, he would. He'd followed her to the stables, trying everything in his arsenal to convince her that riding into James Buchanan's arms, whether he was innocent or not, would create a far darker threat to her dear friend than any general's noose. Evidently, she hadn't believed him, for she marched unfazed to her horse, leaped upon it without so much as a glance in his direction, and thundered out, into the darkness.

Within seconds of mounting and taking off after her, it became apparent to Graham that she was going the wrong way. Gaining speed, he rode her tail, warning her to slow her mount. Chunky ribbons of cool mist were rolling in from the east, already clinging to the treetops and absorbing the scant light from the waxing moon. Soon, the moist fog would creep downward like a gossamer veil, impairing Claire's vision. She was not a Highlander. She did not know how to move about in the mist.

Racing up her left flank, he reached for her reins, then

snapped his hand back and glowered at her as she swatted him away with her sword. He ground his teeth, swearing to himself that if he got his hands on that sword, he was going to ring her bonny throat with it. He found no fault with her wielding such a weapon, but he was damn tired of her pointing it at him! Had a man done the like, Graham would have sliced him open the first time.

Hoping she did not try to lop off his head, he made another grab for her reins as they barreled through the thickening mist. He yanked hard, lurching her forward as her mount came to an abrupt halt. She swung, clearly trying *not* to cause him injury, he realized, when her sharp blade slashed the air a full arm's length away.

Taking no chances, he snatched the hilt out of her fingers and flung the weapon into the darkness. The blasphemy she hissed at him stung his ears, along with the punch she hurled into his lobe. Damnation, he should have this little hellion teach Rob how to use his fists! He reached for her, but she escaped his hold and slipped out of the saddle, cursing him while she stomped away in the direction he'd thrown her sword.

"Pray I do not find my blade, you son of a pig. For I fully intend to cut out your . . ." The remainder of Claire's tirade ended when she glanced up and saw nothing but wispy tendrils of silvery mist swirling around the tree trunks. She spun around. "Troy?" Where the hell was her horse? "Graham?" A chill swept over her nape as her calls went unanswered. She took a step forward, then stopped, not knowing which way she should go. "Graham!" she shouted, now even more furious with him for leaving her unarmed. A sound to her right startled her and she reached for her dagger. Was it Graham? The mist was growing denser. She could barely see the small blade she held in front of her.

"Stay with me—" The shock of Graham's throaty burr at her ear momentarily slowed her reflexes. A moment was all he needed to shackle her wrist and slip his other arm around her waist. "—and I'll teach ye how to fight even when ye're blind."

His warm breath trickled over her flesh. His broad fingers splayed across her belly, holding her firmly in case she thought to resist.

Resisting him did cross Claire's mind, but the satin caress of his voice, his tall, honed body pressed so intimately behind her, tempted her to ask him to teach her more than that. No, she reminded herself, and pulled away. He did not care what happened to her.

Breaking free of his embrace—and noting that he had plucked her dagger right from her fingers—she faced him, and for the first time, she backed away.

"You knew Monck had promised me to a life of obedience to the Campbells' Protestant party, and you kept it from me." She retreated another step when he advanced, breaking through the mist that separated them.

"Aye, and it nearly destroyed me."

Taken aback by the anguish in his admission, Claire fought to keep her wits about her. He had told her that night at the inn that her life was not her own, and that he would fight to gain it back for her if it were against anyone but him.

Robert. His friend.

He'd resisted her that night, and every day thereafter, because she had been promised to Robert. He had betrayed her. But such loyalty to his friend, Connor would have admired—had taught her to admire. God's blood, she could not fault Graham for so noble a quality.

He stepped closer, bathing her in his shadow, his intoxicating heat. He was temptation incarnate. Even the veil of darkness did not daunt his potent male virility. Instead, it piqued her awareness of his scent, his sound, his closeness, a hundredfold.

"Ye will not marry Robert," he promised, closing his arms around her and drawing her into his embrace. "I vow the only man ye will surrender to, is me."

Chapter Twenty-three

Surrender. It is so powerful a word, and none more sweet to the ears of a true warrior.

The silence of the forest amplified his ragged breath. The darkness gave life to every shudder of muscle beneath Claire's fingers. His embrace pulsed with the abandon of his resistance, and she responded with equal measure. She did not think. She did not care. She only wanted him. But she was never one to give up without a fight.

"It is not I who will surrender, rogue," she breathed against his chin.

"Will it be me, then, warrior?

"That depends on what you want."

"Ye," he answered without hesitation. The touch of his hand gliding down her long braid sapped the last shred of her will. "Just ye."

She was certain he would feel her heart pounding in her lips as his mouth descended on hers. She loved kissing him. Each time he had done it, it had chipped away her resolve. He had a right to be arrogant. For who could resist him? His lips caressed and teased while his tongue explored with bold curiosity. His large, broad hands traced a scalding path down the length of her back, then closed around her buttocks. He raked his teeth across her bottom lip, over her chin, biting and suckling the sensitive hollows in her neck until she thought she might scream with the need for something more.

Emboldened by his raw desire, she stroked her palms up his chest, delighting in every well-defined curve. Cupping his face in her palms, she drew him closer, inviting him to take his fill.

He growled like a beast about to plunder his mate, lifted his hands between them, and tore her tunic down the center. Bending over her, he captured her waist in one arm and swirled his tongue over her erect nipple. His hungry mouth made her writhe and clutch fistfuls of his hair when he closed his lips around her and began sucking.

The taste of her . . . the feel of her quivering in his mouth made him so hard he ached. He pulled at the stretched wool of his plaid and groaned with relief as his stiff shaft bolted straight up, unhindered. He gripped himself and drove his hand up and down over his hot flesh to appease his desire. But nothing could satisfy him now, save her. He unclipped her belt and hauled her back to him when he unhooked her trews.

Holding her still, he bent his knees and pressed his mouth to the crest of her pelvis. He licked and kissed her thighs while he pulled her trews down to her ankles. She jerked hard in his coiled embrace when he parted her with his fingers and flicked his tongue over her seething nub.

Rolling her head back, Claire beseeched the saints to forgive her for finding such unholy ecstasy in his tender ministrations. But when his touch became more sinful, sucking her into his mouth, laving his tongue over the full measure of her, she knew she was doomed. Tunneling her fingers through his damp, misty curls, she coaxed him closer, deeper, as wave after thrilling, spasming wave engulfed her.

She collapsed into his arms and drifted on the aftermath of bliss as he laid her down limp upon the moist leaves. Her muscles trembled with spent energy such as she'd never experienced before. Her lungs dragged in short, shallow gasps of cool air. Even after endless hours of practice, or fighting off the crushing weight of a man's blade, she had never felt this alive. She could have died happy right in that spot—if her arse was not so cold. Her eyes shot open and she arched her buttocks in the air and dragged her trews up.

"Pity, I can barely see ye." She heard his voice over her and sat up swiftly as he sat down, leaning his back against the shadowy figure of a thick tree.

The obscurity was a good thing, since he also could not see the fire in her cheeks. "You tore my tunic." She could think of nothing else to say. What was there to converse about after a man did *that* to you? And what happens now? Would he forget her now that his game of hunter and prey was over?

"Ye can wear mine."

He grew silent for a moment, then handed her his tunic. *That* meant that he was sitting two inches away from her bare-chested. How in blazes could that arouse her when she was so exhausted?

"Thank you," she said, accepting his offering. The smell of forest and leather and sweat bombarded her senses when she slipped his tunic over her head. It was maddening how deliriously content she felt enveloped in his musky aroma.

"What did ye mean when ye said that ye cowered to please me?"

Her shoulders scrunched up around her ears while she wriggled out of her tunic beneath. Och, why did he have to bring that up? She certainly did not want to talk about how she had struggled to behave like a lady—and failed miserably—so that he would find her more to his liking. "You misheard me. I said that I desired to kill you."

She felt his hands clamp her waist and her rump rising off the ground. "Tell me," he demanded, planting her down between his thighs and closing his arms around her from behind.

Och, what sorcerer's magic did he possess in that smoky, sexy baritone, in the searing heat of his breath at her nape that persuaded her to tell him all her secrets? Mayhap, it was the way he snatched her up, vanquishing the awkwardness between them, that made her want to share so much more with him. "I will not tell you," she retorted coolly, covertly enjoying the feel of being held so possessively by him.

"Ye take pleasure in defying me, stubborn wench."

"Your blithe arrogance tempts me often to do so."

He laughed, sparking lightning bolts down her spine. "Such a sharp tongue on one so bonny."

"You think me bonny?" When she twisted around in his arms, her hip brushed over his unrelenting erection beneath his plaid. Drawing in a sharp breath, she quickly scooted an inch out of the way.

"There's yer proof."

Hell, she could not argue *that* point. "You do not find me manly, then?"

"How could . . ." He paused, and when he spoke again,

she could hear the grin in his voice. "Ye sought to please me by becoming more like yer sister."

"Don't be absurd." Her spine grew rigid against his chest. "I don't care if I please you or not."

"But ye do please me." The sensual timbre of his voice along her nape made her toes curl. With a slight tug, he heaved her more firmly against all his hard angles. "The bold silhouette of yer hips pleases me." Shifting his hips, he pressed his potent arousal against the sweet swell of her buttocks. He groaned, raking his teeth over her nape. "Aye, it makes me want to do all sorts of wicked things to ye." Claire shuddered in his arms as the memory of him pleasuring himself in the loch invaded her thoughts. She wondered if she might be able to bring him such satisfaction.

When he smoothed his big hands over her breasts, her nipples grew taut. "What kinds of wicked things?" his touch lured her to ask.

She felt him grow even harder against her back, felt him pulse and tremble with desire that made her own body ache with need. He pinched her nipples with excruciating care, rolling them beneath the fabric of his tunic between his fingers while he kissed her neck. Instead of telling her, he showed her, spreading his palms down her belly and then beneath her trews. Cupping her hips, he pushed the snug garment over her buttocks and worked them slowly down her legs, his hands delighting in the feel of her bare skin.

"Kick off yer boots," he commanded on a ragged whisper.

She obeyed, too aroused to bother with blushing. Nestled in his embrace of hard, sinewy thighs and powerful arms, a scintillating awareness of her femininity washed over her. To hell with being a lady, she mused while he helped her discard her trews. He made her feel like a woman, and she loved it. Her tunic, or rather his, went next.

The mist cooled her naked flesh. In the darkness, the delicate tracery of his fingertips up her arms and along her collarbone made her skin burn. She could hear his heavy, strained breathing behind her as his fingers closed around her jaw. Angling her face to meet his, he captured her uneven breath with a slow, intoxicating kiss.

"Yer sassy mouth pleases me," he whispered over her parted lips, then descended again. He ravaged her mouth with his tongue, stroking her, tasting her like a starving beast. When she flicked her tongue over his in response, his muscles jerked. He lifted her in his arms, turning her body to meet his, and cupping his hands under her thighs, spread her legs over his hips.

Claire clutched his shoulders as she straddled him. She should be appalled, even afraid of what he was doing to her, or was about to do. But his hands gliding over her thighs, molding to her backside to drag her closer to his rigid shaft, made her wriggle to get even closer. Some ancient, thoroughly wanton side of her wanted to caress every erotic inch of him. When he caught her nipple between his teeth, she arched her back, offering him more. He suckled her hard, pulling tight little gasps from her throat. He bent his knees to support her and pulled at his plaid.

She wanted to look at him, to see the fire that consumed her in his eyes. But the absence of one sense heightened all the rest. Running her hands over his arms, his chest, she relished every nuance of muscle that sculpted him. He lowered his hand between them, and she followed, feeling him tug at his plaid. He covered her fingers with his and closed them around the solid weight of his erection.

She did not pull away. Though her fingers felt small around him, and she felt a momentary jolt of fear at the thought of him fitting this anywhere but in her hand, she marveled at the extraordinary combination of silk and steel. No sword ever forged was as fine as this one. Boldly, for she was not one to approach anything in life with meekness, she stroked his length, rubbed the pad of her thumb over his engorged tip, exploring, squeezing him until he near burst in her tight grip.

"Come here." His voice was rough, a throaty tangle of demand and need. Gripping her hips in one hand and his cock in the other, he slid the moist tip over her warm niche.

Claire grasped his shoulders as hot, charged energy whipped through her. Instinctively, she spread her knees, wanting him, needing him to quench the flames that threatened to consume her.

She almost grew angry with him when she felt his fingers glide over her taut nub, but his touch was one of ultimate seduction. He fondled, and teased, and dipped within her firm folds until she swayed, wet and ready in his hand.

He entered her slowly, breaking the thin barrier of her sweet virginity with long, torturously measured strokes. She cried out and tried to break free of his embrace, but he held her firm, trailing his lips over hers and whispering how she made him feel. Soon, the pain began to ebb and pleasure so replete, so unrelentingly erotic quaked her to her soul. Every muscular thrust made her more wild, until she felt drunk with want. She rode him with shameless abandon, exulting in the violent spasms that made her tighten around him. She coiled her arms around his neck and kissed him, hard and long, flicking her tongue over his in a dance as ancient as the forest around them.

He ground his hips against hers, impaling himself into her as deep as she could take him. He tugged on the string binding her braid and drove his hands through her luxurious tresses. His thrusts grew more fevered as he pulled on her hair, curving her back and exposing the knotted peaks of her breasts to his hungry mouth until she screamed his name in the rapture of her release.

With one final surge that drove her upward to the clouds, Graham spilled his scalding seed deep within her, groaning with sweet, savage victory. Finally, she was his.

Chapter Twenty-four

I shall gain the victory, but the glory will be yours.

Dawn broke over the treetops, spreading a pool of amber light over the warrior asleep upon the leaf-carpeted ground. Finally clothed and sitting at his booted feet, Claire appraised him at her leisure. Her gaze traveled up his long, powerful legs, lightly dusted with bronze hair. His plaid had ridden up his left thigh while he slumbered, and just the sight of it stalled her breath and made her loins ache more than they already did.

She struggled against the urge to lean over and trace her fingers over his whipcord-tight belly in the daylight, slide her hand up the lean sinew knotting the bare arm flung over his head. His curls fell in impish disarray over his forehead, like an askew halo atop the head of a fallen angel. His sulky mouth was just as devastating relaxed in sleep as it was when he aimed his heady smile at her. When she fought him blade to blade outside the tavern, his quick arm and quicker grins—both of which he did not hold back from her—had nearly cost her her victory. Never had she fought a man like him. She was certain nothing would ever feel more exhilarating. She was wrong. Feeling his body quake and heave with need for her, his muscles bunching beneath her fingers with measured restraint to take her, and then . . . finally, that hot, throbbing lance breaking through her body like a battering ram, felt better. Had she truly made love to such a man last night? Or was it some lust-filled dream sent to make her fall in love with him?

"Satan's balls," she muttered. She was going to have to be more wary of allowing *that* to happen. The rogue had done this countless times before without giving his heart to any woman. She was no different.

"Yer sister would not approve of that mouth."

She cocked a wry eyebrow at Graham as he sat up, coming face to face with her, but whatever retort she was about to fling at him faded when he smiled at her.

"God, ye're beautiful."

It was not his declaration, one she'd heard many times before from men who sought to win her favor, but the way his breath faltered when he set his eyes on her, that felled her heart to her arse. "Thank you," she said softly, feeling a ridiculous smile creep up her lips. "You are beautiful, as well."

The devil beat her! She mewled worse than any kitten! She could have bitten her tongue right off. Did she just tell him he was beautiful?

"And so bold," his voice dipped to a smoky baritone as he reached out and wrapped his index finger around a lock of her loose hair. He tugged, bringing her face closer and sweeping his lips over hers. "I vow there is nae other lass like ye in all the world, Claire Stuart."

Was that a good thing? she thought to ask him, just before he captured her breath with his mouth. The passion in his kiss convinced her that it was.

"I hurt." She pushed against his chest with her palms when he lowered her onto the dewy grass.

Instead of looking repentant, he grinned down at her, quite pleased with himself. "Aye, ye'll need a day or two to recover."

More like a sennight, she thought, but kept it to herself. No need to feed the knave's unrivaled arrogance. And did he think she was his to do with as he pleased now that he'd deflowered her? A day or two indeed. Why, he'd be fortunate if she spared him a second . . .

He pressed his lips to the corner of her mouth, scattering her thoughts like leaves in a storm. The caress of his fingertips against her throat made her tremble in his hands. "I do not know if I can wait so long to have ye again," he whispered, parting her lips with the pad of his thumb. The proof of his desire pushed against her hip, hard, unrelenting, insatiable.

Despite the pain he'd caused her, her nipples went rigid, for the pleasure he'd given her was far greater. She coiled her arms around his neck and opened her mouth fully to his masterful tongue. She did not want to wait either. Shamelessly, wantonly, her body writhed with the hunger to feel him inside her again. She was sure she would have happily given him all he desired if the sound of approaching horses had not startled her so.

She jolted up, mindless of her shoulder smashing into his jaw. She managed to shove a few strands of hair away from her face and pat it back into some semblance of neatness as the intruders came upon them.

"Well then," Angus peered down at them from atop his great warhorse, his stern gaze falling suspiciously over Graham's tunic hanging three sizes too big over Claire's shoulders. "I'm guessin' this means she isna goin' back to Ravenglade."

Claire sprang to her feet, cursing the searing flame spreading across her cheeks. Avoiding her sister's knowing stare, she swiped the dirt from her backside and turned her eyes on Angus. Whatever they suspected had happened between her and Graham, it was high time his men knew that she would do as she pleased, whether their commander approved or not. "Why ever would you assume that, MacGregor?"

"Because Ravenglade is that way," he said, hooking his thumb over his shoulder.

Bristling, Claire pivoted around to Graham. "You chased me for no reason."

"Nae." He grinned, his dimples charming her senseless. "My reason was good enough."

Damn him to Hades. The feral gleam in his eyes revealed to all what his reason had been. Suddenly, she felt naked before their eyes and curtained her gaze behind her heavy tresses.

"Claire." She heard Anne call her and had no choice but to lift her mortified gaze to her. "Does this mean you will not be returning to James?"

She opened her mouth to tell Anne that naught had changed. Now more than ever she believed Monck had betrayed their brother. She would obey none of his commands, including wedding Robert, and she intended to warn James of his treachery. But Graham's voice cut her off.

"Yer sister is mine now, and she'll be coming to Skye with us."

For an instant, Claire was sure she'd heard him wrong.

When the instant passed, and she realized he was serious, she almost laughed right in his face. Almost. Her nostrils flared. Her lips tightened. Her eyes blazed with indignation as she swept her hair away from her face. She was *his* now? "Why, of all the puffed-up . . . insufferable . . . Do you sincerely think—"

Her tirade came to an abrupt end when he snatched her up by the waist and clamped his mouth over hers. Crushing her to him with one arm, he devoured every last shred of her resistance, until she hung weak in the crook of his elbow.

"Find yer sword and mount yer horse, Claire," he commanded huskily, his gaze spilling over her features, basking in his prize. "I'm taking ye home."

Three days later, Claire was still not sure when she had agreed to follow him to the end of the bloody earth. She told herself that she journeyed to Skye in order to keep Graham and Robert from riding back to Edinburgh and alerting Monck to their suspicions regarding James. But she knew she followed Graham for another reason entirely. Was she in love? How was she to know? She'd spent her entire life primping for battle, not suitors. And if it was love, how the bloody hell could she have given her heart to a rogue? Aye, she let him take her, but that didn't mean she loved him, did it? All the men in Connor's garrison had bedded women they didn't love. She could ask Anne, but then she would have to endure endless hours of teasing. Och, why hadn't she given at least some of her attention to the ways of courtly ladies and lords when she was a child?

Whatever it was, it had a grip on her from the beginning. Every plan she'd ever had to slip from his company had been thwarted by the man who rode just a few feet ahead of her, tall in his saddle, his broad, bare shoulders lightly bronzed from the sun. Save for what happened at Ravenglade, he had not used force, or the practiced charm of a rogue, to keep her with him, yet each day she had willingly followed him in whichever direction he led. She had no one to blame but herself for her mad attraction to Graham Grant. And now he thought she was his.

The thought of *belonging* to Graham no longer stirred her temper—at least, not as much as it had when she first heard him announce it. Highlanders were a stubborn, primitive lot with their own set of laws. Cradling her in his arms last night, Graham had explained that he had every right to claim her as his woman if he so chose. And would he fight General Monck's whole army for her? she had laughed at him. Aye, he'd promised, he would. She would have punched him in his ribs if he hadn't been holding her so tenderly beneath the stars. If she'd detected a trace of arrogance in his voice, she would have challenged his claim, called him daft.

But it was she who'd gone mad. Mad because she wanted to believe he could. And mad with desire every time he touched her, looked at her, smiled at her. It shocked her, really, the way she purred like a damned kitten in his trembling embrace. Connor would have laughed at her, insisting that she had finally found a man who could tame her. She would have denied his claim, though, knowing that her Highland warrior had sparked in her a feral, reckless need she never knew existed.

It came upon her whenever they stopped for the night. The urge to lure him into the woods, to steal him away

from the others, peel off his plaid, and mount his sleek
body the way she had in the mist. Never in her life had
she felt such sweet power over a man, such glory in being
a woman. Even now, with little more than a few stolen
kisses between them in three days, Claire felt more alive
and on fire than she ever had in combat. Her nipples flared
to life against the soft wool of her tunic at the slightest
slant of his mouth. When she walked Troy to a stream,
Graham's hooded, hungry gaze made her excruciatingly
aware of the sway of her hips, the feminine contour of her
derrière.

Of course, she did not act on her newly kindled lust,
for she was no trollop—especially with Anne so close by.
But her determination to resist him for modesty's sake
crumbled when they stopped at an inn just before they
reached Glenelg.

"Why, 'tis Commander Grant!" A buxom amber-
haired woman, with a sway in her hips Claire was sure
had to be painful, sauntered straight for Graham. "The
Lord has answered m' prayers."

"And mine," another serving wench called out, hefting
a jug of ale to her patron's table.

Entering the inn at his side, Claire watched Graham
slip off his cap, letting loose his unkempt tumble of honeyed curls. She saw what the other women saw and understood why the mere sight of his dimpled grin ravished
their breath.

"'Tis good to see so many friendly faces, Abby," Graham greeted the woman warmly, but when she lifted her
arms to coil them around his neck, he caught her wrists
gently and stopped her. "This is Claire," he told her turning her in Claire's direction.

Claire smiled, more at Graham than at the woman. What was this? Had the rogue lost interest in his wenches? And was it because of her? With a pang that set her heart to racing, she remembered that he had not bedded Lianne at the inn in Stirling. Could she have captured the heart of this magnificent warrior? How was she to know?

"And will she be sharing yer room?" Abby sneered at her.

Before Graham could answer, and och, Claire wished he had, Anne stepped forward, looping her arm through Claire's. "Of course not." Her smile was as serene as a summer loch when she addressed the dour-faced maid. "My sister is a lady, but should she find you skulking about his, or Lord Campbell's door, she is likely to beat you senseless."

Claire tossed her sister a scrutinizing look while another wench led them to the stairs. There was no visible evidence to confirm Claire's suspicions. Anne didn't stumble or sway on the stairs but glided up them like a swan across a loch, still wearing that ridiculous smile. "That was a tad unladylike, Anne—as is getting drunk with men."

"I am not drunk," Anne discarded her sister's admonishment with a delicate wave of her hand. "I took but one sip to help dull my senses, lest I find myself riding off into the misty eve with Robert." She cast her sister an and-you-know-exactly-what-I-mean look and continued up the stairs even while Claire paused, gaping at her. "We are not like the women here, Claire. We are kin to the king, and must conduct ourselves as such."

Although it was quite shocking to hear her sister's confession about wanting to bed Robert so badly she had to drink whisky to resist him, Claire could not help the sudden surge of laughter rising from her throat. "Och, Anne, we are not so different from these women at all."

"Aye, we are." Turning, Anne stopped and looked down at her over her shoulder. Her tranquil smile held a hint of victory fit for the battlefield. "We have won the men they pray for."

Claire's heart battered wildly in her chest. Had she won Graham? She turned to look at him over her shoulder only to find him looking back.

"Abby," he called out without breaking their gaze, "have someone prepare a bath in my room."

Claire slipped out of her and Anne's bed and into Graham's room without being seen. She paid no heed to her sister's words. Her only thoughts were of him. She shut the door behind her and entered a haven bathed in the rosy candescence of candlelight. His bath had been prepared, its surface glittering like starlight. He moved within the shadows and light, coming to stand behind her.

"What kept ye, lass?" He buried his face in the soft hollow of her neck and grazed his teeth over her rapid pulse beat.

"I arrived as quickly as I could," she said, her breath as short as his while his deft hands undressed her. Her nipples tightened instantly at the stroke of his palm.

By the time his plaid crumpled to the floor, Claire was trembling with unchecked desire for him.

The water spilled over the edge when he stepped into the basin. He sat, gently pulling Claire down to sit nestled between his thighs. Plumes of candle smoke raced across Claire's nostrils as the cooled water caressed her belly, her breasts. Enfolded in the heat of his body, she felt heady and drunk with Angus's potent whisky. Her muscles relaxed and her limbs went numb as he pulled her back against his chest. She watched his fingers skim the surface before her, a seductive dance that made her nipples ache with anticipation.

With his hot breath raking across the pulse at her throat, he cupped her breasts in his hands, squeezing, kneading her gently. But his touch grew more intense, more possessive as his staff hardened against her back.

She drew in a long, languorous sigh when his hands reached for the soap bowl, leaving her alone to savor the tingling aftereffects of his ministrations. He lathered his hands above her, dripping soap onto her breasts. A subtle shift of his hips grazed his erection along her lower spine and pulled a labored groan from his throat. Slipping his legs beneath her, he spread her wider over his knees and arched his back, lifting her pelvis out of the water. Lowering his hand to her eager niche, he flicked his soapy fingers across her, taunting, and then satisfying with more meaningful strokes. His other hand worked her deeper into oblivion, tugging her nipples and caressing her in his rough palms.

He dipped his finger into the water, and then into her, and stroked her from the inside. Claire writhed in his hands as wave upon thrilling wave sluiced over her.

Graham held her firmly, as fiercely aroused by her climax as she was. He slipped his finger out, and sliding it over her engorged nub, he lowered her onto his waiting lance.

Claire thought nothing would ever feel the way his fingers just did, but how could she have forgotten how sinfully good it felt to glide over his cock? She *had* to forget, else she would be mounting him every time he crossed her thoughts. It wasn't just the way he stretched her just enough to almost tear her apart, or the satisfying fullness of having every inch of him inside her. It was the way he moved, as if taking her was his right. The gyration of his hips that drove him deeper, the slow, excruciatingly erotic plunges and retreats that teased her with his length, and the way he clutched her to him, impaling her hard and fast, having his way and making her love it.

Och, but he was as wicked as he proclaimed, taking her lobe between his clenched teeth and telling her how tight and hot she was.

" . . . like hungry flames on my shaft, licking and sucking me dry. D'ye feel how hard I am fer ye, Claire?" He drove into her like a battering ram, soaking her with his seed.

"Aye," she panted.

"How does it feel?"

She told him without reserve, pulling up and dipping down over his throbbing erection until he filled her to bursting and she cried out with the rapture of her release.

Chapter Twenty-five

I have kept my heart's desire silent long enough.

As the sun began its lazy descent in the west, James Buchanan set his bloodshot eyes toward the high, ragged peaks of the Grampian mountain range. He had not slept in over a sennight, plagued by thoughts of vengeance while his men slumbered peacefully round the campfire. Night after night he sat awake, contemplating whom to kill first when he finally reached Skye. Graham Grant, he decided, for smashing his skull into the wall and setting him to bed for days with an ache in his temples that made him wail, a broken nose, and a cracked tooth. The son of a bitch was going to pay dearly for that.

Robert Campbell would be next to feel his wrath. The earl was a traitor to the Parliament. Who on the council would fault him for killing a royalist MacGregor sympathizer? James hadn't liked him from the moment the earl set foot in Ravenglade. He didn't like the way the man's eyes changed color with the direction of the light. Or the way those eyes watched him with open suspicion. As if he knew . . . James had to kill him. He would cut out the tongue that had flapped against him in Claire's ear, and then he would cut out those wolf's eyes.

As he settled his back against the gnarled trunk of a tall pine, his thoughts turned to Connor's sisters. A doleful sigh escaped from the gaping hole where his tooth used to be. He would not take any pleasure in killing them, but now they left him no choice. He ground out a blasphemy through his tight lips, thinking about how easily Claire had turned on him. She took the word of a Roundhead over his. Arrogant cunt. Connor had always given her her way. Even when they had joined the resistance, and Claire insisted on going with them, Connor had confided in him that he had agreed with her decision because he understood her so deeply. His blood flowed through hers. And so it did. She was as much a bitch as her brother was a bastard. Always refusing him, always so serious, with no interest in play.

And James had wanted to play with her. Good and hard. He wanted to hold that tight bitch down and use her until she screamed her allegiance to her new lord and master. And scream she would, just before he cut her throat.

There was still a way to gain Connor's lands with them all dead. When the king was rightfully restored to the throne, and he saw that it was Buchanan who rode at General Monck's side when they took back the kingdom— Buchanan who slaughtered the men who dared to kill his two lady cousins, he would grant the lands and titles to his faithful servant.

James smiled to himself, pleased with his craftiness. He could not lose. Even if Charles never made it back to England, Monck trusted him, and after delivering Connor's head to them on a silver platter, Lambert and Fleetwood did, too.

A disturbance from within a stand of trees to his left interrupted his thoughts. Pouncing to his feet, he drew his sword and kicked the sleeping soldier beside him.

"Who is there?" he called into the twilight shadows, waking a dozen more. "Announce yourself, or die."

"Hold!" a man hailed back. "It is I, Steven, with men from Ravenglade!"

Hearing this, James sheathed his blade and stepped forward. What the hell was the captain doing so far from Ravenglade? James had to leave him and his entire legion behind. For they were not any of his men, but Connor's, loyal to the Stuart line. "What is it? Why have you followed us?"

"A missive." Steven held a folded parchment aloft and leaped from his saddle, joining James in three long strides. The seven men who accompanied him hung behind in the shadows. "It arrived from London by way of Stirling," he said as James tore the parchment from his fingers. "The messenger said it was urgent, and should be delivered to you posthaste." He followed James to the firelight. "Who is sending you missives from London?"

The tone of Steven's question was innocent enough, but when James slipped his gaze to him, he saw suspicion in the thrust of the captain's chin.

"I will tell you who after I myself find out." James cast him a sinuous smile before returning to the missive. He recognized the handwriting right away. Elizabeth Fleetwood, the general's daughter. The stately slut who had shared his bed and many of her father's secrets when James visited London last winter. He scanned the letter quickly, suspecting she wrote to beg him to visit her again. His eyes fell to two words leaping off the illuminated page.

Connor Stuart.

His heart thumped madly in his chest as he quickly scanned the rest. Above the flames, his face went ashen and he stumbled back. Steven caught him by the arm and tried to have a look at the letter.

"What is it that causes you to look like you've seen a ghost?"

He just had. Connor Stuart was alive—imprisoned in the Tower, but alive.

"Who knows of this missive?" he asked, yanking his arm from Steven's grasp.

Steven eyed him warily as he dropped the parchment into the fire. "Just those of us who delivered it to you." He retreated a step when James slid his sword from its sheath.

A short while later, James wiped the blood from his blade, stepped over one of the eight bodies littering the ground, and motioned to his men to saddle up.

"Change of plans. We're going to London. Stuart's alive, and we must remedy that before his cousin returns."

Claire braced her legs and her mettle against the brisk wind tearing at her braid and whipping strands of hair across her face. But it was not the weather that held her breath suspended in her chest, or the surging pitch of the boat beneath her boots that heaved her stomach to her throat. It was the view as they crossed the narrows into Skye. The jagged, mountainous peaks of an isle suspended between the mists of heaven and hell. A place where time meant nothing—the feeling of leaving all she loved behind to enter a world forgotten by man . . . mayhap by God.

"The first time I set my eyes upon *Eilean a' Cheo'*, the Misty Isle, I was certain my sister was dead." Robert joined her at the ship's bow and rested his hands on the thick wooden rail. "For only a man with a harsh, desolate heart would choose to dwell in such isolation."

Claire regarded his sculpted profile as he spread his gaze over the isle looming ahead. "You were brave to come for her, Robert Campbell."

He shook his head, accepting no glory. "I could have done no less."

Claire smiled. She had thought him unskilled, too idealistic to understand the ultimate sacrifice of battle. But she had sorely misjudged him. He might not be willing to die for the deliverance of Scotland, but he would have died for his sister. "You are truly a knight, Lord Campbell. Kate is a fortunate woman."

He turned to her, his fondness for her warming his eyes to deep amber. "Both of our sisters are fortunate."

"Aye," Claire agreed. "And Anne, doubly so, now that she has you looking after her."

His grin flashed, shy, modest, devastatingly sweet. Roundhead or not, Claire was glad he fancied her sister. She would put a good word in for him to Charles if ever he returned to England.

"So what happened when you found your sister? Did you fight the MacGregors?" she asked, returning her attention to the isle.

"I had no intention of fighting them. By the time I entered Skye, I had discovered that we cannot always trust our first impressions. Skye," he said, looking back toward the rugged landscape, "is one of the most magnificent places in Scotland, and the man who chose to dwell here is fair, and compassionate, and very much in love with my sister."

"Did he just call Callum compassionate?" Graham

came up behind them and snaked his arm around Claire's back. "He wanted to kill ye the first time he met ye, and the time after that, Rob."

Claire was instantly, excruciatingly aware of Graham's closeness, the melting warmth of his muscles grazing her frame. His touch was casual, and yet provocatively possessive, washing her away on thoughts of domination and submission. Her blood ran scalding through her veins, directly to her loins. He had not touched her since they left the inn. Claire guessed it was her own fault, because of the way her reluctant gaze darted to Anne—who remained ever at her damned side—every time Graham got too close to her.

She remembered to breathe when Robert's laughter pulled her back to the moment. She grinned when she looked at him, but had no idea what the bloody hell she was smiling about.

"He's never made me shyt in my plaid," Graham said, defending himself against whatever Robert had accused him of.

"You mean to say that when he flung you clear across his barn you did not fear the sting of his wrath?"

Above her, Graham answered with a whimsical smile in his voice. "I rose back up and stopped him from killing ye, did I not?"

"Who?" Claire asked both of them.

"Callum," they replied in unison.

Claire nodded, recalling the topic now. She waved when she spotted her sister stepping on deck. Beside her, Robert's body snapped to attention after following the direction of her greeting. Claire cut her gaze to him, thinking of a way to get Anne out of her hair, and out of the Highlanders' brew. If the young knight knew why his

sweet damsel was half soused every day, he would surely
do something to stop it, and then, mayhap, Anne would
quit lecturing her about the merits of being a lady. "I am
concerned about her dallying in Angus's whisky."

"Aye," Robert agreed, echoing her worried tone. "Has
she always enjoyed spirits?"

"Och, she does not enjoy drinking," Claire assured
him, smiling at her sister's approach. "She does it because
of you."

"Me?" Robert asked, dragging his gaze from Anne to
Claire. "She drinks because of me? Why?"

"I'm afraid I do not know. You will have to ask her."

Robert was off before Claire could even turn to him.
She concealed a little giggle behind her hand, which Graham promptly halted when he leaned his hips against the
rail and hauled her into his arms.

"A clever ploy to get me alone." His green eyes twin-
kled, his seductive smile curled her toes.

"Really, rogue," Claire argued, breathless against him.
"Do you tell yourself that the sun rises each day just to
shed its light on your glorious countenance?"

"Nae," he said, his smile deepening into something
more meaningful. "Because it rises to shine on ye." He
caressed her cheek in his palm and leaned in to kiss her.
Claire knew she was lost to the fullness of his lips, the
erotic dance of his tongue, the drum of his heart against
his chest and hers. She clung to him, opening her mouth
to take him deeper.

"I want ye, Claire." His shuddered breath fell across
her lips while he glided the proof of his desire along her
crux, burning her, branding her. "I will not wait much
longer to have ye."

She gazed into his eyes and quirked her mouth into a rueful smile, enjoying the chase as much as he did. "Unless your Highland claim on me grants you leave to force yourself upon me, waiting is what you shall do."

His mouth hooked into a slow, blatantly sexual grin. "Woman, beware of how ye tempt me, or when this boat docks, I will carry ye deep into the woods and fuck ye senseless."

"Tempt me neither then," she parried, despite the tremor in her voice. She slipped her hand between them and rubbed her palm down the length of him. "And I will not take hold of this pulsing beast and make you forever mine."

Anne would have dropped down dead if she'd heard her, but Claire had never learned to be shy or submissive with men. She knew she sounded like a brazen wench, but as long as Graham found no offense—which his clenched jaw and smoldering gaze proved he didn't—she didn't either.

"I am already yers," he growled, locking her in his steel embrace and capturing her hand between them. "But ye may work the *beast* to yer heart's content if 'tis convincing ye need." He dipped his hungry mouth to her throat, grazing her flesh with his teeth and pressing his thick shaft against her cupped hand.

"Can ye no' wait until we reach Camlochlin fer this?" Brodie grumbled as he passed them. "Everyone's watchin' ye, fer hell's sake."

Claire immediately tried to break away. Talking like a wench when no one else could hear was one thing; rubbing herself all over Graham like a sex-starved harlot while others watched was another. But Graham pulled her back, turning her in his arms and using her body to conceal the strain against his plaid.

"Brodie, go fetch Angus and get the horses ready." The menacing glint in his eyes warned Brodie not to argue. "And ye," he bent his mouth to Claire's ear. "Don't move."

Move? She could hardly breathe with his arousal butted up against her rump so intimately. She tried to remain still even when a tendril of hair fluttered across her face and made her nose itch. She shifted her weight to one leg and felt Graham's body stiffen against her spine. She forced a casual smile at her sister when Anne returned from wherever Robert had just taken her. Anne glared at her in return, clearly angry with her for telling Robert her reason for drinking. Relaxing into the hard wall of muscle behind her, Claire let out a satisfied sigh. Ah, success! The *lady* looked a bit flustered. Her cheeks were flushed and her lips were swollen from being kissed. Mayhap now, Anne would understand the struggle *she* had to endure each day.

That struggle was about to come to a shattering halt, Claire realized when they docked in Kylerhea and were mounting their horses. As she lifted her boot to Troy's stirrup, Graham rode up alongside her, curled an arm around her waist, and hoisted her into his lap.

"We'll catch up with ye," he told the others, whirling his stallion and hers around in the opposite direction. "Angus, tie yerself to Anne when ye reach the cliffs and don't let her fall."

"What cliffs?" Claire gaped at him, and then at her sister, as Graham dug his heels into his horse's flanks. "She could fall off a cliff?"

"She is safe," Graham promised her against the wind battering their faces. "Ye, on the other hand, are not."

Chapter Twenty-six

But soon, the land shall quake at my coming . . .

"We should not have separated from them," Claire complained to Graham as he dismounted. "My sister should not be—" She caught her breath when he clamped his hands to her waist and lifted her out of his saddle and into his arms. "—alone." She tilted her face up to his and his potent gaze set a thousand butterflies loose in her belly.

"She is not alone," Graham breathed, his tawny lashes sweeping downward as he leaned toward her. The lazy stroke of his tongue across her lips made her groin sizzle. "But we are. At last." He closed his arms around her, drawing her to him in an embrace as needful as his kiss. His tongue swept deep inside her mouth, stroking, titillating, vanquishing her every other thought, save for one. He was going to fuck her senseless. And she couldn't wait. She flung her arms around his neck, and driving her hips hard against his, rubbed herself like a languid cat over his full erection. He withdrew slightly, still captive to her eager embrace, a teasing smile dimpling his cheek.

"What is it ye want so, lass?"

She wanted him naked and mad with desire. She

wanted to feel—to see his muscles, sleek and straining while he took her. He knew it, and he deliberately kept it from her.

Dragging his palm over the ripe swell of her buttocks, his hand disappeared between her legs. "D'ye want to spread these creamy thighs beneath me while I sink deep and hard into ye?" With naught but a slow, salacious flick of his finger against the moist wool of her trews, he coaxed her apart. "Aye," he answered for her as she tossed back her head, offering herself up to him.

Graham's control snapped. He snaked his arm around her waist and crushing her to him, lifted her off her feet. His mouth descended on hers, open, ravenous, almost brutally possessive. Claire matched his fervor, biting his lower lip and clawing at his plaid. He broke their kiss only to get her out of her clothes faster, and to unfasten his belt. His eyes shone like smoldering embers as they poured over her bare, beautiful form even while her own did the same to him.

Claire wanted to feast her eyes on him a moment longer. She wanted to let her gaze savor the savage look of him, wild with desire, hard and huge with need. But he would wait no longer. With a low grunt, he heaved her up over his hips as if she weighed nothing and caught her nipple between his teeth. He sucked her while he hefted her thighs up and around him.

The wind wailed across the braes, blending with her cry as he caressed her buttocks and thrust himself inside her. His muscles shook against her palms as she tried to writhe out of his grasp. He held her firm, laving his tongue like a flame between the valley of her breasts, up the smooth column of her throat, all the while moving, grinding his hips against hers. She sought mercy from him, but did not find it as he buried himself to the hilt, driving her upward while his mouth captured her pleas.

She had forgotten the pain, but with each relentless plunge, the agony turned to pure, sinful pleasure. Her body spasmed as shards of green and gold flashed before her eyes. She tightened her legs around him, crossing her ankles at his lower back to clutch him to her, never wanting to let him go.

Graham watched her passion with smoldering eyes and a darkly sensuous smile, basking in the pure, unabashed pleasure she took in him. She swept her tongue over his and he groaned in her mouth, harshly, sweetly, wanting to give her all, and more. His fingers trickled down her braid, singeing her spine, making her muscles jerk and clench around him. Breaking their kiss on a fevered growl, he stared deep into her eyes as he cupped her backside and guided her up and down his long shaft.

She smiled, taking every inch, grasping his sensitive head within her tight folds. Dear God, but he was big, and full, and so deliciously strong holding her up while she milked him like the harlot of harlots that she was. She did not care. He drove her wild and she showed him that he did, without the boundaries of propriety to stop her. Just as he had shown her no mercy, she gave him none now. When he tossed back his head, she followed, licking the sleek, strained cords of his neck. Clutching his shoulders, she nuzzled her mouth to his ear and sucked his lobe.

"You convince me well, warrior."

With a grin as wickedly arousing as the thrust of his hips, he withdrew fully, closed his hand around his glistening rod, and shot his hot seed like a geyser up between them.

When he was done he turned her around, dragging her buttocks against his groin. "Ah, lass," he murmured roughly, bending her forward to take her from behind. "I have not even begun to convince ye."

Graham lay naked beneath the darkening sky, a smile of deep contentment hovering about his mouth. He was home—in the north where the days were shorter with the coming of winter. Home, where the earth beneath a man's bones was harder, less forgiving, until the spring returned and life burst forth anew, more radiant and magnificent than anywhere on the mainland. How had he stayed away so long? This time, he would remain. His travels with Robert were over, but not their friendship. That, they would share always. But he was home, and here was where he wanted to stay.

With her.

He closed his eyes and listened to the sound of Claire's breath while she slept, clutched in his arms. How she had changed his life, he would never know. He did not care. He only knew that the plans he made for his future included her. And that there was no other woman like her in the world. No other woman he wanted to spend the remainder of his days with.

He would have liked to gaze on her face while there was still some light, but he did not want to sever their embrace. For now, he would be content to remember the way she looked in the heat of her passion. How she matched his fervor, or mayhap surpassed it. He had taken her four different times this day, and each time her desire flared anew with his. He'd been with many lasses, but he felt as if he'd never made love to anyone before Claire.

He would awaken her again, for they could not cross the cliffs in the darkness, and the night was going to be a long one. In a moment, he would get up and start a fire and hunt for something to eat. But he was loath to move. He wanted to stay right here with her forever, happy to simply listen to her breath while he breathed in her scent and felt her slow heartbeat pressed to his chest, and her lean, muscular limbs wrapped snugly around him.

He had won her heart. He was almost certain of it, but he felt no arrogance in such a feat. For she had won his heart, as well.

Her sweet kisses around his nipple roused Graham from sleep. He opened his eyes to the morning sun and the glorious sight of Claire's smile.

"I am hungry."

He grinned at her, lifting his hand to smooth her loose tresses off her cheek. "Can nothing sate yer appetite, wench?"

"It is your appetite that worries me, rogue." She turned, presenting him with the alabaster delicacy of her profile while she glanced at his morning erection.

Graham found it amazing and unusual that she would blush now, after she'd taken such pleasure in his body throughout the night. Her innocence was as thrilling to him as the bold, blistering passion he had unleashed in her.

"Well?"

"Well, what?" He trailed his fingers along her collarbone, to the soft swell of her breast.

"Are you going to get up?" She sounded a bit breathless, but when he met her gaze she tossed him an impatient look.

His dimples flashed and her cheeks grew even redder before she pushed him away. "I would like to reach Camlochlin today. I worry for Anne, facing your laird alone."

Graham laughed, springing to his feet. "Aye, Callum may fling her into a vat of boiling oil before the day is through. We should make haste."

"I do not find that humorous." Claire's retort lost its sting as she watched him meander naked toward their horses. Dear God, he'd promised to render her senseless, and he had done exactly that. Why else would she find such joy in the flare of his shoulders, the shape of his firm buttocks, the carved sinew of his thighs? When she awoke, the first thing she became aware of was the soreness between her legs. The second was his body, so hard even in sleep. She'd wanted to touch him, to run her tongue over all those chiseled angles. She hated pushing him away, but it was either that or climb atop him and spend another day away from Anne. Ah, God, he made her forget what lay ahead and care only about being with him now.

She almost rethought her decision to make haste to Camlochlin when Graham retrieved a pouch of dried berries and turned back to her. She suddenly understood how Eve must have felt each morning when she awoke to find Adam in all his glory, traipsing around in the garden. She looked away when he smiled, catching her silent appraisal.

"How long will it take to get there?" she asked when he sat beside her.

"A few hours, if ye can keep yer hands off me."

Damnation, was her lust for him that obvious? "It will be difficult, for even now I am tempted to strangle you."

He cut her a sidelong look that was brimful of amusement and popped a berry into his mouth. "If killing me is what ye want, Claire, then I suggest ye stick to last eve's battle plan. Yer wee hands around my neck would do naught but excite me."

She knew he was teasing her, but it was the matter-of-fact tone of his voice that made her laugh. She felt his eyes on her, as profound as a physical caress while he delighted in her mirth.

"Ye don't laugh much." He leaned closer to her and reached out to brush his fingers over her lips. "I will teach ye how to enjoy life."

"By becoming a lady-rogue?" Her laughter faded when his hand curled around the back of her neck and his mouth descended on hers.

"*My* lady-rogue."

There was nothing ladylike in the way Claire spread her legs when he pushed her down and covered her body with his. Nothing genteel or demure about how she bucked beneath him, clawing at his rippling shoulders. When she rolled with him and came up on top, she pressed her palms to his glistening chest, tossed back her wild mane, and rode him as if she owned him. She was no damned lady, and she did not want to be one.

Chapter Twenty-seven

. . . and the man who has lost everything shall gain it all back.

"Dear God in Heaven, my sister is dead." Claire chanced opening her mouth to say, even though she was sure her heart would leap out of it when she saw the next turn.

Perched high upon a narrow ledge of Elgol's honey-combed cliffs, she near fainted when Graham peered over the edge at the jagged rocks below. "Nae, she did not fall. Ye'll thank Angus fer that later."

"Should I not be tied to you?" she asked, taking no comfort in his teasing smile. A wave of nausea churned her insides. As if her eyes had a mind of their own, they darted to the edge, only a few meager inches from Troy's hooves.

"Claire."

"What?"

"Open yer eyes."

Och, hell, she did not want to. Couldn't she just keep them shut until Angus came to get her?

"Claire," Graham said more forcefully. She obeyed

this time, and scowled at him. "Stay behind me and follow my horse's steps. The ledge is wider around the next
turn. Ye're going to have to dismount when we come to it
and sit with me."

Did he say dismount? "You're mad if you think I'm
getting off this horse."

He turned in his saddle to look at her more fully.
Claire's pulse raced hard enough to make her feel light-
headed. She wanted to scream at him to be still lest he
fall. "Ye're too fearful," he said. "Ye're making Troy
nervous."

"I do not want to get off," she insisted even as Troy
grew anxious between her legs.

"I see yer sister—and Robert's—possess more courage than ye," Graham said, turning forward again. He
smiled when he heard the string of mumbled blasphemies
flowing from her lips and the clopping of Troy's careful
hooves behind him.

She saw, almost as soon as they rounded the next bend,
why he was wise to make her ride with him. A slow, gossamer mist rolled down the wind-beaten precipice, its
dewy moisture clinging to her hair and skin. They had to
ride through it, in it. Visibility would be poor, and without the steady, confident pace of a good horse, one would
likely fall to one's death.

Dismounting—carefully—she reached for Graham's
hand and let him lift her to his saddle. She waited without
moving, barely breathing, while he tore off a strip of his
plaid and tied Troy to his horse.

It astounded her how safe she could feel in a man's
arms, but when the cliffs finally fell away, the view below
her left her truly breathless.

A castle, as black as pitch, rose out of the behemoth mountainside at its back, its serrated turrets piercing the hovering mist.

"'Tis worth the challenge of getting here." Graham dragged in a ragged breath behind her. "'Tis Camlochlin."

It was starkly beautiful, brutally isolated, ominous and foreboding, like something pulled from the imaginings of a mad poet. A jagged cluster of towers loomed above its inhabitants below and within like a sentinel.

It was safe from intruders, to be sure. Monck was clever to have her and Anne brought here. No one would ever find them, and if they did, they would likely be too afraid to get any closer. Suddenly panic engulfed her. How would she ever escape when Monck sent word? Trying to would likely get her and Anne killed. Returning to her horse, she turned to look around. Could she make it back over the cliffs?

"'Tis more colorful in the spring, but ye will like it here."

She would have to if they tried to force her to wed Robert, she thought, while Graham disappeared over the crest. And what about him? She had thought, had hoped that he would help her stand against Monck. But she had the feeling that following Graham these last few yards would change her life forever. Camlochlin was not a shelter meant to keep her safe from a traitor—for the traitor had sent her here. It was a prison where she would wait out her days until Monck forced her to wed.

"Claire."

At the sound of Graham's voice, she flicked her reins, helpless, once again, to do anything but follow him.

"Is there no other way out?" she asked him, catching up

and looking around at the thatch-roofed bothies scattered about in no particular pattern, their inhabitants peeking at her through narrow doorways, cautious, untrusting.

"Aye, to the east, over those hills. But 'tis the long way 'round. The cliffs are easier."

A ray of hope bloomed in Claire as she surveyed the sweeping hills to her right. Her hope vanished an instant later when she spotted the guards pacing the battlements. From their vantage point, they could see in every direction.

Connor would have applauded the outlawed Mac-Gregor for building such an impenetrable fortress.

"It is no surprise to me how your laird managed to elude his enemies for so long. Even if the army found this place, they would be seen coming for leagues."

Graham agreed cheerfully and raised his hand in greeting to a group of men training in a wide, open practice field just off the western wall.

One lad, who appeared younger than the rest, saw him, dropped his sword, and bolted forward. His hair was as pale as Claire's, and his eyes, a lighter shade of blue. He looked so much like Connor that Claire's heart halted in midbeat until he reached them. When he did, he immediately bowed before her as if she were royalty.

Until that moment, Claire had forgotten that she was.

She felt other eyes on her and turned to see a small group of men and women venturing out of their homes. When Claire's gaze met theirs, they bowed before her. These people, so far from the laws, were Royalists, loyal to their king.

"Rob said ye were comin'," the lad said, turning to Graham. He smiled up at him and a ray of sunlight pierced the gloom. " 'Tis good to see ye again, brother."

"'Tis good to be home, Jamie." Graham leaped from his horse, clutched his brother's forearm, and dragged him closer into a tight embrace.

Ah, Jamie, Claire thought, dismounting next. *The devoted husband of the Devil's sister, Margaret.* "M'lady," he said turning back to her, washing her in warmth. "'Tis an honor to meet ye. We've never had the king's relations here at Camlochlin. Yer sister is inside with my wife and Kate. I will tell them that ye have arrived." He spun on his heel before she could answer and charged for the castle. "Rob's been tellin' us of yer adventures," he called over his shoulder at Graham. "But I wait to hear them from—" He crashed headlong into the chest of another man exiting the doors just as Jamie reached them.

"Callum," Jamie went on as the man held him steady on his feet. "Graham has returned!"

"Aye, I can see that."

Claire watched, torn between running the other way and staring at the chieftain in open, blatant appreciation, as the legendary laird moved Jamie out of his way and began walking toward her and Graham. She almost laughed at herself for thinking him beautiful. The man was glorious; the perfect embodiment of a warrior, unmatched and unbeaten. His colorful plaid draped shoulders a league wide. The heavy claymore at his side added more swagger to his long, masculine strides. His dark hair glistened with moisture from the light fog around him and fell well past his shoulders with two strands plaited at his temples. His face might have been fashioned from the unyielding rock hovering behind and above them. When he stood just a few inches from her, Claire could not help but tremble at his presence. His eyes were the color of fire, blue speckled with ruthless shards of gold. He fastened them on her first, a slow, grueling assessment from her boots to the sword dangling at her waist. She raised her chin in an effort to appear less affected by him, but the sheer power of his gaze, when it finally settled on hers, sapped her confidence and she looked away.

"Our king's cousin is welcome at Camlochlin."

She looked up as he straightened from a slight bow, meeting her gaze with one of respect. Then he swept past her, smelling of heather and mist.

He gathered Graham into a bone-crushing embrace. "Welcome home, ye bastard. Dinna stay away so long next time."

Graham pounded him on the back as he withdrew and turned to Claire.

"Claire Stuart," he presented her with a smile and reached for her hand.

Callum noted the possessive gesture and cast his friend an amused look. "I understand ye're skilled with a blade," he said, fixing his gaze on her again.

"I . . . I . . . my brother . . ." Och, how the bloody hell was she supposed to answer that? Was she to take pride in ambushing men and cutting their throats, when before her stood a battle-hardened warrior whose great skill at killing made even Oliver Cromwell retreat?

"She has fought blade to blade against the realm, Callum," Graham answered for her.

"Fer what purpose?" the laird asked, sizing her up with a different kind of admiration.

"To restore the monarchy," Claire said, unaware that the pride she took in her cause was evident in the tilt of her chin.

Callum saw it and his approval shone in his eyes. "'Tis a good cause, and one that I support."

She believed him. This man was not in cahoots with Monck. He was not holding her prisoner in his fortress, but meant to protect her in it.

"Graham!"

The woman's voice yanked away Claire's thoughts and dragged her eyes to a raven-haired beauty hurrying toward them with a babe on her hip.

"Robert told us you were coming," she said, stepping into Graham's waiting arms. "It is so good to see you again, dear friend."

Claire would have been worried if this woman was one of his wenches, for she was positively radiant, with sparkling eyes as dark as onyx and a tumble of riotous waves framing her creamy complexion. But the way the laird's face went soft looking at her told Claire who the woman was.

"Ah, Kate, ye grow more bonny each time I see ye. Let me have a look at this babe." Graham took the babe from Kate MacGregor's arms and cradled him against his chest. Watching him, Claire imagined him holding their babe with such care and felt a rush of warmth course through her.

"He's a fine lad," Graham said first to Kate, and then to Callum while the two drew closer to each other, as if pulled by something far greater than pride over their son. "What do ye call him?"

"Robert."

When Graham heard Kate's reply, he gave the babe a mournful pout. "If yer parents had named ye Graham, yc would have grown into a strapping man."

"My brother is quite strapping," Kate said, swatting his arm before accepting her son back. "Lady Anne thinks so too, which is one of the reasons I love her as a sister already." This set up the perfect opening to introduce herself, since it seemed to have skipped her husband's and his best friend's minds. Kate smiled at Claire and reached for her hand. "It is a great honor to have such a lady in our home."

Before Claire had time to blush over the unfamiliar reverence given her, Kate closed her fingers around hers and led her away. "Come, let us get out of the cold and go inside and get acquainted, though I feel as if I know you already. Anne told me that you fight as well as a man. I have never met any woman besides myself who—"

Graham, Callum, and Jamie picked up their steps behind the two chattering lasses and followed them into the castle.

"Is it true then, what Robert says?" Callum asked Graham, cutting him a casual glance.

Graham shrugged. "What does he say?"

"That ye may have finally lost yer heart to a lass."

On the other side of Callum, Jamie peered across the laird's chest at his brother, his eyes wide awaiting Graham's answer.

"Aye," Graham said, smiling at Claire's long braid swinging down her back. "I may have."

The inside of Camlochlin was infinitely more welcoming than the outside. Tall candle stands and sconced torches lit the long corridors. Thick tapestries depicting battle and biblical scenes alike draped the walls, providing warmth to the drafty halls. Heavy Highland burrs permeated the peat-scented air with melody as Camlochlin's many inhabitants made their way to and fro.

But it wasn't until Claire saw her sister that she allowed herself to relax. Kate brought her to the main solar, where Anne sat conversing with Robert and another woman before a roaring hearth fire. At least Claire thought she was a woman. She was small enough to be a child, lost in the huge, high-backed chair where she reclined, her feet dangling a few inches from the floor.

When Anne saw her sister, she sprang to her feet and rushed to the door. "I was worried for you. Are you well?"

"Of course I am." Claire's cheeks flushed a bright shade of red, hoping, praying her sister did not ask for an explanation of why she and Graham had stayed behind for a full day.

Fortunately, she did not ask, but she did not have to. It appeared, by the impish grin curling the corners of her mouth, and the careful scrutiny narrowing her brilliant blue eyes, that the small lass already knew.

"Lady Stuart," Kate said, ushering her into the room. Robert stood up immediately and took the babe from her arms. "This is Callum's sister, Maggie."

The wee woman rose from her chair, the slight hump of her back bringing her no higher than Claire's ribs. Her grin softened into a welcoming smile while she sized up Claire as closely as her brother had.

"Hmm," she voiced, making Claire feel as if she were being appraised for some higher purpose, but no conclusion could yet be made of her worthiness. "I'm saddened by the news of yer brother."

Claire blinked at the sudden change of direction, and then nodded.

"As am I." Kate took her hand and squeezed it. "I cannot begin to fathom how difficult his loss must be for the both of you."

"Nor can I," Maggie agreed with a weighty sigh.

Claire caught the loving smile Kate offered Robert while he made cooing noises at his nephew. Why the hell did she suddenly feel like weeping? She cleared her throat, but it was no use. Her eyes misted with tears. Why now? she beseeched the heavens. She'd had months to cry over Connor's death. Why would her body betray her now in front of these women whom she did not even know?

Because they understood. They each had brothers as dear to them as Connor had been to her.

"It has been profoundly difficult," she admitted for the first time.

Hearing the emotion in her voice, Robert looked up and Anne rushed to her side. "I miss him, too," she said. "I have longed to speak of him with you, but you . . ."

"I know," Claire quieted her, stroking her sister's cheek. "Forgive me. I sometimes forget that you lost him, too."

Anne shook her head, spilling tears over Claire's hand. "He was your twin, and your dearest friend. I have always understood the bond between you, and have never felt slighted by it."

Claire hugged her as the door opened and the men stepped inside.

"Well, look what the winds have dragged home." Maggie set her fists on her hips and aimed her most disapproving scowl at Graham.

"Come here, ye wee she-devil, and admit that ye missed me."

Without turning at first, for she did not want Graham to see her tears, Claire closed her eyes and let the sound of his voice soothe her. A moment later, she looked at him, helpless to do anything else. He'd brought laughter and purpose back to her life. Part of her had died with Connor, but Graham Grant made her feel alive again. She smiled, watching Maggie rush headlong into his arms.

Hell, but she wanted to be next.

Chapter Twenty-eight

But know this, that I am a soldier with a need for nothing more.

The private chamber Claire was given boasted two monstrously big wardrobes carved from deep brown walnut with wrought-iron hinges. The two women who escorted her remained silent while they dusted cobwebs from the corners and fed wood to the giant alcoved hearth. Kate had introduced them as Glenna and Lizbeth, the tanner's daughters. They were twins, sharing the same rich auburn hair, scalding green eyes, and pinched lips. Pretty, but sour-tempered. Claire shrugged, sitting on the edge of a massive four-poster bed. She sighed with delight at the soft feathered mattress beneath her rump. Och, but her arse was killing her from being in the saddle for so long. One of the maidens—Claire couldn't tell who was who—stomped over, snatched up a pillow, and gave it a hearty whack. A small cloud of dust erupted and made Claire sneeze.

The twin reached for another pillow, but Claire reached forward and laid her hand on top of it. "I can manage the rest," she said with a caustic smile. "That will be all."

The twin straightened her spine and wiped her hands

down her skirts. Her glare was razor sharp and Claire wondered what the hell she had done to anger the wenches so. She looked as if she wanted to say something, or mayhap spit in Claire's direction, but her sister's voice stopped her.

"Come, Glenna, leave her be. He will tire of her soon enough."

He? Satan's balls. Claire pounded the mattress, expelling more dust. She should have known. Would she be plagued everywhere she went by Graham's lovers? And twins! Och, the lusty bastard. Did his decadence know no bounds? Tire of her, indeed! She fumed as the twins left the chamber, slamming the door behind them. He would be fortunate if she did not tire of him and his lecherous appetite first.

Finally alone, she looked around and took stock of her situation. So far, save for the twins, Camlochlin was proving to be quite pleasant. Everyone was painfully nice to her. Kate had done much to make her feel at home, and she liked the spark of belligerence in Maggie's eyes. Anne seemed to take to them well enough. Where the hell was Anne, anyway? Did Camlochlin have so many rooms that everyone had his own?

Hell, she needed a bath.

There came a knock at the door and Claire looked at it, wondering if the twins had returned with a pair of matching daggers. She felt inside her boot for her own and left the bed to swing open the door.

This time a quartet of beaming beauties, each with hair a slightly different shade of blonde, met her wary gaze. They curtsied almost in unison, calling her m'lady.

"Och, well then," one of them said, looking her over. She frowned at the kirtles draping her arm.

"Look." Claire had had enough. She fisted her hand on her hip and glowered right back at them. "I did not force any of you into the rogue's arms, or his bed. If I have to endure one more sneering look from his slighted lovers, I swear I will kill him myself and end all your suffering."

One of the four gave the rest a worried look. "Does she mean Graham?"

"That is exactly who I mean," Claire railed. "He told me he was wicked, but I had no idea . . ."

"Poor child." The tallest and eldest-looking of the group clicked her tongue, gave Claire's shoulder a sympathetic pat, and stepped past her into the room. "We are no' Graham's lovers," she said, resting the gowns on the bed. "We're his sisters. I am Murron." She swung around and smiled at Claire. "That is Sineag, Mary, and Aileen."

Claire turned to the other three, wishing a bed as big as the one in her room would fall on her. "His sisters . . . Forgive me for . . ."

"There's nae need," Sineag assured her, entering next.

Aileen followed, her pert golden curls bouncing against her buttocks. "Aye, we understand. Sometimes even I think Graham deserves a knife to his innards."

"Aileen!" Mary charged in next, grasping at her throat in horror. "Ye dinna mean that!"

"Well hell, of course I dinna mean it." Aileen waved away her sister's concern. "But ye know as well as I do, Mary, that our brother has rutted every—"

"Aileen," Murron cut her off with a stern glance. "Why dinna ye go have some steamin' water prepared fer Lady Stuart's bath."

"But I want—"

"Aileen." Murron's tone was serene, but the warning to her sister not to argue was unmistakable.

Claire caught the flare of Aileen's nostrils as she stormed out of the room. She had some fire in her, that one. Immediately, Claire liked her. She turned to Murron—who thought she needed protection from the truth.

"I know of your brother's—" She paused, searching for the appropriate word. "—adventures."

"But ye dinna want to be reminded of them, aye?" Murron turned back to the kirtles without waiting for an answer.

No, she did not, Claire thought with a clearer understanding now of Murron's thoughtfulness.

"We thought ye might enjoy a hot bath and a change of clothes after so long a journey," Murron said, holding up one of the kirtles, dyed in the palest yellow. The bodice was cut high to the waist, with thick, luxurious woolen folds cascading to the floor. "Alas," she said inspecting Claire's trews again, "I fear they willna suit ye."

"Nae, they are lovely," Claire hastened to assure her, still feeling terrible about mistaking the four women for Graham's lovers. She hurried to the bed and swept her hand over two more kirtles of rich emerald and ruby red. There were long shifts to wear underneath, crafted in soft white linen, both long-sleeved and short. "Truly, they will suit me well."

Murron and Sineag gave her knowing smiles, their gazes dipping to the sword hanging from her hip.

Mary curtsied again, wringing her hands in her apron. "We pray fer the king's return soon, m'lady."

Claire smiled at her. "You have my thanks."

"Kate will bring ye some earasaids to wear over them

if ye venture outdoors," Murron told her. "It gets a fright-ful bit nippy this time of year."

The sisters remained with her until Aileen returned with more men and women carrying a large basin and buckets of steaming water.

They told Claire about the kinship between the Grants and the MacGregors, and shared with her some advice about getting along with Maggie. They loved their sister in marriage dearly, but she sported a wicked temper. For-tunately, there were only two things that ignited it, con-suming an animal and scolding Callum and Kate's son.

"She spoils that babe as if 'twere her own," Mary said with a disapproving sigh while the water was being poured into the basin.

"Och, where is the harm in it?" Aileen mumbled, shaking her head at her sister. "She has yet to conceive her own bairn, so she lavishes wee Rob with love. 'Tis understandable."

"Aye," Sineag agreed solemnly. "I doubt she will ever give Jamie a son. She and Callum were tortured by Kate's grand-faither when they were bairns," she explained to Claire. "Her body still suffers the effects, though her mind has healed since her brother no longer wars with the Campbells."

"It was torture that misshaped her so?" Claire asked, horrified.

"Aye," said Murron, "but 'twas long in the past and our laird and his sister prefer to ferget it."

"Speakin' of sisters," Aileen ventured, stepping closer to Claire. "I have met yers and she seems to be naught like ye. If I may, m'lady, is it true that ye can wield a blade bet-ter than a man?"

"Better than some, and as well as most," Claire replied.

If the lass was bold enough to ask such a question in spite of her sisters' exasperated expressions, meant to silence her, she deserved an honest answer.

"Truly?" Aileen's deep-blue eyes lit up. "I have been practicin' my swordplay with Kate, but since Rob was born she takes little interest in honin' her skills. Mayhap, ye would consider . . ."

"Aileen, leave her be now." With a chastising scowl, Mary ushered her toward the door. "Heavens, what man will ever want ye fer his wife if ye're swingin' a sword in his face?"

Their exit came to a halt when Graham stepped into the doorway, blocking the way.

"A man who appreciates a braw lass." He flicked his gaze to Claire and smiled.

Claire felt a rush of warmth throughout her entire body. He had accepted her for who she was from the day they met. He enjoyed her belligerence, had made a cat-and-mouse game out of trying to win her until he learned of her betrothal to Robert. Even when he discovered that it was she who had fought Monck's men, he had not called her daft. And when she feared she was too much like a man for his liking, he showed her with his kiss, his touch, his body how much of a woman she was.

She could not be angry with him over Glenna and Lizbeth, and however many other women were out there wanting him. Not when she looked into his eyes and saw such genuine tenderness gazing back at her from across the room.

"Are ye certain ye want her to stay here in yer chambers?" Murron stepped forward as Graham entered. "I think 'tis goin' to stir trouble."

"Aye, I'm certain," Graham said, never taking his eyes off Claire as he crossed the room to her. "None shall protest."

His chambers? Claire's eyes darted around the room and came to rest on the bed he had shared with other women—with the twins! Satan's balls, she could not sleep here.

"Ye should abide *her* laws." Mary tugged on her brother's plaid, glancing at him nervously. "She is not some village wench, but the king's cousin."

Claire had no idea why Mary would speak of her laws. She was too busy feeling her cheeks burn at the thought of how she'd flung herself into Graham's arms and met his fervor more eagerly than any tavern wench. She was used to the disapproving stares when people understood she was a warrior. But she was no wench!

"I protest!" She shot out her palm, halting Graham's advance. "I will not sleep in your chambers."

Graham covered her hand on his chest with his own and slanted his mouth into a devastating smirk. "Would ye prefer to sleep with me beneath the stars?"

Hell, he was a danger to her good senses, to her virtue. She had known it from the very first time he touched her. She hadn't understood the value of what she'd given him, the way a lady of the court would. But being here reminded her that she had a noble name to uphold.

"I would prefer to share a chamber with my sister. I'll not have these people think me a trollop," she added in a whisper when he creased his brow at her.

"Of course not," he said indulgently, then turned to his sisters. "Lady Stuart will be sharing Lady Anne's chambers, tonight."

"Every night," Claire corrected.

Graham pivoted on his heel, looking a bit more worried. "Every night?"

Nodding, Claire spared him a thankful smile, stepped around him, and headed for the door. "I shall see you at supper."

Chapter Twenty-nine

I do this not with the hope of achieving greatness, but with fear that should I submit, nothing more shall be secure.

Lifting his cup for the fourth time in a toast that had no true importance, Graham downed his whisky and thanked the saints for bringing him home. He could travel to the three kingdoms, but there was naught so good as drinking with his kin in Camlochlin hall.

"To Robert," Angus held his cup aloft again, waiting for the others at the table to do the same. "Fer survivin' so many arse beatin's."

"There were not that many," Robert contended, drinking to himself.

"There were eight," Graham reminded him, patting him on the back. "'Tis much to take pride in."

"Were any bones broken?" Callum asked, dipping a hunk of bread into his mushroom-and-turnip stew.

"Aye, my nose. Twice."

That earned Robert another round of toasts, in which he joined merrily.

Sitting at her husband's side, Kate sipped a cup of warm

milk and eyed Callum's commander over the rim. With curiosity arching her brow, she noted how many times his eyes returned to the entrance of the hall. She knew Robert fancied the younger Stuart sister, for she had spoken with her brother privately the night before and he had told her of his plans to wed her. Kate could not be happier for him. Anne was delicate and mild-mannered, courtly and intelligent; perfect for Robert. Indeed, she seemed to have stepped straight out of one of the storybooks Rob used to read to her when they were children.

But Graham was a man devoted to the pursuit of pleasure, unchaste and unfettered. To see him taken so with one woman piqued Kate's interest. What kind of woman was Claire Stuart to have captured his heart?

"Ladies ofttimes take a long while to primp and preen, Graham."

He stopped tapping his boot under the table, cut his glance to her, and then laughed softly, as if he knew something she did not. "Aye, Kate, ladies ofttimes do."

"He's got eleven sisters," Maggie scoffed on the other side of Kate. "He knows about the habits of women. He keeps lookin' fer Claire Stuart because he has fallen fer her."

Kate smiled behind her hand. Leave it to Maggie to speak the truth without pretense or honey coating.

"Are ye truly happy with this viper fer a wife?" Graham asked Jamie, and winked at Maggie, whose grin was just as devilish as her brother's.

"Jamie," Robert said, wiping his mouth on his serviette. "I've been meaning to ask you, where do you find all the heather you pick for your lovely bride? Graham will be needing some."

Graham cut him his foulest look. "He doesn't pick heather, Rob. Callum does."

Brodie snickered into his cup before Callum quieted him with a warning glance.

The conversation at the table turned, as it usually did, to fighting, but Graham had stopped listening when Claire finally appeared at the entrance.

He wanted to go to her, but he could do naught but gape at her, counting his thrashing heartbeat as it kept time with her footsteps. He'd always found her bonny in her manly garb, but seeing her for the first time with skirts flowing around her slippered feet and a bodice clinging to her maddening curves stalled his heart and made him all the more eager to carry her back to his chambers where he could undress her.

He didn't worry overmuch about her wish to sleep with her sister. She feared what others might think of her here, but there was no need. Soon he would make it clear to all that she was his, and his alone. Until then, she could easily slip unseen into his chambers as she had at the inn.

"Please forgive our late arrival," Anne offered politely after the men rose to greet them.

"The fault is mine," Claire said, taking the blame. "I'm afraid my hair has a will of its own."

Her hair looked glorious swept up into an elaborate crown of knots and plaits, loosely woven with amber ribbons. Graham smiled at her and practically pushed Angus, who was sitting to his right, out of his chair. "'Twas worth the wait."

"Do I look utterly foolish?" she whispered to him, taking Angus's seat and tugging on the stiff bodice cutting off her breath.

"Ye're the bonniest lass here," he promised, wanting to touch her.

She offered him a grateful smile, then turned to the others at the table.

Graham watched her while she reacquainted herself with the laird and lady of Camlochlin. When she laughed with Kate and Anne, he found himself thinking how right it felt to have her here among his kin, a part of his life, and theirs. She even won Maggie over when she politely refused the trencher of roasted beef set before her.

"Callum says his men need the added nourishment for the coming winter months," Maggie told her, biting into an apple. "But I would rather be boiled in oil than eat anything that once looked back at me."

"I had not thought of it that way." Claire cast her trencher a repugnant look and pushed it farther away, much to Maggie's delight, and gave the laces at her waist another yank.

Aye, Graham mused, she would fit in well here. Reaching for her hand, he realized what a fool he'd been to fear his feelings for her. She . . .

She pulled her hand away and shot him a chastising look, which he returned with a crestfallen look of his own. A few moments later, he curled his arm around the back of her chair and rubbed his thumb along her shoulder. She shifted, moving away from his intimate touch.

After that, the conversation turned to General Monck, and she avoided Graham's gaze as ardently as she declared her mistrust for the governor of Scotland.

"What cause has he given ye to suspect him of such treachery?" Callum asked her, giving her full leave to speak her mind.

"So he could wed us to men of his choosing and gain our lands."

"And ye believe Robert wants yer lands?" Callum asked her.

"Well, nae . . ."

"And tell me," Callum cut her off gently, his eyes on her sharp. "Why he would go to all the trouble of gettin' ye here to wed a man who doesna even want yer land, when he could have ordered Rob to bring ye to Edinburgh when ye were so close, and forced ye to wed there?"

Claire stared at him for a moment as if that thought had never occurred to her.

"And what of James Buchanan? Does yer brother's death no' benefit him as well?"

Claire cut Robert a heated glance.

"Aye, he told me of Buchanan's desire to wed ye and no' yer sister," Callum said, dragging her attention back to him. "He stands to gain no' only lands, but the king's favor if he takes ye as his wife, nae?"

"He will not be wedding her," Graham said flatly. When Claire finally turned to him, he stared directly into her flashing eyes, daring her to challenge him on it.

She didn't, but severed her gaze from his again. "Lord Buchanan loved my brother," she told Callum. "Graham and Robert do not know him as I do."

"We have no proof against either man," Robert reminded the laird, having already informed Callum of his concerns about Buchanan.

"Then we can do naught fer now."

"And what is to become of Anne and me in the meanwhile?" Claire asked, tugging, more angrily now, on her bodice. "When Monck deems it safe to send for us, he will make decisions that I cannot abide."

Callum eyed her, then, with a hint of amusement dancing across his eyes, looked at Graham.

Aye, Graham knew she was a hellcat. He did not need reminding. She probably did not even realize she was glaring at the Devil MacGregor. Most lasses did not dare give him any cheek, save for his wife and Maggie, but Claire had a mind of her own—which, Graham had begun to fear from the moment she pulled away from him—might not go well for him while they were at Camlochlin.

"In the meanwhile, ye will enjoy yer stay here and no' fret over what the governor decides," Callum told her in a tone that ended the conversation.

"With respect, my laird, I would know what you—"

"Claire!" Anne tried to kick her under the table and hit Graham instead. Her eyes told him she was sorry, but her smile was tight when she turned it on her sister. "Let us not badger our gracious host. It is late, and we should retire."

Claire smiled just as tightly, but nodded and rose from her seat.

Graham leaped from his as well and swept his fingers lightly over her wrist. "Claire," he said quietly.

She looked up, and without so much as a quirk in her lips, bid him good eve.

Claire did not come to his chambers that night, or any night thereafter. When Graham saw her in the great hall, or the solar, or even in the halls, she was always accompanied by a flock of women. It seemed as if even his own sisters were determined to keep her from his arms.

After four days of not touching her, of barely speaking with her, he was ready to smash some heads. After seven, he seriously considered tossing her onto his horse and leaving Skye. When she had tried her hand at being a lady during their journey here, it was to please him. She was not pleasing him now.

He finally came upon her on a day that was as foreboding as his mood. Aileen was with her in the bailey, toting a sword as long as her legs. While his sister looked exhausted, Claire appeared revived and invigorated, her cheeks flushed despite the brisk, overcast weather.

When she saw him, she waved as if nothing at all was wrong between them. Was she daft? He clenched his jaw as she sauntered closer, Aileen at her side. When she moved to pass right by him, Graham stepped into her path.

"Aileen, leave us." His burr was thick with checked anger and frustration. When his sister hesitated, the dark warning in his eyes encouraged her to move her arse.

"How are you, Graham?" Claire asked pleasantly.

His brow shot up. "How am I? *How am I?*" He took a step closer to her and she backed up. "Claire, what the hell is going on?"

"Going on?" She brushed a stray tendril of hair off her cheek, looked down at her boots, and then at everything else in the bailey but him. "I don't know what you mean."

"Aye, ye know exactly what I mean," he growled. "Ye've done everything in yer power to avoid me. Why?"

Claire couldn't tell him the truth. That in order to resist him, she had to keep completely away from him, because just looking at him made her insides burn and her head feel light. She had to resist him because one touch and she would lose herself, careless of what anyone thought of her. She'd had days to think about the consequences of her actions with him. She was King Charles's kin, ruined by a Highland rogue who had not once been faithful to any woman. "I cannot speak to you right now. Kate has been reading Malory to me and I am already tardy." She tried to push past him but he snatched her wrist and pulled her back.

"What have I done to displease ye?"

"Nothing." She tried to pull her arm back, but he held firm. "I told you I would not have these people think me—"

"I don't care what they think, Claire. Ye belong to me."

"Graham, stop it." She pushed away from him, using her free hand against his chest. "Where I come from a woman does not simply 'belong' to a man because he wants it to be so. And if you want to know the truth, I find it a bit barbaric and insufferably arrogant, and I will not—"

Her words and her breath came to an abrupt halt as he seized her waist and dragged her mouth to his. His kiss was hard, demanding, utterly possessive, leaving her with no doubt of his claim.

He broke their kiss on a ragged breath and pressed his lips to her temple. "If it is a priest ye want, then I'll send fer him, Claire."

She went still in his arms, and then looked up at him slowly. Her eyes were so bonny blue and clear that just gazing into them made Graham want to pledge his heart, his life, and his sword to her.

"Are you asking me to actually marry you?" she asked breathlessly.

"Aye." He smiled down at her. "If that will make being here easier fer ye."

"Easier for . . ." Her eyes darkened to a smoky indigo.

•

Her jaw tightened, and her nostrils flared. "Let me go, you careless lout!" She broke free of his embrace. "You offer to marry me to get me into your bed!"

"Would ye rather I just demand ye into it?" his voice dipped to an angry growl.

She looked like she was about to punch him. He was tempted to take a step back.

She didn't move to strike him, but squared her chin and glared at him—though Graham was certain he saw a hint of hurt in her eyes. "After all our time together do you still think you can order me about? Do you still not know me, Graham? I *do not* belong to you, and I tell you if the power was mine to choose what man to take for a husband, I would not choose you!"

She stormed away, leaving him to stare after her, the heart-wrenching pain in his guts reminding him of why he'd sworn never to fall in love with a lass.

Chapter Thirty

Shall I be stripped bare on the battlefield or be clothed in righteousness and readiness?

"D'ye truly want to wed her?"

Graham refused the cup Callum offered him and watched his best friend recline in the chair next to him before the roaring hearth fire.

They were alone in the solar, a place they used to come to discuss the next Campbell raid. Now they were here to discuss lasses.

"Aye, I do."

Callum tossed him a skeptical look. "If ye had to think that long on it, then mayhap ye're no' so certain."

"The idea of it terrifies me, if ye need to know the truth. But I'm certain."

"She is the king's cousin," Callum reminded him.

"Aye, I know. But she is mine by Highland law."

Stretching his legs out in front of him, Callum rested his head on the back of his chair and closed his eyes. "If Charles is restored he willna agree."

"That's why I wanted the bloody priest."

His friend smiled. "Think hard on this, brother. There are many lasses in Scotland."

"Aye, and I vow, Callum, every one of them confounds me."

"They are no' so difficult. They all just want to be cared fer."

"Nae, not Claire," Graham argued, kicking off his boots. "She is convinced that she does not need a man to protect her. She is fiercely independent—a fault I lay at her brother's feet."

"And this fiercely independent lass . . . ye demanded her into yer bed?" Callum laughed, pulling a frown from his friend.

"She accused me of wanting to wed her simply to get her there. I was just letting her know I didn't need to."

He did not sound arrogant, but so pained, Callum almost took pity on him. But it would do his commander good to ponder his heart for once, instead of thinking with the rest of his body.

"As ye say, she doesna understand our Highland ways. Ye'll need to apologize to her." Callum's eyes were still closed, so he did not see the foul glare Graham aimed at him.

"D'ye apologize to Kate often?"

"More than I'd like to, aye."

"Hell, ye have turned into a pansy like my brother."

Unfazed by his friend's banter, Callum yawned. "I shall prove to ye at first light what a pansy I've become."

"Will Kate let ye out at first light?"

"Mayhap, no'. She may insist that I keep our bed warm until our son awakens. But dinna fret, if I am tardy, ye will have the dogs in the hall to keep ye warm." He lifted his lids, offered Graham a triumphant grin, then closed his eyes again.

Hell, he had no heart for banter tonight. His heart was with her, damn him. He would apologize if that's what she wanted.

"Part of who I am tells me it does not matter if she cares fer me. 'Tis long been our way to take a wife without the church's vows, since the church denies our rights. But another part of me," Graham said quietly, proving that he'd been pondering his heart for quite some time now, "one that I only became aware of this night, wants her to *want* to be with me always."

Now Callum sat up and gave Graham his full attention. "Ye love her then?"

Only with this man, his best friend since boyhood, could Graham confess the truth and how it scared the hell out of him.

"Does love make ye feel like there are nae limits to what ye're willing to do to please her? Then, aye," Graham said when Callum nodded. "I do. And I fear the vulnerability it brings. 'Tis like being on a battlefield without a sword or even a shield to protect ye."

Callum agreed. Indeed there were times when love felt that way. "It makes a man want to give up his defenses and surrender his life."

"Aye." Graham nodded. His friend understood.

"But if she loves him in return," Callum pointed out, "there is nae longer any need fer his defenses."

Och, hell, Graham brooded, remembering her final words to him in the bailey. He was indeed doomed. "Then now more than ever, I need to hold fast to mine."

*   *   *

Claire sat in the solar listening to Kate tell of King Arthur and his noble knights. Satan's balls, she was miserable. The more Kate read about those tender, romantic warriors of the realm, the more miserable Claire became. Damn that insufferable knave, Graham Grant. Why could he not be more like Lancelot, whose love for Guinevere was so strong it brought down a kingdom? Love! Ha! She snorted aloud. Graham did not know anything about love.

"Claire?"

She blinked at Kate and offered her a questioning look. "Aye?"

"You are not paying attention. Is there something you wish to talk about?"

Hell, Claire didn't need to see the knowing spark in Kate's eyes to figure out that Graham had likely told Callum what had transpired between them, and Callum had told his wife.

"He is a rat!" Claire sprang from her chair and began pacing a short path between them. "Nae, he is lower than a rat!"

"Graham?"

"Aye! I thought . . . I had hoped . . . I let him become important to me, and then because I withheld my affections, he asked me to marry him."

"I am still astonished by that bit of news," Kate admitted, wide-eyed.

"Don't be." Claire whirled on her. "He is a scheming rat who will do anything to get what he wants, and if his wiles are unsuccessful, he resorts to bullying. Och, I do not want to speak of him anymore. I am going to change my clothes. I need to swing at something. Preferably Graham's head."

"I'll come with you," Kate dropped her book and practically leaped from her chair. "Rob is asleep and I have not practiced my swordplay in ages."

"Aye," Claire said, turning to her as they left the solar. "Robert told me you could wield a sword. Are you any good?"

Ten minutes later, Claire stood beneath a vast expanse of pewter clouds, her sword at the ready. Her opponent bore no resemblance to any warrior Claire had ever fought. Even in practice, Aileen looked more powerful than this wisp of a woman in her woolen kirtle and lady's earasaid.

"Do you wish to tie up your hair first?"

Kate flicked a spray of ebony waves off her shoulder and clasped her hilt in both hands. "It is nae bother."

"Truly?" Claire asked, circling her. "It is so long. Mine distracts me."

"Aye, yours is thick," Kate agreed, eyeing the other woman's braid. "I noticed the other night at supper when you wore it loose." She took a swipe at Claire's abdomen.

"And your skirts?"

Kate shrugged her petite shoulders. "I've always practiced in skirts."

Their swords met in a clash before their faces.

Impressive, Claire thought, as she jabbed at Kate's legs and missed.

"So, do you love him?"

"Who?" Claire asked, neatly avoiding a blow to her shoulder.

"Och, for hell's sake! Graham!"

"Nae," Claire said quickly, then she bit her lip. "Aye. I did. I think."

"You are not certain, then?"

Claire shrugged. "I have never been in love before."

Kate stopped swinging for a moment to smile at her. "You both have much to learn."

"Mayhap." Claire readied herself again. "But I will no longer practice on that rogue. I will not be ordered about by General Monck or by Graham Grant."

"I understand." Kate brought down a chopping blow. "But do you truly believe Graham wants to wed you just to have you in his bed?"

Claire paused, blushed, and parried a jab aimed at her ribs.

"He follows Highland laws, Claire. And if he has already claimed you, he does not need a priest to make your union lawful. It already is. He has the right to take you to his bed as any husband would."

The tip of Claire's sword dropped to the ground. "Do you mean we are already wed?"

"I know it seems a bit barbaric, but it is their way. Especially since the MacGregors and their sympathizers are denied the sacrament of marriage in the church."

"But the priest . . ." Claire said, trying to understand. Graham had called her his woman, not his wife!

"Father Lachlan is our friend. He married me and Callum and Maggie and Jamie, also. So you see, Graham did not offer to send for him so that he could bed you. He offered to send for him . . ."

"To make it easier for me while we're here," Claire finished, recalling Graham's words to her. Dear God, she was his wife! For an instant, she didn't know if she was furious with him or elated. He should have told her. He should have asked her! Her anger faded as another thought occurred to her. According to his laws, she was truly his, and he had not demanded her to his bed in all these days, as was his Highland right. Satan's balls, he was being thoughtful!

"The king will not be pleased," she said an instant later, worrying her lip.

"Aye, Callum worries over that, as well," Kate confided. "But your union means nothing in England. It will not be recognized, so you are not bound once you leave Skye."

Their union meant nothing? Like hell it didn't!

"Och, there is Callum. Quickly, Claire, sheathe your sword!"

"Why? Does he not want you to practice?" She already knew the answer. Most men did not approve of women in arms.

"He has forbidden it while I am with child."

Claire went pale, forgetting Graham for the moment. With child! Blast her, she should be resting, sewing, whatever women did when they were with child—not swinging a claymore! "You should have told me. I would never have lifted my blade to you!"

"What the hell d'ye think ye're doin', Kate?" Laird MacGregor demanded as he strode toward them.

"Just a little harmless practicing, husband."

"I have forbidden it, lest ye ferget, woman," he said harshly, then turned his blistering gaze on Claire. "Did she tell ye she is with child?"

"Not until—"

"I am weary of sitting around all day growing fatter and fatter still." Kate sniffed, pulling his attention back to her. "I fear that my loving husband will soon grow tired of seeing me swell like a calf fattened before a feast."

God's toenails, she is good, Claire thought, watching every trace of anger on Callum's face fade into utter remorse. When he gathered his wife up in his arms, swearing that he loved the swell of her belly and would spend the next six months proving it to her, Claire returned Kate's victorious smile over her husband's shoulder.

So this was what love did to a man. It made him regret his thoughtlessness, toss away his arrogance without caring who witnessed it. It softened his gaze, gentled his hands, and made him pick flowers. Watching the laird and his lady, Claire suddenly felt as if she'd been missing something intensely profound in her life.

With a sigh, she sheathed her blade and turned to head back to the castle. She halted in midstep when she saw Graham standing a few yards away with Rob and Anne.

Did love make a man sacrifice his own desires without even understanding why he was asked to resist them?

His eyes were already on her, drinking her in as if he had not seen her in years. His stance was casual until she met his gaze and he moved forward as if he could not stop himself from rushing to her.

But Claire's pounding heart almost ceased beating when somehow, he managed to.

Chapter Thirty-one

Shall I let the faithful child die while the wicked man prospers?

Standing there staring at the woman he loved, Graham had never felt more defenseless in his life. How was he to ignore the suffocating tightness in his chest, calm the violent crashing of his heart, or quell the maddening desire to take her in his arms and promise her anything when she was just a few feet from him? He did know her. She was a stubborn wench who did not like being told what to do. He could live with that. Hell, her strength was the thing that had drawn her to him from the beginning. But had she refused his offer of marriage because she was angry, or because she did not love him in return? He wanted to know, but when he saw her, he wasn't certain he had the courage to hear what she would tell him.

He had almost reached her when he stopped, his eye catching sight of a rider breaking over the crest. Callum saw him, too, before he disappeared into the castle, and stopped to wait when the rider flagged him down. Graham made a move to go to his laird but slowed when he saw Claire coming toward him.

"I feared mayhap you had gone off and wed someone else," she teased lightly when she reached him.

Graham smiled, missing the slightly husky pitch of her voice, the way those stray tendrils of flaxen hair eclipsed her bonny blue eyes. "Who the hell could ever compare to ye, Claire?"

He'd meant to sound unaffected, not like some smitten squire who'd just found the courage to speak to a goddess. He almost laughed at his inability to control his own mouth. Hell, he was a damned good warrior, but he never had a chance against her. Better to just accept defeat and quit running.

"Then you're not angry with me?" She sounded hopeful and looked utterly beautiful.

God, he missed her. Every day without her in his life felt meaningless and dull. All he had done to win her before this day he would do over until he won her heart. "I was not angry with ye." His body trembled with the need to snatch her up in his arms and vow to fill her days with joy and adventure if she would only have him. "I was thoughtless and a coward." He took a step toward her. "But I'm telling ye now, Claire, I lo—"

"Graham, Robert!"

Graham looked over Claire's head at Callum waving him over with a parchment clenched in his hand. The rider was gone.

"Bring the ladies with ye," his friend called out. When they reached him, Callum held out his hand, offering the missive between his fingers to Claire. "It has just arrived from Kylerhea, sent to us by General Monck. Ye need to read it."

Claire took the letter with a tentative hand. Why did

she need to read it? If it was about her marriage to Robert she would tear it to pieces and fling it to the four winds. The cracked seal confirmed that it came from the governor. She glanced up at Callum, but his hard expression gave her no indication of what was inside.

Unfolding it, her eyes were at once drawn to the brown smudges covering most of the correspondence.

Blood.

The writing was faint, as if penned by a weary hand. A bolder hand had written an addendum in the uppermost corner of the parchment. She read this first.

Found in Wallingford House in London. Unknown when it was penned. Possibility that author still lives, moved to Tower. Make haste. Use caution.

Somehow, Claire knew who had written the rest of the letter, though the weak strokes and jagged lines bore no resemblance to her brother's strong hand. Her fingers quaked and she brought them to her mouth to silence a shuddering sob. Connor had not been killed on the road, but had been taken captive—taken to the Tower—tortured before he wrote this.

When she finished reading, she wiped her tears and handed the missive to her sister. She turned for the stables when Anne began reading it aloud, but Callum clasped her forearm.

"Let me go," she warned him. "I will not be hindered again from saving my kin."

"No one will stop ye, but first we will discuss what course of action is best to take."

"Saving my brother is the best course of action."

"Claire." Now it was Graham who spoke, setting a gentle hand on her shoulder. "It could be a trap."

"Aye, and ye will not leave Camlochlin until I am certain 'twill no' get ye killed."

Claire's eyes glistened with tears as they turned to Kate for aid, but the laird's wife only nodded, telling her silently to trust him. Frustrated that she had no other choice in the matter, Claire shot the laird a venomous glare. She could not fight him. She did not want to. But every instant Callum kept her from riding away to London grew more unforgivable. She nodded stiffly and let Anne finish reading. Her eyes darted to Graham listening, but she looked away. There was no time to go soft, to ponder what he'd tried to say before Callum interrupted him. She would not let him stop her this time. No matter what he wanted to tell her, she was leaving Camlochlin by nightfall.

"He knew he was betrayed, then," Robert said when Anne was done and everyone had grown quiet.

"But by whom?" Callum paced before them. "If this is a trap set by Monck, why wait until ye're all here in Skye? Why did he no' send ye to London when ye were in Edinburgh?"

"Because it is not a trap," Robert said. "Connor was betrayed by James."

"For the last time," Claire said gritting her teeth. "You cannot be sure of that. He makes mention of a friend. Both James and Monck are his friends. We do not know who he meant." Satan's blasted balls, they were wasting time!

"I do," Anne said faintly at first, and then lifting her tearful gaze to her sister, she repeated more firmly. "I know who he meant and so does the general. It is why he urges us to use caution."

"Anne, for hell's sake. James deserves more loyalty than—"

"Connor used to call me the flower of Scotland, Claire. Do you not remember?"

Claire's face went pale as the first truth hit her. She snatched the missive from Anne's hand and reread it.

—— *the flower of Scotland crying* —— *Save me from the kiss of the devil!*

"Connor promised me to James before his best friend betrayed him."

Dear God, Claire thought, feeling sick as her sister's words found their way to her heart. Anne was right. They all were. It was James. She met Graham's warm gaze and fought a fresh rush of tears. She had almost caused his death by confiding in James. If Ravenglade's guardsmen had ambushed them in Killiecrankie . . .

"It still does no' explain why Monck believes Stuart still lives."

"Aye, mayhap it does," Robert told Callum, and took the missive back from Claire. She surrendered it with a nod, offering him her sincerest apologies for doubting him.

". . . *warrior arrayed in the frost of—*" Robert read from the missive and held it closer trying to make out the words. "It looks like 'winter'. *Warrior arrayed in the frost of winter —— has perished. And yet, he lives.*" The young earl looked up with regret coloring his eyes to glittering gold. "General Monck thought Connor was speaking of himself. But the warrior he mentions is you, Claire. His twin, fighting in his stead."

Claire shook her head. "Connor did not die on the road. He could still be alive now."

"I agree."

Claire could have leaped over her sister and flung

herself into Graham's arms. She offered him her most grateful smile instead. "I will need you to help me kill James when this is over."

He flashed her a knee-melting, dimple-inducing grin. "I thought ye would never ask." He turned to Callum next. "I will accompany her to London."

Immediately, Robert stepped forward. "I will go also."

"Nae," Graham refused his offer. "Claire and I will travel alone."

"D'ye think 'tis wise?" Callum asked him.

"Rob is the Earl of Argyll. Fleetwood will recognize him, and nae matter how we garb Angus and Brodie anyone with good vision will know they are Highlanders. I don't want to alert the Tower garrison of our arrival or our intentions before we even reach London."

"Ye have a plan, then?" Callum asked. When Graham nodded, the chieftain smiled, knowing his commander better than the rest of them did. "D'ye need coin?"

"I have it."

"When will ye be leavin'?"

"Now," Graham said without hesitation. "They may be keeping him alive to get to Monck. He is the only one who knows on whose side the general truly stands. If that is the case, then time, right now, is vital."

Claire listened with a swelling heart while Graham discussed saving her brother with as much passion and determination as she felt, and in that moment she could no longer deny how deeply she had fallen in love with him.

"Then ride swiftly, brother." Callum placed his hand on his friend's shoulder. "I shall see ye again soon, and Claire as well."

"Soon," Graham agreed, and bent to embrace Kate.

Anne gaped in horror while Kate went to her sister next to offer her good wishes. They were daft! Her sister might know how to wield a sword well enough, but two against two hundred could never prevail. "Claire." She rushed to her sister's side. "Reconsider, I pray you. You and Graham do not stand a chance against Fleetwood's army. Please do not do this foolish thing. You are all the kin I have left."

Claire smiled at her sister, her and Connor's joy, his flower of Scotland. "You still have a brother, and I am going to bring him back to you."

"Rob." Callum slipped his arm around his wife's waist and hooked his mouth into a chilling smirk that Claire was certain added to his frightening reputation over the years. "Ease yer woman's fears. Tell her how Graham brought yer uncle's garrison to an end with naught more than his wretched smile and well-learned Lowland speech. I have other needs to see to at present."

When the four of them were alone, Rob vowed to tell Anne the tale later that evening, even though, he admitted, it was not a tale he enjoyed telling. For now, he gave her his word that her sister would be safe with Graham. He took her hand in his and leaned closer to whisper something in her ear. When she nodded, giving him her consent, he set his wide hazel gaze on Claire.

"We were going to tell you at supper. We have sent for Father Lachlan. When you return to Skye, your sister will be my wife."

Claire simply stared at him for a moment, taking in the firm resolve etching his handsome features. He was not asking for her permission, but hoped for her blessing. Claire would give it, and she would make certain her cousin gave it as well. Aye, her sister was going to wed a Roundhead, but this young lad, whom Claire had thought so inexperienced, had proven his worth, his courage, and his honor to her more than any man she'd ever known.

"My sister is a most fortunate lady, indeed," she told him, and laughed when Anne threw herself into her arms. "You love him," she whispered close to Anne's ear.

"With my whole heart."

"Then I shall happily tell our brother that we have chosen for ourselves."

Anne smiled at Graham a few steps away, oblivious to what they spoke. Claire had fallen in love with him—the poor man.

Chapter Thirty-two

Nae! I shall ride forth and obliterate the shame that has been brought upon the father.

The stench of rotting corpses and moist mold had stopped turning Connor Stuart's stomach months ago. He'd sworn never to grow cold to the terrible wailing from the other prisoners in the cells around him, but he'd had to in order to save himself from going mad. Most days— or nights, he could not tell the difference—he prayed for death to claim him. But still he lived, as if his sole purpose for being on the earth was to frustrate Lambert and the rest of the generals. He was no longer afraid of his punishment for not telling them what he knew. He welcomed it, hoping the next blow would be the one to finally kill him.

He'd even stopped worrying about his sisters. It took him a long time, but he'd finally come to accept the fact that he would never see them again, could not help them. The paths he had chosen for them had already begun. But dear God, why had he not given Claire to James, instead of Anne? At least then, he could die knowing Claire would kill the bastard—most likely a few hours into the marriage.

There was one other thing keeping him alive. Revenge

scored his heart, slashing it afresh with each and every endless moment of his miserable existence. He ate, drank, shyt, and slept thinking up different ways to repay his closest friend for what he'd done, not only to him but to his sisters.

A rat scurried across his foot and he kicked it away as the heavy wooden door of his cell creaked open. The light from the single candle flame on the floor beside him flickered. He knew it wasn't the guard with his gruel by the polished sheen of the wearer's boots clicking across the floor. Which general was it today? he wondered, not bothering to look up.

"How are you today, Connor?"

Lambert. Connor smiled into his bent knees, remembering how many of this general's men he had killed.

"Do you hunger?" He crouched before Connor, stinking of the sweet perfume of noblemen, his sharp features illuminated by the flame. "I purloined this from Fleetwood's own plate." He reached into a pouch on his shortcoat and produced a half-eaten pear. "Would you like it?" When Connor nodded, Lambert handed it to him without hesitation. "There is more," he said while Connor sank his teeth into the ripe fruit. "Puddings and warm tarts lathered in honey, fresh venison and cool ale to wash it down. Anything you desire, and all you need do to have it is tell me why Monck kept company with rebels."

"I cannot speak now. My mouth is full."

Lambert laughed, but the sound grated like sandpaper against Connor's ears. "Come now, Stuart. You must realize by now that your cause is hopeless. You are going to die here, and for what? Some false sense of loyalty to a man who betrayed you?"

Connor chewed quietly, unfazed by Lambert's words, for he knew who had betrayed him.

"Why do you not simply tell us what we want to know? What were your secret meetings with General Monck about? You are Charles's cousin, a Royalist rebel to the death, aye? What have you and Monck in common?"

Satan's rancid balls, could not even one of these sons of whores think up a fresh query to put to him? It was always the same thing, day after day, sennight after sennight. Could they not get it through their thick skulls that he was not going to tell them anything? No matter how they tortured him, no matter what they promised him, he would not betray his king. Tossing the pear core to the side, he gave the same answer he'd been giving since they locked him up in this Godforsaken place. "You have been misinformed. There were no meetings."

Lambert stood to his feet, his sickeningly sweet tone replaced by rage when he spoke again. "Buchanan has told us . . ."

"Then ask Buchanan, for hell's sake, and leave me alone."

The boot to his gut almost brought what little of the pear he had eaten back up. "Still an arrogant son of a bitch," Lambert growled above him. "I am going to enjoy watching you hang."

Connor fought to keep from passing out and finally raised his gaze to his enemy. There was no fury, no promise of retribution burning in the fathomless clear blue depths of his eyes, only the calm satisfaction of a truth Lambert and his minions had revealed to him. "As much as I enjoy learning how desperately you fear Monck?"

Lambert was a small man, but his fist came down like

a hammer on Connor's bearded jaw. "I fear no man," he snarled, clutching handfuls of Connor's filthy tunic and lifting him off his rump. "I shall prove it to you when I bring you with me on my march into Scotland." He sneered into Connor's face. "We shall learn then how much Monck values your life when I take it before his eyes. Aye, that will be quite telling indeed. If he supports the king's rebellion, as he does Parliament, I will see him hanged." He yanked Connor forward and then smashed his head against the damp wall behind him, knocking him unconscious. "Guards!" he called out over his shoulder. "Take him to the stables." He stepped away, smiling, as he left the Tower. "Mighty rebel, indeed."

Claire swept her earasaid across her thighs in an effort to drive out the chill of the dark November night and the bleak despair it brought with it. They'd left Skye three days ago, and with each league that brought them closer to England, her hope of finding her brother alive faded. How long ago had he penned his letter to her? She had no way of knowing. She wanted to believe he still lived, but it had been three months since he'd been captured. What if it was too late? What if she'd been too busy seeking revenge on Monck and trying to save Anne, while her brother was being hanged? And if he was still alive, how much longer would he remain so? It would take them at least three weeks to reach London, two if they continued traveling as they did.

It was Graham's idea to ride through the night without pause. Fortune, he'd told her, was on their side. The full moon provided enough light to travel safely while she slept cradled in his arms for a few hours, after which time he woke her, secured his horse to hers, and slept in his saddle while she led them over the moonlit moors.

Claire was glad he was with her. By day, his light conversation and warm smiles kept her thoughts off the fate of her brother. When she did voice her concerns to him, he was quick to reassure her that he believed Connor was alive.

They did not speak of what had happened between them in Skye. In fact, he avoided the topic of marriage altogether when she'd brought up Robert and Anne's nuptials. For the first few days of their journey Claire was too occupied with thoughts of Connor to care. But at night, as now, when she rested against his chest, his strong arms wrapped so snugly around her, keeping her warm in her thick earasaid, she wondered if his claim on her had less to do with arrogance, and more to do with his heart. What would become of them after they found Connor and killed James? Would Graham let her ride out of his life when they were no longer in the Highlands and their union was deemed invalid? She didn't care about General Monck's plans for her to wed Robert. He might truly be Connor's friend, but he was not her king. And besides, Robert and Anne were likely married by now. But what of Charles? If he was restored, would he allow her to wed Graham? Would Connor? Aye, her brother would help her convince the king that a union between the Stuarts and the Highlanders was in the kingdom's best interest.

The thought of never seeing Graham again was more agonizing than when she'd first learned of Connor's death. And now she knew why. She loved him. Damn it to hell, she loved him more than she could have ever thought possible, more than she would ever admit to him. How many women had whispered that they adored him in his fickle ear? How many times must he have had to pry their needy fingers off his heart and make a mad dash for the nearest door?

She sighed against him and closed her eyes, praying for sleep to overtake her troubled heart.

"All will be well, Claire," he spoke tenderly behind her, smoothing his hand over the top of her head before he pressed his lips there. "Ye'll see yer brother again, I vow it."

He spoke of Connor and she smiled, wanting, needing to believe him. But . . . "What if you are wrong?"

"I am not. Monck has long been silent on the issues that plague England, setting himself apart from the others. The army captured, but did not kill the leader of the resistance, the only other man who—they were informed by Buchanan—knew what Monck might be planning. Would yer brother break upon torture?"

Claire's eyes darkened with the threat of a torrential downpour of tears, but she held them back and shook her head. "Nae, he would not."

Graham's voice went soft along her ear. "Then he is not dead."

He was right, Claire thought, heaving a great weight off her shoulders. Pitiful or not, she would always love Graham for coming with her, for never once chiding her for who she had chosen to be, and for not letting her believe the worst about her brother's fate.

"They are keeping Connor alive because what he knows is too valuable."

"Aye." Claire smiled and nestled closer against him. "You have been a good friend to me, Graham."

She felt him go stiff behind her. He moved his face away from her and made a sound as if her words caused him pain.

"Can ye not sleep?" he asked a moment later, shifting uncomfortably.

"Nae, I cannot. Why do you not sleep first? I can see perfectly well and will not lead us into a tree, like last eve."

Immediately, his arm curled tighter around her middle. "I am fine where I am."

"You sound weary."

"I am not."

"And short-tempered."

He tossed back his head and muttered something that sounded suspiciously like "blasted stubborn wench." When her spine went straight, he dragged her back hard against his chest. "Cease arguing with me."

Claire pushed off him and tossed her head around to offer him a pointed look. "Are you trying to distract my thoughts away from Connor by tempting me to hurl you off my horse?"

He smiled, then laughed quietly and bent his face to hers. His breath warmed her mouth and she parted her lips, waiting, wanting him to kiss her. But he moved away, leaving her with the alluring scent of his neck.

"Ye speak of yer fears regarding yer brother, but ye do not speak of him. Tell me of the man who came into the world with ye."

She hadn't spoken of Connor with anyone, and she needed to. Saints, she needed to. "What do you wish to know?"

"How did he gain such favor in yer heart?"

Leaning her head back against Graham's shoulder, she closed her eyes remembering. "My childhood was difficult. I had nothing in common with the other young ladies at court. Not even with Anne. While they were learning how to embroider and play the lute in their immaculately fitted gowns, I was being tossed, with my brother and his friends, at my father's feet, accused and guilty of bullying the other boys of the parish. My punishments were harsh but swift, for I believe that beyond my father's shame of me, it pleased him to know that I was as courageous as his son. He never admitted it, though, and always insisted that I behave more like Anne. I confounded my mother and every other mother in our household, and finally they began to keep their daughters away from me, lest they develop the unnatural desire to wear their brothers' clothes and swing a sword.

"The only place I fit in was with Connor, and he took me with him every day without complaint and without quarrel. He was pleased with me the way I was."

"He knew ye were perfect, then."

Claire opened her eyes and smiled at him. "He knew I wasn't, and he still loved me."

"I think I will like him," Graham whispered against her temple.

"I think so, too," she answered, loving him all the more for his steadfast belief that they were not too late to save Connor.

At Camlochlin, she had not gone to his bed, trying, for the first time in her life, to behave like a woman of nobility. Graham would never know how difficult it had been for her to stay away from him. How she had lain in bed next to Anne, night after night, thinking of him. He had not touched her since the day they'd arrived in Skye. And now, with their time together possibly nearly at an end, she wanted more than anything to kiss him again, to feel his hands on her. She didn't care if she was a pitiful wench, a royal trollop, she wanted to make love to him one more time, whether he loved her or not.

"Is there an inn close by?"

"Aye, there is one a few leagues from here," he told her. "D'ye want to stop? 'Twill slow us down, but . . ."

She silenced his words with a tender kiss along his jaw line, and then another, until she felt his heart beating hard against her. "Take me there." She smiled when his mouth descended over hers.

Aye, she loved him more than anyone else in her life, and if she was too afraid of his reaction to tell him, then she would show him.

Chapter Thirty-three

Be patient. Be vigilant. For there is as much honor gained by suffering wants patiently in war, as by fighting valiantly.

The crackling flames in the hearth bathed the room in a rosy hue that matched the soft blush of Claire's cheeks. Graham watched her as she stepped around the bed, tracing her fingertips over the fur blanket. He stood at the door, hesitant, mystified by the sultry invitation in her smoky blue gaze. He'd intended to court her properly, not making love to her again until he claimed her heart and she agreed to wed him. It was the right thing to do. When she had called him friend, his hopes of ever winning her shattered. But even then he was not willing to lose her. If he could never be anything more than a friend to her, then a friend he would be.

Hell, she confused him. Was she up to something? he thought, while she pushed her earasaid off her shoulders. She had not kissed him like a friend, but like a lover, making his loins ache for what she wanted to give him. It felt as if a century had passed since he last touched her with any intimacy. Both his body and his heart ached for her.

His gaze devoured her as she pulled her braid free and set loose her glorious mantle of pale flaxen. He rethought his first decision as he stalked around the bed after her. If she wanted a friend, there were plenty in Skye. He was going to take her . . . in every possible way.

She turned in his arms when he reached her and the spark of warmth, of excitement in her eyes made him as stiff as an iron rod against her.

She rose up on the tips of her toes, stretching her luscious curves over the length of him to whisper along his prickly jaw, "Would you like to undress me, warrior?"

The sensual hook of his mouth gave her the answer she sought. His muscles knotted with the restraint it took not to tear her garments away, butt her up against the wall, and fuck her until she could no longer stand. He reached for her belt with his hands and seized her lower lip with his teeth, pulling her closer. But she broke free, teasing him with a daring smirk as she backed away. Her gaze dipped to the long hump stretching his plaid taut between his legs, and she licked her lips.

His cock throbbed when he thought of that tongue licking him, that mouth sucking him until he . . .

"Though you have claimed me, I have not yet decided if I want you."

He laughed at her coy game. She liked the chase as much as he did.

Kicking off his boots, he shed his plaid and took his huge erection in his hand. "Whether ye want me or not, ye're going to have me."

She arched her brow at him. "Am I?"

"Aye," he promised in a rich, throaty baritone and moved toward her. He slid his hand up his shaft, to his engorged head, and then down again. "I've been patient long enough." Every muscle in his body tensed, and he grew harder, more defined in the firelight.

He reached for her belt again, and this time, she did not resist. "But first, I want to taste these ripe breasts." Bending his head, he sucked her nipple through the fabric of her tunic. When she gasped his name, clutching his shoulders, he pulled the tunic over her head, capturing her wrists in her sleeves and holding her still while he caught her nipple between his teeth and flicked his tongue over the sensitive tip.

When she strained toward him and bit his neck in response, he let out a low growl, released her, and tunneled his fingers deep into her hair. With one hand and a little pressure he guided her hungry kisses over his abdomen while he closed his other hand around his lance and guided it into her mouth.

The feel of her soft, wet lips around his head was pure ecstasy. But when she began to suck, he almost came in her mouth. He pulled her up, tugged off her trews, and spread her beneath him on the bed. With a curl of his mouth that promised utter surrender and complete domination, he impaled her to the hilt.

Later, Claire lay in his arms beneath the thick fur bed covering. Their lovemaking was perfect, raw passion blended exquisitely with tenderness. It was everything she had wanted to give him, and more.

And yet, she felt like weeping. Satan's arse, she had thought she was stronger than this. She had thought she could live with the memory of him alone. But now, in the dreamy aftermath of their intimacy, she knew it was not enough. The future was too uncertain. She could deal with Charles and Connor. It was Graham's decisions that frightened her, his lifestyle that plagued her notions of love, and family, and a life with him. Could he surrender his heart to one woman? Could he ever love her enough to stand before the king and proclaim it?

She closed her eyes against the hard angles of his chest and listened to him breathing, memorizing the sound of his strong heartbeat, the scent of him, the feel of him. It might be all she had left.

"What troubles ye, Claire?"

She opened her eyes but did not move, letting the deep melodious burr of his voice seep into her bones like warm mead. "Nothing troubles me," she lied. How could she tell him the truth? She was fairly certain that if she told him she wanted to bear him a dozen bairns, he would leap for the door and she would never see him again.

"Then why are yer fingernails tearing holes in my arm?"

She loosened her grip on him and murmured a soft apology. A few moments later she wiped a tear from her eye and swore an oath under her breath.

He sat up immediately, pulling her with him. "Claire, are ye weeping?"

"Don't be ridiculous," she replied, sweeping away another tear and keeping her gaze averted from his. "We should get moving."

"Aye, we should," he agreed, stroking his hand down the length of her hair. "But first ye'll tell me why ye weep."

"I was thinking of my brother. He will be in your debt." She moved to swing her legs off the bed, but Graham caught her, stopping her before she left him. "I will make certain that he grants you whatever you want."

"I want ye."

As much as it pained her to do so, she looked at him, feeling as if she needed to burn his image into her mind. God, he was beautiful sitting there wearing naught but a fur blanket and a tender smile. Firelight flickered around his features, kindling the ever-present sultry glitter in his eyes.

"You have had me," she said with a note of defeat ringing in her voice that made his smile fade.

At first, alarm passed over his features, but it quickly changed into anger. "I see. So this meant naught to ye?"

If he didn't look so dangerous sitting there about to pounce on her, Claire would have laughed right in his face, or burst into tears. "To me?" She raised her hand to her chest. "Do you jest?"

"Not about this," he said, his voice an octave above a growl, his green eyes boring into her.

"Very well, then, I will tell you." She tilted her chin, ready to have out with the whole pitiful truth once and for all. "It meant everything to me. What I gave you, I never gave to anyone else."

His hard expression faltered. "I know."

"Do you?" Her eyes searched his. She no longer cared that tears were spilling from them. "You have touched me in a way that no one else has and no one else ever will again, and I fear I have been naught but a victory for you."

"A victory?" Now he sounded as pitiful as she had a moment ago. "Woman, I have thrown down my arsenal at yer feet and allowed ye to pierce my heart. Where is the victory in that? D'ye think I wanted to fall so deeply in love with ye that the thought of a day without ye is worse fer me than the thought of surrendering on the battlefield? I—"

"What did you say?" Claire sniffed, cutting him off.

He stared at her as if his heart might leap from his chest and he was powerless to stop it. "The thought of . . ."

"Nae, before that." She inched closer to him, unsure of her own ears. "The part about falling deeply in love with me. Have you? Fallen in love with me?"

"Aye." He raked his fingers through his hair and scowled at her. "Why else d'ye think I've turned into such a pansy?"

Instead of answering, Claire hurled herself into his arms, pushing him down onto the bed. She kissed him senseless within the veil of her thick pale locks. When she finally withdrew, just enough for them to share their breath, she looked into his eyes and smiled. "If you've gone soft—and let me assure you, you have not—I have been too busy falling in love with you to notice."

His dimples flashed and Claire melted all over him. "Ye could have saved me a sennight's worth of anguish by telling me that sooner."

"And we could have been wed by your priest if you had told me." Claire bit his lip gently and laughed when he rolled her onto her back.

"Then let me tell ye now," he said tenderly, poised above her. "I love ye, Claire." He kissed her, and then spent the rest of the night showing her how much.

Chapter Thirty-four

Let a soldier's resolution be never so great, and his courage invincible in the day of battle.

James Buchanan waited in an uncomfortable chair with a high, cushioned back that tilted him forward. The chair looked inviting from the door, but when he sat down the elaborate wood carved along the edges poked and pinched and made waiting for his audience with Charles Fleetwood slightly unbearable. He sat back and shifted restlessly. When he noticed his hands shaking slightly, he cursed himself. He had no reason to be afraid. He'd proven his value to Fleetwood, and to Lambert, as well. They would not dare lay a hand on the man who could end the Scottish resistance with but a word. They would be angry with him for coming here to London, but it was a risk he was willing to take. If Connor was alive when the king returned—if the king returned—James knew his death would be swift. Why the hell were they keeping the bastard alive?

He looked around the spacious study, hoping Elizabeth would come to him before her father did. She would help him, mayhap even sneak him into the Tower. He was thinking of the quickest way to kill Connor when the huge wooden door at the other end of the study creaked open.

Tall and middle-aged, General Fleetwood had piercing dark eyes that had seen their share of battle, though these days he preferred to act more as a politician than a warrior. "Ah, Buchanan, what brings you to Wallingford House?" He strode into the study, his long auburn curls bouncing spryly around his shoulders.

James rose from his chair to properly receive his host, then sank back into it when Fleetwood's heels clicked past him. He heaved a silent sigh of relief when the general gave no indication of anger at his arrival. "I have been informed that the traitor Connor Stuart still lives," he said, feeling a bit more at ease.

"And what has that to do with you?" Fleetwood looked up briefly as he poured himself a drink.

"I am curious as to why he was not killed as we discussed."

"So you came here to question me." The general cast James a cool sneer and sipped his wine.

"Nae, I—"

"Nae? Then why did you come? To kill Stuart yourself, perhaps?" He laughed, but the sound held no mirth as he took a seat behind a massive table of carved wood. "Fear often follows the vilest of men. It is what drives them. But I would know *why* you fear him so much that you would forfeit the safety of your anonymity and ride all the way to London to ensure his silence. Do you worry that he will escape and seek you out? Or is it someone else entirely that you fear?"

"My lord," James eyed the cup in Fleetwood's hand

and swallowed, wishing for a swig of the spirit to calm his nerves. "I am sure I do not know who else you speak of."

"Why, I speak of the king, of course. I believe you know more about what Monck is up to than you told us." He smiled, ignoring James's emphatic denial. "Our friend, the governor, has openly declared himself ready to uphold the Parliament's authority. The Parliament we dissolved. For weeks now, his representatives have been engaged in negotiations with the Committee of Safety to resolve the matter without bloodshed. Yet, at this very moment, he has amassed an army of several thousand and marches toward England. Does he support the king as well? We had hoped to gain information from Stuart, but he has remained stalwart despite our many . . . creative attempts to draw the truth from him. You were the only other man who was present during Monck and Stuart's clandestine meetings."

"Nae, I told you I was not privy to their conversations," James insisted, swiping his sleeve across his brow. Hell, something was wrong. Terribly wrong. "I only know what Connor told me in confidence. That General Monck had agreed with him about the civil unrest here in England and he planned on doing something about it."

"Restoring the king to the throne, mayhap?"

"Mayhap," James answered, starting in his seat when the door opened again. "I . . . I do not know for certain." When he saw Elizabeth enter the study accompanied by two of her father's guardsmen, his heart stalled in his chest.

"You know my daughter." Fleetwood's voice lowered to a chilling pitch. "She agreed to aid me in bringing you back in return for my forgiveness for sleeping with so loathsome a creature as you. I suspected the moment you learned that Stuart lived, you would show up at my door.

Now tell me why you are so eager to see him dead, or you will be hanged along with him."

"I know nothing!" James recoiled in his chair when the two guardsmen left Elizabeth and moved toward him. "Nae, you cannot kill me. You need me! I am the one who—"

"You are correct." Fleetwood motioned with his hand for his men to seize James. "I need you to tell me everything you know about George Monck. You will have plenty of time to think on it in the Tower. My only regret," he called out as James was led out of the study, "is that you will not be reunited with the man who dreams of killing you." He smiled pleasantly when James paused and looked back at him over his shoulder. "Stuart is on his way back to Scotland with Major General Lambert."

When they were alone, Fleetwood raised his sickened gaze to his daughter. "Swear to me that you did not give your heart to a man so contemptible that only the death of his closest friend will satisfy him."

Elizabeth looked toward the door one last time, then lowered her eyes to hide the truth from her father. "I swear."

Dear God, she was tired. The brisk chill numbing her cheeks wasn't helping. Claire knew the effects of winter's seductive fingers. Connor had made her practice doubly hard in the winter months when the air was so cold it singed her lungs and sapped her strength. Succumbing to exhaustion in a fight—or to the lure of sleep on some snow-blanketed hill—would kill her, so he made her learn how to keep awake. But hell, this was different. She did not feel weak or confused, and she was barely shivering, but she felt like hell. She turned slightly on her horse to glance at Graham, wishing for the comfort of his arms.

Highlanders, she thought, with a well of warmth creeping up from her chest and ending in a smile. He barely felt the effect of the coming winter.

"Ye look a wee bit pale," he said, slowing his pace. "D'ye want to stop in the next village and sleep in a bed tonight? Mayhap purchase some shifts fer under yer tunic?"

"Nae, I do not want to stop again. Wherever Connor is, I am sure he is colder than we are. He needs us to make haste."

They rode hard for another hour before slowing their weary mounts. While she chewed a slab of dried meat—thanks astonishingly to Maggie, who had insisted on packing what was left of the beef for their journey—Claire prayed for the hundredth time that her brother was still alive.

"Connor will not approve of your Highland claim on me," she said, breaking the comfortable silence while they ate.

Graham shrugged and licked his fingers. "Then I'll wed ye properly. We will send fer Father Lachlan when we return to Skye."

"Will we live there then?"

"Aye," he answered without hesitation, then lifted his eyes and cast her a worried look. "Ye do want to live there, d'ye not?"

It was his home; where his kin were. Claire knew he loved living there, and she wanted to be wherever he was. Hell, she had to be daft to agree to spend the rest of her days in such a dreary place. "My brother will be living in our home in Athol, and Anne will go to Inveraray with Robert, so aye, Skye is as good a place for me as any."

His face lit into a grin she found exhilarating and heart-wrenchingly sexy. "'Tis a good place to raise bairns."

She stopped chewing and looked at him, feeling suddenly misty-eyed. The thought of having his son or daughter thrilled her—and yet here she was on the brink of tears. Och, what was wrong with her? Her emotions were playing havoc with her. "I would love a son like Rob." When Graham frowned at her, she hastily corrected. "Callum and Kate's son."

His easy smile returned. "Will ye not miss the life of a rebel, then?"

"Och, I'll always be a rebel, Graham." She cut him an impish smirk and he laughed, and then looked up beseeching the heavens for the strength it was going to take having her for a wife.

"How about you? Will you miss your . . . adventures?"

"Nae, I can barely keep up with ye. But if I feel the need fer a journey off Skye, ye'll be with me."

"I . . ." Claire swooned slightly on her horse and then clutched her belly.

"What is it?" Graham rode to her side, concern etching his features.

"It is nothing," she was quick to assure him. "I think mayhap the beef has gone bad."

He gave her a worried look and offered to hunt for some live game. When she grew pale and clamped her hand over her mouth, he glanced down at her belly.

"What?" Claire queried curiously when she caught his faint smile.

"It could be the meat, but I think mayhap we will be having a bairn sooner than we expected. I have enough sisters to know what happens to a lass when she's carrying a babe."

Claire's eyes opened wide, as did her mouth when her hand fell away from it. "But how can that be?"

His mouth hooked into a slow, sensual grin, reminding her how.

"I know how." She rolled her eyes at him. "I meant . . . Och, never mind. Will it get worse?"

"Aye, it will."

"Satan's balls."

Graham leaned in to kiss her. He began to tell her how happy she made him, then pulled back, looking as sick as she felt.

"What is it?" she asked, reaching to cup his face in her palm.

"I was not thinking," he said, his voice a hollow drum as his horrified gaze poured over her. "Everything has changed. Ye are carrying my bairn. I cannot let ye come with me to London."

Claire stared at him, trying to decide whether to laugh or scream. "Not *let* me?" she repeated, tight-lipped, her hand falling away.

"I cannot. Ye'll wait fer me outside the city in the safety of an inn while I free Connor. I'll not have ye jeopardize the life of our babe, or yer own."

"We do not even know for certain if I am with child, Graham!" she argued.

Pushing back the cap on his head, he faced her with the unyielding power of a commander in his emerald gaze. "Ye'll wait fer me."

With flaring nostrils and a determined set in her jaw, Claire watched him whirl his mount forward—toward England. Like hell she would.

Chapter Thirty-five

For men wear not arms because they are afraid of danger, but because they would not fear it.

Claire thought she was dying while she leaned against a tree expelling her breakfast. She'd lost track of how many times she had done the like over the past sennight. Everything she ate came right back up. She could barely ride for more than a quarter of an hour before swooning in her saddle and forcing them to stop. If that wasn't terrible enough, she had actually wept like a babe two nights past for no reason whatsoever, other than that they had finally crossed the border into England.

Graham was wonderfully patient, but more insistent than ever about leaving her at an inn when they reached London. Claire did not argue—most of the time. She felt too ill, but there was another reason for her silence. Every day she watched her lover transform more and more into a commander, alert, aware of every nuance around them, set afire with a single purpose—to get them in and out of London alive. She would not defy such a leader.

Entering the city in his Highland plaid would gain too much attention, so he'd purchased a high-waisted doublet of dyed mulberry and breeches from an innkeeper in Northumberland, both of which fit a bit snugly, and left a drunken Puritan patron slumped over his chair in naught but his tunic and undergarments. With a few more coins, Graham acquired two linen shifts and a coarse mantle of dark wool for Claire.

"How will we do it?"

Riding at an easy canter at her side now, Graham swung Claire a hard look. "*I* will gain entrance into the Tower. Ye will—"

"How?"

"I'm going to dangle a lure before the generals; one that is too tempting for them to resist. I'm going to tell them that I know General Monck's true intentions."

Claire bit her lip and shook her head. "They will not believe you."

"They will when I tell them that I accompanied Connor Stuart and James Buchanan to their meetings with Monck, meetings no one else knows about save yer brother, Buchanan, and the generals." When Claire smiled, seeing his point, he continued, with a spark of devilment firing his green eyes. "That is how I will gain entrance. Once I am in, I will have yer brother out by the following morn."

She did not question him further. The man was a snake, able to coil around even the most mistrusting heart. She needed no further proof of it. But still, she worried for him. She did not want him to do this alone.

"What if they—" The rumble of many horses approaching halted her in midsentence.

Claire reached for her sword, but Graham stopped her. "They are soldiers. Be still."

She narrowed her eyes on the first group to break through the trees. "They are General Monck's men. Look, they carry his banner."

Graham nodded, seeing it snapping in the wind. "A call to war against the military, mayhap?"

"Let us go ask him." Without waiting for his response, Claire flapped her reins and dug her heels into Troy's flanks, leaving Graham to gape after her.

He caught up quickly, risking an arrow to his chest should an order be given to shoot the madman charging toward them. But no such order was issued. Instead, the lead rider raised a gloved hand and called a halt to the men behind him.

"General Monck," Claire greeted him coolly as she faced the man she'd hated for months.

Looking mildly ill, the general swept his plumed hat, a remnant from his days when he served King Charles I as a Cavalier, across his chest and dipped his head. When he lifted it again, a flash of affection warmed his steel-gray eyes and then passed, leaving his gaze hard and sharp. "It has been many years since I last saw you, Lady Stuart, but the gleam of rebellion still shines brightly in your eyes."

"Brighter than before, General," Claire assured him, proving her claim with a slight curl of her lips.

"Does that explain why you are not in Skye where you belong?"

"I am where I belong," she replied succinctly, then, without further explanation, she looked past his shoulder and surveyed his troops. "Have you rallied so many men to save my brother?"

"Nae, I sent a missive to Robert Campbell that he might do so. He assured me that you were in his care." He cut a cautious glance at Graham. "How did you come to be separated from him?"

"I left Skye once your missive was received," Claire told him. "You have my—"

"You left?" Monck stared at her, horrified, and then enraged. His attention snapped to Graham. "Who are you? Tell me Argyll did not send you alone to do as I bade him."

Graham opened his mouth to reply, but Claire did it for him. "He is not alone. I am with him."

"You . . ." The general worked his mouth around words he could not bring himself to utter aloud. Finally, he ground his teeth. "You were to be kept safe. I see now that Argyll was a poor choice for a husband. He allows you to—"

"A poor choice, indeed," Claire agreed with the snap of impatience in her voice. "But that is something we can discuss after I get my brother out of London."

Monck's complexion went milky white. "My dear, I will not allow you to do this."

Graham would have told him that there was no cause for concern. He was not going to let Claire anywhere near London. But once again, she cut him off.

Her nostrils flared with belligerence, but when she spoke, her voice was surprisingly calm. "I'm afraid that choice is not yours to make, General. We are going to London to save Connor, and if you worry that I am not skilled enough to see the task done, then bring your best soldier forward so that I can demonstrate my competence and determination, and ease your apprehension."

For a moment, General Monck simply gaped at her, astonished and taken aback by her brazen declaration. Then, because he recognized the same unshakable resolve in her eyes that he'd seen in her brother's, he expelled a great sigh of resignation. "I've no doubt you believe you are fully capable of entering London with . . ." He shifted his gaze to her companion, waiting for the introduction he had been denied the first time.

"Graham Grant." Graham bowed slightly in his saddle. "First commander to the clan MacGregor of Skye."

Looking at least somewhat relieved, Monck continued. ". . . with Commander Grant and saving Connor. But I can assure you your quest will fail."

"Why?" Claire asked softly, afraid to hear his reply, but needing to know. "Is he dead?"

"Nae, my dear, I am assured he is alive. But he is not in London."

"Then where is he?" Claire demanded.

Instead of giving her an answer, General Monck turned to Graham, and with doubt and disquiet still etched in his expression, asked, "Are the two of you truly his only hope? Is your army not on its way?"

"I would not lead an army of three hundred against a number nae man can count."

"Then how do you hope to rescue Stuart?"

"With cunning."

Monck looked vaguely amused at such a foolish, arrogant statement, but then his careful gaze narrowed on the Highlander garbed in Lowland attire. "You are the MacGregor commander who infiltrated Duncan Campbell's holding in Inveraray a few years ago."

"I am."

"I know the tale well. You gained the trust of your laird's enemies and then led them all to their deaths."

"Not all," Graham corrected.

"Ah, aye, you left young Robert Campbell alive and tied to Kildun's portcullis. Why?"

"Because he was no longer my enemy."

General Monck returned Graham's smile. "Very well then, I will tell you where Connor is. Only you must give me your word to guard Lady Claire with your life."

"You have it," Graham answered immediately.

Monck nodded and then cut one last concerned glance to Claire. "Stuart rides with General Lambert as his prisoner. Lambert set out for Scotland some time ago with roughly ten thousand men."

"Ten thousand?" Claire echoed and cast Graham a wilting look.

"Take heart, fair lady," Monck said gently. "Faced with the severe weather conditions and lack of pay, most of his men have since deserted him. I am told that a mere hundred remain with him in Newcastle."

"Then to Newcastle we shall go," Claire announced, turning to Graham.

"My men have not been out of the saddle in two days and begin to grow weary," Monck told them. "We will make camp here for the night. Please, remain with me for a little while longer. Eat and refresh yourselves for the journey ahead. You will need to be strong."

"There is no time." Claire refused his offer, but Graham moved his mount closer to hers and rested his hand on her arm.

"Ye need to rest. I'll not go until ye do."

Making camp ended up taking over two hours. Tents that were too numerous to count were set up among the sparse trees, and inside the temporary sleeping quarters, hundreds of candles provided soft light. Outside, fires were built to offer warmth and heat water. After stationing over two dozen men along the perimeter to keep watch over the camp, General Monck finally entered the spacious tent where Graham and Claire waited.

"Are you comfortable, my dear?" Monck asked Claire, handing her another blanket before he folded his legs and sat across from her on a thick woolen pallet.

"Ridiculously so," she replied, nibbling on a square of hard black bread. "I have not been this warm in over a fortnight."

Graham smiled at her while Monck poured him a cup of ale. "Why did Lambert come to Scotland?" he asked the general, accepting the drink.

"Fleetwood and some of the other generals have sought my support in their bid to rule the country, but I refused to give it. For it seemed all too likely that England would fall under the most abhorrent and debasing kind of government, one of complete tyranny. Indeed, since the expulsion of Parliament it is occurring already. I have openly declared that I will reduce the military power in obedience to the civil. Lambert has come in a last campaign to persuade me to follow him rather than fight him."

"And . . ." Claire barely had time to bring her hand to her mouth to cover her gaping yawn. "Pardon me," she said, oblivious to the smiles of the two men watching her. "He intends to use Connor to persuade you?"

"He intends to use your brother against me in some way."

"Is that why you do not bring your army to Newcastle?"

"It is part of the reason," Monck told her. "I do not believe Connor has told him what he wishes to know."

"I agree," Graham said quietly.

"I cannot risk Lambert finding out before I reach London."

"Finding what out?" Claire yawned again and leaned her elbow on her pallet.

"It is best that you do not know." Monck cut his gaze to Graham, hoping the clever commander had not already discerned the truth himself.

"So Connor knows what no one else does," Claire surmised, trying her best to keep her eyes open.

"Aye, and should I ride to Newcastle, I've no doubt Lambert will use Connor's very life to compel me to tell him."

"Would you tell him in order to save Connor's life?"

The general met her sleepy gaze with a solemn one of his own. "I am afraid I would."

He watched her cool sapphire eyes grow warm against the golden light of the candle flames, the ever-defiant tilt of her mouth relax into the softest of smiles. "I was wrong about you, General Monck," she confessed, closing her eyes. "I am glad I did not kill you."

When the sound of her breath grew slow and even, Monck looked away from her to Graham, but the commander merely shrugged, reading the question in his eyes. "She believed 'twas ye who betrayed Connor. But she knows now 'twas James Buchanan."

"Aye, I surmised that he was the traitor when I read Connor's letter. I will see that he is dealt with properly." Monck poured them each another cup of ale and handed Graham's to him. "Do I have you to thank for stopping her from breaching my fortress walls and slitting my throat while I slept, Commander?" When Graham cast him a doubtful look, the general tugged at his collar to reveal a small scar on the side of his neck. "It is precisely where I found Connor four years ago; hovering over my bed with a dagger at my throat. It was only by the grace of God that I possessed a single piece of evidence to offer him, convincing him that I was not his enemy, that stayed his hand. After that night we became friends, though he never told me how he made it past my guards. I'm certain she knew how he did it."

Graham smiled looking at her, so angelic in her slumber. He remembered her determination to save her sister when he first met her, her bold confidence in gaining entrance into Edinburgh, despite the hundreds of guardsmen patrolling its high cliff walls. Could she have breached its mighty defense as her brother had? He knew she would have given her life trying. He shook his head. Hell, she was braw, a force to be reckoned with, and he loved her more than his heart could bear.

"You are in love with her."

Graham downed his ale and swiped the back of his hand across his mouth. "Is the surrender of my poor heart that obvious?"

"She is promised to another."

Graham laughed and leaned back on his pallet. "General, you will have to kill me to see *that* promise through. Besides, Robert Campbell's heart belongs to Anne."

"To Anne?" Monck mused. "Hmm, I wonder what Connor will think of that. He had hoped to gain a strong alliance with the Campbells for the future."

"He will have it," Graham told him. "And with the MacGregors and Grants, as well."

Glancing at him from beneath his heavy brows, Monck's eyes shone like swords against the firelight.

"And if the king should return to England, will you swear your allegiance to him and bid the other Highland chiefs to do so as well?"

"Aye, without question."

The general cut his glance to Claire. "Interesting," he murmured absently. "We had not considered a Highland alliance." Looking back at Graham, he said, "You do realize what it will mean for you if the king accepts this offer."

"What will it mean for me?" Graham asked, canting his arms behind his head.

"Since Connor is alive, you will not gain his lands, but you will become a lord by taking Claire as your wife."

Closing his eyes, Graham smiled. "I can live with that. Just so long as nae one tries to make a lady out of my woman."

Chapter Thirty-six

And it is most sure, the valor of a few may surmount the numbers of many.

The flame flickered. The man crouched in the corner rushed toward it on his hands and knees, praying as he crawled. *Don't let it go out. Please.*

James Buchanan's anxious gaze darted upward to the iron grate in the stone ceiling, and then back to the lone candle. *Please.*

Stumbling forward, he reached the illuminated corner. Hope provoked a smile as he drew his body over the flame to protect it from the draft. He'd been careful to place his candle far away from the overhead grate, but the slight gush of cold air bounced off the walls and always found its way to the flame. He would have shielded his candle with his shirt, happily giving up the little warmth it afforded him, if there was a way to secure the fabric to the wall. But there was nothing in his cell save a small bucket for his waste, and his candle.

Dear God, how had Connor resisted giving his captors the information they sought? Fleetwood said that Connor had remained stalwart. How? How, when just the threat of darkness tempted James to scream and never stop?

He lifted his hands to cup the waning flame and damned Connor to hell. If the bastard had given them what they wanted, James would be at Ravenglade right now enjoying the comfort of a willing wench's embrace.

The light grew smaller. He watched with helpless desperation until it became a tiny spark of blue.

Fighting the urge to scream, he crumpled against the cool wall. It would do him no good if his resolve broke down, for his throat was too dry, his vocal cords too sore to utter even a moan.

The rats would come soon, courageous in the darkness and as hungry as he. Panic engulfed him, washing over the resentment he felt toward Connor. He closed his eyes, awaiting the battalion of squeaking, scurrying rodents and their sharp teeth that nipped and bit, testing his flesh and his sanity.

But his cell was silent, save for the foreboding drum of footsteps echoing outside his door.

"I know nothing," he cried out in a low whisper, turning his face into the wall as the key grated against the lock and the door opened. "Please, do not hurt me again."

The footfalls rushing to him were light, the voice, dulcet—like angels calling his name. "James, oh, my dearest, James."

He stopped whimpering and opened his eyes to the face illuminated by the torch held beside it. Elizabeth.

"Come, my darling," she said in a hushed voice, casting a frightened look over her shoulder. "I am getting you out of here."

* * *

From a low, tree-lined hill a few hundred yards away, Graham surveyed what remained of Lambert's massive army as they marched north along the river Tyne. He smiled slightly against the brisk wind that tore at his mantle. There were no more than fifty soldiers. The slumped posture of almost half their number told Graham that they were weary and inattentive to their surroundings. They'd been traveling long on little food and less pay. Whatever promises of glory their leader had made had been chiseled away by the frigid weather. With fifteen of Monck's men at his flanks, he could ride straight at them and likely cut down ten men before their comrades had time to react. But Connor was somewhere among them, and Graham would not risk Lambert's using him as a shield. He'd promised Claire when he left her this morning, guarded by five of the general's fiercest soldiers, that he would bring her brother back alive. He meant to keep that promise.

"Ready yerselves," he told the men around him. "And remember what I've told ye. We must take them by surprise. Catch them off guard. Even if 'tis by but a few moments, 'tis our best chance. And nae matter what happens, protect Connor Stuart at all cost."

"Do you think Lambert will believe that we've come to aid him, Commander?" a soldier to his left asked.

Graham nodded, grazing his astute eyes over the troop trudging along in the distance below. "Aye, he will believe it." He pulled off his bonnet and dug his heels into his horse's flanks. "I will make him believe it." He took off, leading his army of fifteen down the hill, in plain sight of his enemy.

He did not slow his thundering pace until Lambert's men began throwing off their mantles to unsheathe their blades. There were few, but those soldiers who had remained with Lambert were his most loyal. They proved it by immediately reforming their ranks and shielding him on every side.

"My lord," Graham called out, raising his empty sword hand in a gesture of submission as he slowed. "We've come from Scotland to offer you our service."

Though he was short in the saddle, John Lambert lacked no arrogance in his proud stature as he sized Graham up with a wary sneer. "Scotland, you say? I have no supporters in Scotland."

"Aye, you do, my lord," Graham said with flawless English inflection, bowing his head in deference. "There were a little over one hundred of us under Governor Monck. Recently, he relieved us of duty and station for our disloyalty to him and his support of Parliament. He is a soldier, and yet he denounces military rulership of the kingdom."

Lambert's lips pinched into a scowl, but Graham's careful eyes had not missed the subtle nod of agreement, the hint of satisfaction that passed over Lambert's face while he listened. "What makes you think I want what General Monck has thrown away?"

"With all due respect, Major General, it is not what you want that is important. It is what you need."

"You presume much . . ." Lambert arched his brow waiting for Graham to give his name.

"Major Alan Hyde," Graham told him. "To my right is Major Richard Lindsey. To my left, Captain Charles Cosworth. The good men you see at our rear are our most loyal soldiers."

Lambert did not look impressed. In fact, he snickered and flicked his reins to leave. "Return to me in three days with a few thousand more men and I will consider allowing you to ride with me."

"In three days General Monck will have reached London. Aye," he said when Lambert stopped, his dark pupils dilated with rage. "He set out for the city weeks ago. Allow us to ride with you now and we can cut off his troops before he reaches the Thames. He rides with less than a thousand men."

"Even if I believed you, what makes you think we can stop him, you fool? We are less than one hundred."

The slow grin creeping along Graham's lips was enough to convince at least some of Lambert's men that what he said next was true. "You will not need more than that with me at your side." When Lambert threw back his head and laughed, Graham smiled with him, then motioned with his chin to the largest and most alert of Lambert's men. "Allow me to demonstrate."

Lambert sighed, but his curiosity was piqued. With a slight wave of his hand, he signaled his man to come forward. "Make a quick end of him, Lieutenant—"

Graham did not wait for him to finish giving his order, but reared his stallion up on its mighty back legs, freeing his claymore at the same time. He brought the horse and the flat end of his flashing sword down on the lieutenant's temple.

"Tell me that was not your best soldier," Graham said as his opponent crumpled from his saddle and fell unconscious to the ground.

Lambert, too, watched his third in command slip to the hard earth, then blinked his astonished gaze back to Graham. He snapped his fingers and two of the men guarding him rushed toward Graham. They went down as quickly as the first.

"Tell me who you are," Lambert demanded, sidestepping his mount out of Graham's reach.

"I told you . . ."

"Nae, you claim to be English, yet you fight like the Scots and you carry their sword."

"A gift," Graham said, holding his bloodless blade up to admire it, "from a MacGregor, after I removed his head." With a flick of his wrist, he turned the sword in his hand and offered the hilt to Lambert. "The craftsmanship is superb. Here, feel its weight and how well it fits in your hand."

Lambert backed up, suspicion narrowing his eyes into slits. "Is it my trust you seek to gain, or my arse on the ground with the rest?"

"Only your trust, my great lord," Graham told him earnestly.

But Lambert was still not convinced. "If, as you say, I need only you at my side, then gain it by cutting off the arm of one of these men."

"As you wish." Graham readied himself once again, but no soldier came forward. Instead, Lambert called out Connor Stuart's name.

Hauled from his horse, Claire's brother almost fell to his knees as he was shoved forward by another soldier. Keeping his expression stoic, Graham marveled at the raw determination Connor possessed to remain upright. Clothed in rags, his tattered mantle snapping in the frigid wind, he lifted his ice-blue gaze to Graham, a gaze charged with the same defiance, the same stubborn refusal to surrender that his sister possessed.

"What is this?" Graham drawled with mild disgust. "You mock the skill I pledge to you by bringing me a broken peasant to fight?"

"This is Connor Stuart, leader of the Royalist resistance," Lambert sneered. "A rebel movement that reaches deep within Monck's camp. Prove to me that the general has not sent you to aid him and I will make you my second in command."

Graham smiled and dismounted. He circled the prisoner, sliding the edge of his blade gently along Connor's collarbone. "I have heard of you, Stuart. A warrior arrayed in the frost of winter told me of your great skill."

Connor's breath faltered slightly, but that was the only proof he gave that he understood of whom the man behind him spoke.

Lambert spat at Connor's feet. "Aye, show Major Hyde how brave you are now."

"Aye," Graham came face to face with Connor, whose eyes now shone with hope and disbelief, and tossed him an easy grin. "Show me." He handed Connor his sword even as Lambert stammered his protest.

"You do not expect me to fight an unarmed man, do you, my lord?" Graham cut Lambert a disapproving glance. "I do have *some* honor, which—" He turned back to Connor while he pulled a dagger from beneath his belt. "—your sister will flatly deny." Connor smiled as Graham slashed a wide gash into the chest of the soldier standing closest to him—and the men around them suddenly came alive.

As Graham had suspected, Lambert's army was weak and weary, and more than half fell within the first ten minutes of battle. Connor, Graham was pleased to see, fought relatively well, considering his poor condition. But he would not last much longer against Lambert's better fighters. Graham had to get him away from the fray.

While Monck's men hacked away at the rest, Graham tossed Claire's brother over his shoulder and ran for his horse. He heard Lambert shout his false name as he hurled Connor over his saddle and leaped up behind him. He did not slow, knowing Monck's men would stop anyone who tried to follow him.

He had almost made it to the tree line when a shot rang out. Pain seared his chest and arm like a molten flame. He looked down to see darker red drenching the fibers of his mulberry doublet. Hell, the bastard had a pistol! Still, he did not stop but broke through the trees like an arrow being shot through hay. He heard a shout; a female voice, but his mind refused to register who it might be. She wouldn't! She couldn't have disobeyed him! No man had ever disobeyed him in battle. Then he saw her, her long pale braid snapping out behind her, her sword raised and ready to cut down anything or anyone in her path as Troy crashed through the trees.

Graham felt his heart fail him as she whipped past him. "Claire!" he roared, then set his murderous glare on the five men following at her heels. He swung his horse around, vowing to kill every one of them for not keeping her safely hidden.

"My brother," Connor yanked on his reins, slowing his horse. "You cannot return to the fight. We will surely die."

Graham ignored him and drove his heels into his horse again. Dear God, she was fighting! He would not reach her in time.

"Look!" Connor lifted a bony finger to the fray. "Your men are behind and in front of Lambert's. The general himself retreats! Let her fight. She is my best man."

"She is not a man!" Graham screamed at him. "She is my wife!" He tried to reach her, but, following his orders, three of his men used their horses to block his path, protecting Connor at all cost.

He could do nothing but watch her, both horrified and in awe of her skill and strength. The melee lasted only a few moments, but it seemed like eons to Graham, helpless to get to her. She blocked, jabbed, and swung, slashing her victims with vicious expertise. Finally, when only a handful of their enemies remained, she shouted an order and Monck's men immediately retreated.

Graham stared at her as she rode to him, a mixture of blind fury and sheer terror darkening his features. Without pausing in her gait, she snatched his reins and yanked him into moving.

They rode in silence, surrounded on every side by General Monck's men, of whom none were lost, until they were safely away. The moment they stopped, Claire leaped from her mount and helped Graham lower her brother into her arms.

"I thought you were dead," she cried over and over while she washed his face in kisses and in tears. "I thought I would never see you again."

Dragging his sister into his arms, Connor closed his eyes and held her as if he would never again let go. "I prayed each day to see your face one more time. To hear you argue with me."

Hearing them, Graham almost smiled.

"Tell me, sister," Connor withdrew and looked deeply

into Claire's eyes, "where is Anne? Tell me she has not been given in marriage to James Buchanan."

"She has not. Graham and Robert suspected his treachery and followed Monck's orders to take her to Skye."

"Thank the saints," Connor breathed with profound relief. "Do you speak of Robert Campbell, the Earl of Argyll?"

"Aye."

Connor nodded and looked up at the man who saved his life. "I knew Campbell was a good man who could be trusted. Might I assume that you are Graham?"

"Aye," Claire answered for him. "He is Graham Grant, commander of . . . Dear God, Graham, your shoulder! You are hurt!" She tried to tug him off his horse, but he only shook his head, his gaze hard and unblinking on her.

"'Tis nothing. A minor wound. The shot went straight through. I am fine."

"Nonsense," she argued, sounding close to hysteria. "Get down here so I can get a look at it."

"I said I am fine."

She stared at him, confusion and concern marring her flaxen brow.

Seeing her distress, Connor leaned in close to her ear. "Your husband is angry with you for rushing into the fight. Give him time to—"

"I am not her husband," Graham corrected him woodenly.

"But you called her your wife."

"A wife of mine would not disobey me."

Bristling in her spot, Claire folded her arms across her chest and glared at him. "And a husband of mine would not give me orders."

"He would if he believed ye too ill to fight because of. the babe ye carry but have nae regard fer!"

"Babe?" Connor blinked at his sister first and then at Graham. "You are carrying a babe?"

But Claire was too busy gaping at Graham in mute fury to give her brother a response.

"He would," Graham continued, his voice growing louder, more fevered with emotion, "if the verra thought of yer lifeblood being spilled upon the ground drove him to madness! I have never felt terror on the field before this day, thanks to ye, ye stubborn wench! I vow, 'twas the last time!"

He whirled his horse around to leave her, but stopped when a small rock struck him in the back. Turning slowly, he glowered at her, then dismounted and stalked toward her like a predator after its prey.

"In case ye have forgotten, I was shot."

"You said you were fine." She faced his most lethal look and fisted her hands on her hips. "Do you think to leave me?"

"D'ye think to stop me by hurling rocks at me?"

"Aye; I will do whatever it takes to keep those I love at my side." As he came closer, her anger melted at the blood staining his doublet. The scent of him, the sight of him, and the sound of him all worked at chiseling away her defenses, as they had from the beginning. Her heart gave in, surrendering all she was to him. "I am sorry I disobeyed you, but I heard the shot of a pistol and the thought of losing you drove me to madness, as well."

His expression went soft, his green eyes warmed like a summer glade as he reached her. "What did ye say?"

"I said the thought of losing—"

"Nae, before that."

When she realized what he meant she quirked her mouth at him. "I said I was sorry."

Graham looked at her brother. "Ye heard that, nae?" Then he slipped his arms around her waist and drew her close, careful of his wound. "Does this mean ye will obey me from now on?"

Claire tilted her face to kiss him, then leaned up on her toes and spoke softly against his ear. "Graham, my truest love, I will do as you say from this moment on. Now please, let me see to your shoulder and clean your wound."

When his sister returned to her horse to retrieve some water, Connor Stuart caught Graham's satisfied smirk and shook his head with pity. "You do not believe all that about her obeying you, do you?"

Graham flashed his dimples at Claire when she turned to smile at them both. "Of course not. If I must fight again while she is in her delicate condition, I will tie her to a tree."

Connor laughed softly. "She will only chew her way through the ropes." He caught an apple Claire tossed him from her saddle. He bit into it and groaned with pleasure, then turned back to Graham. "So, are you sure you can tame her? Many have tried before you and failed."

"Nae," Graham admitted, settling his loving gaze on her. If she ever again frightened him the way she did today, he would throttle her, but he . . .

"Satan's blasted balls!" Claire cursed, spilling the water and interrupting his thoughts.

He could not help but smile. "I've nae intention of taming her. None whatsoever."

Epilogue

The time has come to let the truth be known. Everything you desire will soon be in my hands. Surrender. It is so powerful a word, and none more sweet to the ears of a true warrior. I shall gain the victory, but the glory will be yours. I have kept my heart's desire silent long enough. But soon, the land shall quake at my coming. And the man who has lost everything shall gain it all back. But know this, that I am a soldier with a need for nothing more. I do this not with the hope of achieving greatness, but with fear that should I submit, nothing shall be secure.

Shall I be stripped bare on the battlefield or be clothed in righteousness and readiness? Shall I let the faithful child die while the wicked man prospers? Nae! I shall ride forth and obliterate the shame that has been brought upon the father. Be patient. Be vigilant. For there is as much honor gained by suffering wants patiently in war, as by fighting valiantly. Let a soldier's resolution be never so great, and his courage invincible in the day of battle. For men wear not arms because they are afraid of danger, but because they would not fear it. And it is most sure, the valor of a few may surmount the numbers of many. And so I go, Your Majesty, not to bring

war, but to bring your people a taste of the sweetness of
peace, and the benefit of a Civil life.*

King Charles II finished reading the missive sent to him
from General George Monck. With a heart that felt lighter
than it had in over five years, he folded the parchment and
hid it inside his trunk. Finally, he was going home.

General George Monck's army restored Parliament in
the Spring of 1660, whereupon Charles Fleetwood was
deprived of his command and called to answer for his
conduct. On March 3, 1660, Major General John Lambert
was sent to the Tower, from which he escaped one month
later. In May of the same year, England's Civil War ended
and Charles II was restored to the throne.

   England and her people were finally at peace—
everyone that is, save for James Buchanan, who found
himself hunted by a most tenacious warrior whom he had
betrayed.

   But that is another story.

---

*Portions of this passage are taken from *Observations upon
Military & Political Affairs,* written by General George Monck,
1644–46. Published 1671.

About the Author

PAULA QUINN has been married to her childhood sweetheart for seventeen years. They have three children, a dog, and too many reptiles to count. She lives in New York City and is currently at work on her next novel. Write to her at paula@paulaquinn.com.

THE DISH

Where authors give you the inside scoop!

♥ ♥ ♥ ♥ ♥ ♥ ♥ ♥ ♥ ♥ ♥ ♥ ♥

From the desk of Carolyn Jewel

Dear Reader,

What was that line Shakespeare stuck in one of his plays? Oh, yeah. *Hamlet*, act 1, scene 2. "There are more things in heaven and earth, Horatio, than are dreamt of in your philosophy." Even if you're not Horatio, and chances are you're not, that's a true statement. When things go bump in the night, maybe it's not the cat knocking stuff over.

Maybe there really is a monster drooling under your bed.

Right. There are things out there maybe you don't know about. Say, for example, the mages in MY WICKED ENEMY (on sale now). A mage is a person who can do magic. Real magic. The kind that can get you killed. Or save your life. Depends on your point of view, I guess. Then there are demons and, more specifically, fiends. They're not people, but they can do magic, too. My advice is watch out for both. Here's the thing you need to know about fiends, though: most of the time they look like normal people. You could walk down the street and never realize that wicked-hot cutie sitting by the coffee shop window isn't human and that if he wanted to, he could destroy your life. Could be your boss isn't human (I've had one or two bosses I'm convinced didn't have a check mark in the human category). For a fiend, learning how to pass for normal is a survival skill. Didn't used to be that way, but it is now. That's just a heads-up for you. Here's another one: they're good at it because they have to be. They end up enslaved to some effing mage if they're not careful. And sometimes even if they are.

With the magekind, it's hard to tell where you stand, mostly because they started out human. They don't have as much trouble pretending to assimilate. Human but not very, if you see what I'm getting at. It's enough to make you wonder, isn't it? I mean, do you even know who you are? Really and truly? Be honest. Maybe you just wake up one day and realize your entire life has been a lie. The man who raised you is a mage who crossed over to evil centuries ago, and now everybody and their brother wants you dead.

Maybe you get headaches. Bad ones. You know, a flash of pain from the supraorbital process down to your maxilla. Hurts like heck. And they're getting worse. And worse. Then you see stuff that turns your stomach. So you run.

Right into the monster's arms.

It could happen. It happened to Carson Philips in
MY WICKED ENEMY.

Watch yourself out there. That's all I'm saying.

Carolyn Jewel

www.carolynjewel.com

♥ ♥ ♥ ♥ ♥ ♥ ♥ ♥ ♥ ♥ ♥ ♥ ♥ ♥ ♥

From the desk of Samantha Graves

Dear Reader,

When I wrote my first romantic suspense, SIGHT UNSEEN, I discovered that I loved exotic locales. The research was intense, but that only made these amazing places more amazing.

In my latest book, OUT OF TIME (on sale now), I got to visit Mexico with all of you. I have never been there, but someday I'd love to see it for myself. In lieu of that day, I did the best I could with guidebooks, videos, travelogues, maps, photos, and even an online Speed Spanish class. What did we do before the Internet?

My fascination for Mexico turned into Jillian's passion, as well. She embraced this culture and its people with an open heart. Her wide-eyed appreciation became a symbol for how she viewed life and people—seeing the beauty in everything.

Simon's dislike for Mexico has nothing to do with the country itself, but with the betrayal he experienced there—a betrayal that marred him with a cynicism that shaped the rest of his life.

During the story, both characters must face the truth as Jillian begins to see the ugliness and Simon begins to see the beauty. It could have been Mexico or Guatemala or Santa Barbara—all places contain both ugliness and beauty. What you choose as truth is up to you. What you do with that truth defines you.

In the end, Jillian didn't let the ugliness change the fact that there is beauty, and Simon didn't let the beauty change the fact that there is ugliness. They simply found their common ground, accepting both as part of life and choosing to see the truth in their love for each other.

I hope you enjoyed both.

All the best,

Samantha Graves

www.samanthagraves.com

P.S. In case you were wondering, *"Quite mis ropas"* means "Take my clothes off." Happy reading!

♥ ♥ ♥ ♥ ♥ ♥ ♥ ♥ ♥ ♥ ♥ ♥ ♥ ♥ ♥

From the desk of Paula Quinn

Dear Reader,

Few authors get to see their characters come to life before their eyes, but I did. You met Graham Grant, the hero in A HIGHLANDER NEVER SURRENDERS (on sale now), in my previous release, LAIRD OF THE MIST. I met him in Grand Central Terminal. The Scottish Village there hosts a fashion show that was about to begin. I like kilts. I'll watch.

Donning a kilt of black leather and matching jacket that he held closed at his chest, model and former rugby star Chris Capaldi stepped onto the stage like he owned it. His tousled mop of deep amber hair eclipsed killer green eyes that sparkled with confidence and a hint of wickedness. All he did was smile and a horde of women behind me started whooping and cheering in a dozen different languages. Oh, yeah, he knew the ladies were digging him, and he fed the frenzy by sliding the jacket off his bare bronze shoulders and curling his sulky mouth into a grin so salacious I swear every woman in attendance sighed at the same time. Grand Central was never so hot.

There was my Graham Grant. Six feet three inches of pure rogue.

Chris has graciously agreed to star in my next Grand Central Publishing release about a notorious rogue and a beautiful rebel he can never have. From the moment Graham meets the bold and passionate Claire Stuart, he wants to take her, claim her. But Claire has far more dangerous undertakings ahead than surrendering to a wickedly alluring Highlander. Amid betrayal, honor, duty, and ultimately love, she must put this vision in his place in order to save her sister's life, and her own. Pick up a copy of A HIGHLANDER NEVER SURRENDERS and journey with Graham to a place that has remained untouched until now—his heart.

Enjoy!

All the best,

Paula Quinn

www.paulaquinn.com

Want to know more about romances at Grand Central Publishing and Forever? Get the scoop online!

GRAND CENTRAL PUBLISHING'S ROMANCE HOME PAGE

Visit us at www.hachettebookgroup.com/romance for all the latest news, reviews, and chapter excerpts!

NEW AND UPCOMING TITLES

Each month we feature our new titles and reader favorites.

CONTESTS AND GIVEAWAYS

We give away galleys, autographed copies, and all kinds of fun stuff.

AUTHOR INFO

You'll find bios, articles, and links to personal Web sites for all your favorite authors—and so much more!

THE BUZZ

Sign up for our monthly romance newsletter, and be the first to read all about it!